Innocent Blood

Innocent Blood

Raymond Haigh

ROBERT HALE · LONDON

© Raymond Haigh 2009
First published in Great Britain 2009

ISBN 978-0-7090-8828-8

Robert Hale Limited
Clerkenwell House
Clerkenwell Green
London EC1R 0HT

www.halebooks.com

2 4 6 8 10 9 7 5 3 1

Typeset in 11/16pt Janson
Printed in Great Britain by
the MPG Books Group, Bodmin and King's Lynn

ONE

Rooks were circling the tall trees that bordered the shrub-bery. Busy repairing old nests, building new nests, the birds and their untidy constructions were ragged black shapes against a limpid blue sky. When I stepped from the car and slammed the door the colony took flight and a raucous cawing shattered the morning stillness. Set midway up a rise from the road, the house was imposing. A steep roof of blue-green slates swept down over pebble-dashed walls, shading windows that nestled beneath wide, overhanging eaves. Large semicircular bays, two storeys high, projected at each end of the frontage. Tall chim-neys rose out of the roof. Massive chimney stacks buttressed high gable ends.

My best black Oxfords crunched over gravel as I strode towards the entrance. Having driven there straight from court I was wearing a double-breasted blue pinstripe, a blue shirt and a wine-red Dior tie with matching pocket handkerchief. The clothes and the Jaguar XJ8 were appropriate. Well-heeled clients expect you to look professional and arrive in a decent car.

Oak posts, grey and weathered, supported a slate roof over the porch. I stepped under it, thumbed the bell, then let my gaze wander over the hinge straps and iron studs that decorated the massive door. Glancing up, I saw a blue and white plaque, about as big as a dinner plate, in the shadows above the lintel. The words *Barfield Civic Trust* ran around its ribboned edge. Its centre was inscribed: *Tanglewood House was designed by Charles Francis Annesley Voysey and completed in 1907*. I heard a key grate in the lock, then the door swung open.

'Mrs Brody?'

The woman smiled and nodded. 'And you'll be Mr Lomax. I'm so relieved your secretary managed to get a message to you. I couldn't possibly have waited another day.' She opened the door wider. 'Do come in.'

I stepped on to a large Persian carpet that almost covered the polished floor. When the door slammed the sound of the rooks faded, and so did most of the sunlight. Some still filtered in through a tall stained-glass window on a landing half-way up the stairs. It gleamed on oak panelling and dappled plates on a Delft rack with splashes of bright colour.

'Come through, Mr Lomax. My husband's in the library.'

We crossed the hall, went through a door and along a passageway where the smell of wax polish was strong and sunlight sparkled on tiny window panes. Walking behind her, I was able take a more leisurely look at the woman in the blue and white print dress. Even in her serviceable low-heeled shoes she was fairly tall; maybe five-eight or five-nine. Slender, but some way from being thin, her bare arms and legs were lightly tanned. I guessed the colour had come from a bottle, but it could have been the fading memory of a winter holiday. Her dark hair was cut very short and combed back, almost like a man's. It was frosted with grey.

She led me into a room where a grand piano projected from one of the big semicircular bays. Its lowered lid was strewn with music scores. There were a few books on some low shelving – Mrs Brody was being fanciful when she'd said the collection amounted to a library. Logs were burning in a green-tiled fireplace that had an oak surround with a mirrored upper panel. A metronome and a clock in a brass case stood amongst photographs ranged along its wide mantelshelf.

'This is Mr Lomax, Daniel.' When Mrs Brody stepped aside I could see a heavily built man. He was sitting on a long and rather baggy sofa, eying me over a copy of the *Financial Times*. Greying hair and a neatly trimmed moustache gave him a military look that was helped along by a khaki sweater with leather elbow patches. I rounded a low table and held out a hand. Pale blue eyes went on staring at me over the pink newspaper. When I realized he was going to ignore the gesture, I swept my hand up, toyed with the handkerchief in my breast pocket and said, 'It's a pleasure to meet you, Mr Brody.'

A voice behind me murmured, 'Won't you sit down, Mr Lomax?'

I turned. Mrs Brody was pointing towards an armchair. I lowered myself into it, then she sat in a chair facing mine. Glancing from wife to husband, I smiled and said, 'I understand you have a problem you want to discuss: something you think I might be able to help you with?'

Mrs Brody gave her spouse a nervous look. He sniffed, pursed thin purplish lips, then inclined his head towards me. I guessed he was telling her to do the talking. She folded her hands in her lap and leaned forward. 'It's Jason. We're ...' – she glanced at her husband – '... *I'm* very worried about him.'

'Jason?'

'Our son. He's at Birmingham University; in his final year.' Mrs Brody faltered and darted another nervous glance at her husband.

Daniel Brody turned to the back pages and began to study the stock market returns. I guessed he was distancing himself from the proceedings; letting me know he thought his wife was worrying about nothing. His corduroy trousers were tight over plump thighs, his brown shoes highly polished, his thick woollen socks khaki coloured, like the sweater.

Giving her another encouraging smile, I said, 'Why are you so concerned about him, Mrs Brody?'

'Well …' She paused, looked down at her hands, then worry surfaced in her voice and she began to speak quickly, almost blurting out the words. 'I've not been able to contact him for more than a week. We used to talk on the phone every other day and he'd come home at least once a month, but he's changed this year. He doesn't contact me any more; it's always me chasing him. And he seems so distant. When I met him in Birmingham last month he wasn't himself at all. He insisted there was nothing wrong, said he was just working hard for his finals, but he's never worried about exams before. And I've usually been able to contact him on his mobile phone, or on the phone in the house he shares, but no one answers any more. It's nine or ten days since I last spoke to him. I'm quite worried.'

'He's twenty-two,' her husband muttered, without looking up. 'He's a man, not a boy.'

She flashed him a reproachful glance. 'I'm worried, Daniel. You hear of such dreadful things happening. And I've never lost contact with him before.'

Daniel didn't respond, just sniffed through his moustache and went on scowling at the share prices.

Looking back at me, she said, 'We … I … wondered if you could go to Birmingham, locate him and make sure he's all right. I really am so desperately worried.'

Daniel Brody gave another derisory sniff. His wife's lips were trembling now. It was becoming embarrassing. They should have agreed what they wanted to do before calling me in. 'How about you and your husband driving over to Birmingham?' I suggested. 'Go to the student accommodation. If your son's moved out, the people he shared with should be able to tell you where he's gone. If you can't trace him, have a word with the police.'

Still glaring at the paper, Daniel muttered, 'Told you he wouldn't want the job, didn't I? You're wasting the man's time.'

Ignoring him, she said, 'I don't think I'd care to go there myself, Mr Lomax. I drove him home after we'd had our last meal together. It's not England any more: it's just row after row of houses in shabby streets where no one can understand a word you're saying. I couldn't go knocking on doors in a place like that.'

'And it's a waste of time going to the police,' Daniel muttered, carrying on where he'd left off. 'Try talking to them about a 22-year-old male student you think might have gone missing and they'll laugh in your face.' His refined voice was brisk, almost hectoring. He punctuated the outburst with another moustache-trembling sniff.

'I'm sure they'd listen to you, Mr Brody,' I said gently. 'They'd make enquiries. It's what you pay taxes for.'

'Taxes!' The word seemed to rouse him to fury. Hairy nostrils flared. He gave his wife a baleful look.

Mrs Brody pushed her shoulders back and made her voice defiant. 'I'm worried sick, Daniel. You know how worried I am, and you're not helping.' She turned to me. 'You don't mind trying to find Jason for me, do you, Mr Lomax?'

Missing persons wasn't the sort of thing I'd normally bother with, but business was quiet and I might as well charge time to the Brodys as sit in the office. So I said, 'Of course I don't, Mrs Brody. But I have to be sure it's what you and your husband really want.' I trotted out details of hourly rates and travelling expenses.

'Cost isn't a problem, Mr Lomax.'

Her husband's eyebrows lifted when she said that and his lips made a wry smile.

'I just want you to locate him,' she went on. 'Make sure he's safe, and persuade him to get in touch with me.'

'Addresses,' I said. 'I'll need what addresses you have, and a photograph.'

Daniel Brody folded his newspaper and tossed it down on the table. 'That's decided, then,' he said briskly. He scowled at his wife. 'You can sort out the details. I'm going back to the workshop.' Small, pale-blue eyes fastened on mine. 'Like you to come up and see me before you leave, Lomax. Maria will show you the way.' He pushed himself to his feet and disappeared behind my chair. I heard the door open and close, his footsteps loud as he crossed the hall, then fading as he climbed the stairs.

Maria's body relaxed when her husband had left the room. Smiling at me, she said softly, 'Thank you, Mr Lomax. You can't imagine how worried I am. I lie awake at night, wondering if something's happened to him. Daniel thinks I'm being stupid, but Jason's never gone this long without phoning me.'

'I'll need a photograph,' I reminded her.

'Of course.' She rose and crossed over to the big fireplace, held her skirt against her legs to prevent it being caught by the flames while she studied the framed pictures lined up along the mantelshelf. She selected one and brought it over. 'This was taken at Christmas.'

I studied the long, bespectacled face. He had his mother's refined features, and his fair hair was untidy and needed cutting. Smiling grudgingly for the photographer, he was standing beside a blonde girl who was wearing a black dress with a sequined top. 'Who's the girl?'

'His cousin. She's my sister-in-law's daughter.'

'Either she's short or he's tall.'

'He's about as tall as you,' she said. 'Six-one; perhaps a little more.'

I looked up. 'May I have the photograph?'

'Of course. Let me take it out of the frame.'

I handed it back to her and she began to fiddle with clips on the velvet back. 'Does he have a girlfriend?'

She slid the photograph from behind the glass and handed it to me. 'A week ago I'd have said no, but when I became worried I looked through his room and found something that made me wonder.' She put the dismantled frame on the low table and headed across to the piano. I rose and followed her. She picked up a leather manuscript case, lifted the flap, and began to leaf through papers and music scores.

From the huge bay window I could see the expanse of lawn at the front of the house and the rooks circling over the treetops, their incessant cawing faint and somehow ominous through the tiny panes of glass. Newspaper had been pushed into gaps where the iron window frames had been distorted by corrosion. Mrs Brody must have followed my gaze, because she said, 'The windows have given us a lot of trouble. We did the other bay last year; we'll do this one in the summer. A firm comes and takes them out, gets the rust off and repairs them, then they're galvanized before they're put back. It costs a fortune and they're still cold and draughty. It's a Voysey house. Grade One listed. Can't change a thing, inside or out.' She laughed. 'Don't ever buy a listed house, Mr Lomax.'

I smiled at her across the piano. Architectural Heritage would probably give me an award if I demolished my shabby little bungalow. Making conversation while she searched amongst the papers, I said, 'Have you lived here long?'

'About twenty years. We came here after Jason was born. We used to live in Felsham. I taught music for a while, at the Ladies College there.'

'*You're* the musician. I thought it might be your husband.'

Laughing, she took an envelope from the document case and handed it to me. 'The only music he understands, Mr Lomax, is the clang of a forge hammer. He was an engineer.'

'Was?' I opened the envelope.

'He inherited the family business when his father died. They made parts for the aerospace industry. Five years ago Aerospace Systems made him an offer for the firm he couldn't refuse. He sold up and retired. He's regretted it ever since.'

I was looking down at a small piece of blue notepaper and only half listening. In a rounded, feminine hand someone had written:

Darling Jason,
Your poem was so beautiful. It made me cry. Thursday afternoon will be OK. I'll meet you at the usual place at two. Please don't text me again. Things are becoming even more difficult here.
Love and lots of kisses, Halima.

I glanced up at Maria Brody. 'No address, no date.'

'I found it in a book he bought in February, so he was probably involved with her as recently as that. What sort of a name is Halima? Would it be Spanish?'

'Could be almost any nationality,' I said. 'Halima's a popular Muslim name.'

Maria smiled. She had a shapely mouth and big hazel eyes. They made her look feminine and vulnerable despite the shortness of her hair. 'You're very knowledgeable, Mr Lomax. Are you a Muslim?'

I laughed softly. 'They'd stone me if I went near the mosque. It's the job: I pick up all sorts of information.'

'You'll want Jason's address,' she said. 'I listed everything I could think of while I was going through his things. It's on the desk in his room. Can I take you up?'

We crossed the hallway and began to climb the wide, dog-legged stairs. The handrail was supported on balusters that were square and plain, and at every turn massive newel posts rose to the ceiling. As we rounded the landing with the stained-glass window, she glanced over her shoulder and said, 'Your secretary's very glamorous. Daniel couldn't take his eyes off her. He likes blue-eyed blondes. He was very much against involving you until he saw her.' Mrs Brody's tone was faintly mocking and I thought I detected an underlying bitterness.

'She's not my secretary, Mrs Brody. She owns the photocopying and printing business on the ground floor. She just watches out for clients and takes calls on an extension when I'm out. My offices are on the top floor.'

The strip of red carpet that protected the stairs continued down a corridor that ran along the back of the house. Through mullioned windows I could see a well-tended garden that rose to the crest of the hill. It was neatly laid out with shrubs and flower beds. A couple of cherry trees were clouded with blossom.

Mrs Brody stopped by an open door. 'This is Jason's room.'

When I stepped inside I saw some more rugs on polished oak boards; maybe Architectural Heritage frowned on Axminster, wall-to-wall. There was a single bed with a blue-striped duvet, a tallboy and a wardrobe, all in the Arts and Crafts style. The desk was modern. Shelves on either side of an iron fireplace in the end wall were sagging under the weight of tightly packed books.

She brushed past me, crossed over to the desk and came back holding a sheet of paper. 'Everything I could think of is on there, Mr Lomax. I sat at his desk while I wrote it all down. I was going to take it with me when I went to the police, but a friend suggested I contact you.'

I glanced at the neatly written notes: Jason's personal details, the college he was attending, the address of the house he shared, his mobile phone number, the name of his tutor. 'What happens when you dial his mobile?'

'It just rings until the voice-mail girl asks you to leave a message. He never answers.'

'Have you contacted his personal tutor?' I glanced down at the notes. 'What's his name … Maynard: Vincent Price-Maynard.'

'I did manage to speak to him. He was very elusive. I had to phone half-a-dozen times before I got through. I needn't have bothered. He hardly knew who Jason was and he couldn't remember whether or not he'd attended his tutorials. Then he started telling me not to worry. God, he was so patronizing. Worse than Daniel!' She paused, looked at me for a moment with the big hazel eyes, then her voice became childishly pleading as she asked, 'When will you go to Birmingham?'

'Today, Mrs Brody.'

Her body relaxed with relief. 'Is there any more information you need? I don't think there's anything else I can tell you.'

I folded the sheet of paper. 'Your phone numbers are on here. I'll call you if I need to.' As I was pocketing it, I asked, 'Who was the friend who recommended me?'

'Emma, Mrs Emma Pearson, the magistrate who chairs the bench. She's heard you giving evidence in court. You seem to have impressed her. Her husband was murdered last year, in his office. It was absolutely ghastly. And Daniel tells me not to worry!'

I smiled. I'd done much more for Mrs Pearson than give evidence before her in court. 'I'll phone you tomorrow, Mrs Brody.'

'Tonight,' she insisted. 'No matter what time it is, phone me as soon as you have anything to tell me. Call me on my mobile. Don't use the house phone.'

'Try not to worry if I don't call. These things can take a little time.' I moved towards the door.

'Don't forget, my husband wants to see you before you go.'

I patted the sheet of notes in my pocket. 'You've told me all I need—'

'He wants to show you his playthings, Mr Lomax. He doesn't

want to talk to you about a son who's been such a big disappointment to him. Daniel was scathing when Jason said he was going to
read English; mocking when he began to have his poems
published. He wanted a practical son, someone who did things and
made things, not a dreamy intellectual. He thinks I'm just a silly
woman, worrying about nothing.' Her plaintive voice suddenly
became loud and corrosive. 'And everyone who comes here has to
go up and admire what he's got in the attic. I'll show you the way.'

* * *

I could feel a tremor in the floor, hear the rumbling, before I
reached the top of the attic stairs. Maria Brody had told me to go
through the door on the right, so I lifted the latch and entered a
room within the roof that was around thirty feet wide and maybe
sixty long. Brick chimney stacks rose through it, and a waist-high
timber decking, some six feet wide, had been formed around the
perimeter. Lamps in green coolie-hat shades, the sort of things
they used to hang over billiard tables, illuminated it. There were
enough of them to make the light gleam on bright metal rails. A
model railway locomotive, more than a foot tall and maybe five
long, enamelled green and black and lined in red, was moving
slowly along the outer track.

Daniel Brody was sitting at a control panel half-way down the
long room, his gaze locked on the engine and its tender. When it
rumbled past the small space just inside the door, he saw me.
'Lomax! Thanks for coming up. Duck under the tracks and come
over.'

I crawled for a distance on my hands and knees, then rose and
headed towards him. The locomotive had rounded the end of the
room and was moving down the far side, keeping pace with me.

He hooked his foot around the pillar of a swivel chair and pulled it from under the decking. 'Take a pew.' He was concentrating on panel lights and controls. He flicked a switch. When the locomotive and its tender rounded the other end of the room it changed tracks. He brought it to a halt beside the console, then turned and looked at me. 'The Duke of Gloucester. What do you think?'

I gazed at the huge model. It was incredibly detailed: every rivet, every pipe, all the oil-slicked rods and levers that, in the real thing, transferred power from pistons to wheels. 'It's perfect,' I murmured, making my voice suitably reverent. 'Absolutely perfect.'

He chuckled, then sniffed through his moustache. 'Finished her last year, on Christmas day. Made six since I retired, all classic English locos. Got to do something or your mind and skills atrophy. Only parts I don't make are the wheel castings and the electric power unit. Firm in Manchester supplies those.'

I shifted my admiring gaze from the model to his florid face. 'Was there something you wanted to tell me before I left, or did you just want me to see—?'

'Do you think my wife's right to be concerned, Lomax?' He picked up a yellow duster and began to caress the roof of the locomotive's cab.

'She could be, but it's more than likely your son's too busy with his own affairs to return her calls.'

'Maria's worried about Jason, and I'm worried about her.' I watched him rub the yellow duster to and fro along the boiler casing. Presently he sniffed, then turned and looked me in the eye. 'I think she's having an affair.'

'How long have you been thinking that, Mr Brody?'

'Almost six months. It's eating me up. I hardly think about anything else.' He refolded his duster and began to polish the cab sides. Talking about it seemed to be embarrassing him, but he'd probably reached the stage where he had to confide in someone.

'What's made you suspicious?'

He shrugged. 'Just a feeling. There's no closeness, no intimacy anymore.' His pale-blue eyes flicked up and met mine again. I was frowning at him thoughtfully. Satisfied I was taking him seriously, he went on, 'She's not interested in me any more; hardly listens when I'm talking; doesn't want me near her; flinches when I touch her.' He wiggled his moustache. Fine veins, like purple threads, were visible beneath the skin of his nose and cheeks. Tugging open a drawer under the edge of the decking, he lifted out a tray of small tools and picked up a photograph that had been hidden beneath it. 'James Hamilton, chap I meet at the club, passed that to me and told me to be careful.'

I studied the image of a man of about thirty. Curly blond hair fell around broad muscular shoulders, and hard shapes beneath a white cotton vest said he was seriously into body building. The face was intensely masculine, but large-eyed and gentle looking. He was wielding a chainsaw. Glancing up at Daniel Brody, I tapped the photograph. 'Your friend's suggesting your wife might be involved with him?'

'He was warning me. He caught the blighter with his wife on the bed in their spare room, stark naked and going at it hammer and tongs. She wasn't contrite; just ranted on and on about what an awful husband he'd been and what did he expect? She said it was only a physical thing; that the man was doing it with most of the wives at the houses where he worked.'

'Where he worked?'

'Grow Well Gardening Services. They do a lot of gardens around Stanhope. He's one of their employees. He's worked here.'

'And what did your friend do?'

'Decided to keep it quiet. Gave his wife a dressing down and told the gardening firm he didn't want them to call any more. Couldn't give the bloke a hiding: the randy beggar's more than six feet tall and strong as an ox. And if James had gone for a divorce his wife would have kept the house and half the marital assets. What's a chap to do?'

'Have you done any checking yourself?' I asked.

'Went out on the days I knew he'd be working here and came back unexpectedly.'

'And?'

'Nothing. He was working in the garden. Maria was in the house.'

'Then why go on worrying, Mr Brody? Your wife doesn't seem to be the kind of woman who'd become involved with—'

'Revenge fling,' he muttered. 'I'm worried about her having a revenge fling. If it's not him, it's someone else. And she's out of the house a lot. I've no idea what she's doing.'

'Revenge fling?'

He sniffed through his moustache and looked away, unable to meet my gaze. Then he said, 'When I sold the family firm the new owners kept me on the board: advisory capacity, part of the deal. About a year ago I went to a directors' meeting. Bumped into an old employee, Olga Johnson, and we had lunch together. One of Maria's chums must have seen us. She told Maria how lucky she was to have a husband who took her out to lunch in expensive restaurants: a discreet word to the wise, if you know what I mean. Couldn't mistake Olga for Maria. Olga's a blue-eyed blonde, in her forties now, but a smart dresser and very striking. I was quite open with Maria when she tackled me about it, but I could tell she wasn't happy.'

'And how can I help you with this, Mr Brody?'

'Check her out; find out whether or not she's having an affair.'

'I'm a little unhappy about a possible conflict of interest.'

'Don't follow you, Lomax.'

'She calls me in to find your son, then you instruct me to check her out because you think she's having an affair.'

'Don't see any problem. If you discover she is, just give me the details and I'll confront her. I'll say I've been watching her.'

I didn't like it, but business was slow and probably going to grind to a stop. Abandoning my scruples, I said, 'Shall I bill your wife for locating your son, and you for checking your wife?'

'Makes sense,' he said. 'But no need to bill me. Just let me know the damage and I'll pay cash, OK?'

Nodding, I pulled out my notebook. 'You said your wife's out of the house a lot. Can you give me some details?'

'She's a member of a string quartet; plays the violin. They give concerts. Involves a lot of practising. They used to do most of it here at Tanglewood, but they seem to meet at the other players' houses now.' He mentioned a Dr Janet Smith and a Clarise Cunliffe, gave me their addresses and promised to telephone through the details of the remaining player when he found them.

'And she's involved with St Edmund's Church,' he went on. 'Plays the organ when the regular organist is away and runs a thing called Tiny Tots, every Thursday afternoon, three 'til four.'

'Tiny Tots?'

'They sing songs about Jesus, read Bible stories, make things out of coloured paper; then they have orange juice and biscuits.'

We exchanged a long look.

'You think I'm wasting your time and my money, don't you, Lomax?'

I shrugged. 'She doesn't seem the most likely woman in the world to be cheating, Mr Brody, but I've known vicar's wives who've kicked over the traces.'

'Exactly! And I've got to find out. Can't stop myself imagining her with another man. It's never off my mind.' He pursed his lips and his moustache bristled.

'St Edmund's Church,' I said. 'Where is it?'

'Back towards Barfield: about a quarter of a mile. Turn left and you'll come to a village called Stanhope. Church is there.' He handed me the photograph of the muscular gardener. 'You may as well take this. I've been told he's called Jack. Don't know his surname.' He tugged a wallet from his back pocket and took out a piece of card. 'Programme of concerts for the Eressian String Quartet. They're giving a performance in Barfield Town Hall, Friday evening. And there's a meeting of the Barfield Theological Society tomorrow night; she's a member of that. They listen to lectures in a hall behind the parish church.'

'St John's, Barfield?'

'That's the place: it's opposite your offices.'

'What car does your wife drive?'

'Vauxhall Astra.' He gave me the registration number.

'Don't tell me it's silver.'

'How did you guess?'

'Any colour you want, so long as it's silver. Have you checked the phone accounts?'

'Her mobile's pay-as-you-go, so she's not billed. I've scrolled through the names and numbers on the screen. Apart from Jason and the vicar at St Edmund's, they're all women. And there's nothing unusual on the bill for the landline in the house.' He gave me a smug little smile. 'If it was that simple I'd have done the job myself.'

I smiled back and rose to my feet. 'Unless there's anything else, Mr Brody, I think that just about does it.'

'When will you—'

'I promised your wife I'd drive over to Birmingham this afternoon. Give me two or three days.'

He nodded. 'You'll be discreet? I wouldn't want Maria to know I'm having her followed.'

'I'll be discreet, Mr Brody. What's your mobile number?'

He recited it, watched me note it down, then began to lead me past the chimney stacks that rose up through the roof space. When we reached the far end of the long room we ducked under the decking, he opened a door, and we descended a flight of stairs. Then he stood aside while I stepped out on to a small landing at the top of some rough wooden steps and found myself looking down on the roofs of his wife's Vauxhall and a black BMW.

'Come in this way if you want to see me without disturbing Maria. Door at the end of the garage is open throughout the day. I'm usually in here or in the workshop. Workshop's through the other door at the top of the stairs.'

I extended a hand. He shook it this time, and said, 'Thanks, Lomax. Get back to me as soon as you can.'

Rooks took flight when I slammed the car door. Their frantic cawing was audible over the whine of the engine as I accelerated down the drive. Glancing in the rear-view mirror, I saw Maria Brody standing in one of the big bay windows. She was watching me leave.

TWO

The landlord of the offices had just redecorated the entrance hall. White woodwork, cream walls and dark-grey carpet extended up the stairs to the accountants on the first floor of the converted Georgian town house. The accountants sublet the attic to me: two small offices and a washroom hardly big enough for a dwarf; freezing cold in winter, baking hot in summer.

I took the mail from the box behind my slot then glanced through Melody Brown's reception window. Girls were tapping away at keyboards and a big machine was spewing copies of a brochure into a tray. There was no sign of Melody, so I headed up, padded over carpet as I circled the accountant's landing, then tackled the last flight of stairs. They're still covered with brown linoleum. I've left them that way. You can hear the scrape of approaching feet and it can be useful to know someone's coming up, especially when it's late and the old building's in darkness.

I unlocked the outer door, crossed a waiting room I'd never needed, and stepped into the office. Spring sunshine was fighting its way through grime-streaked dormer windows, and the glazing bars cast hard shadows across a cluttered desk and along a row of old filing cabinets. The cabinets had been abandoned by the accountants when they'd got tired of the arctic winters and quit the place.

St John's, the parish church, is just across the pedestrianized area at the front of the offices. Through a dormer window behind a gap in the parapet wall I can see the clock on the tower. Mrs Brody was supposed to be attending a Theological Society lecture in the church hall tomorrow evening. It wouldn't exhaust me to stroll over and check her out.

Stepping behind the desk, I began to open the mail: a cheque from a London firm for some local legwork, a swatch of junk mail, and a letter from the Benefits Agency. I'd been expecting it. They were telling me benefit fraud in the area had been dramatically reduced and they'd no longer be calling on me to investigate bogus claimants. The account for that morning's court attendance would be the last. I'd been right not to turn away the Brody's business.

Light footsteps approached up the linoleum-covered stairs, high-heels thudded over cord carpet in the waiting room, then Melody breezed in, carrying a tray. 'We've all had pizza, but I thought you'd be late back so I told Rachel to get you a sandwich from the deli. Ham and salad; that OK?'

'Thanks,' I said. 'Ham's fine.' I let my eyes browse over blonde curls; the feminine form under the stylish hounds-tooth patterned suit. Melody's vividly blue eyes had been discreetly made up and her crimson lips were full and shapely, like the red sweater peeping out between the lapels of her unbuttoned jacket.

'Did you visit the Brodys?' Melody wrapped a napkin around the handle of the coffee pot and began to pour. 'The wife seemed quite agitated.'

I nodded. 'Big house, just beyond Stanhope. Two jobs: missing person and a suspected cheater.'

'He looked like a philanderer.' Melody slid the cup across the desk. 'Such lecherous little eyes and that silly moustache he kept wiggling at me. It wouldn't have been quite so embarrassing if his wife hadn't been watching.' Melody suddenly frowned. 'Why did she bring him with her when she was going to talk to you about him cheating?'

'It's the other way around. He thinks his wife's cheating; she thinks their son's missing. He got me on my own before I left; asked me to take a look at his model railway in the attic so we could talk in private.' I bit into the sandwich. Decent ham, crisp salad, plenty of mayonnaise: it was pretty tasty.

'Toy trains in the attic? Sounds a bit nerdy. Is she?'

I gazed into Melody's baby-blues. She was smiling down at me, the kind of condescending smile women give men they've grown accustomed to. 'Is she what?'

'Cheating.'

'After she's practised the violin, given the occasional recital, played the organ at church and read Bible stories to tiny tots, she's probably too bushed for hanky-panky, marital or otherwise, but you never can tell.' I took another bite out of the sandwich. Mayonnaise began to ooze down my chin.

Melody tut-tutted. 'You're going to spoil that nice silk tie. You should take smaller bites.' She picked up the napkin, leaned over the desk and wiped away the dribble. Her eyes suddenly met mine. 'Please don't look at me like that, Paul.'

'Look at you like what?'

'With that longing look. You promised me you wouldn't.'

'That was Christmas. Time passes. You might have had a change of heart.'

'I'm not going to have a change of heart, Paul. You're spoiling things being like this. I want us to carry on just the way we were: a laugh and a joke, a little flirty conversation, nothing serious.'

Dropping the sandwich back on the plate, I said, 'What's wrong with serious?'

'Don't, Paul. You're tormenting yourself and upsetting me.'

Fixing her in a steady look, I said, 'If you don't like serious, why did you invite me over to your place for Christmas?'

The question made her uncomfortable. She brushed a strand of hair from her face and looked down at the tray. 'Because you'd been injured and you were ill, and because I couldn't bear to think of you all alone in that sad little bungalow.'

'I know it's not going to make *Homes and Gardens*, but I wouldn't call it a sad little—'

'It needn't be a sad little bungalow. It could be quite a neat little bungalow. And it's on a nice quiet estate. But you've been a widower for seven years, Paul. Curtains get washed once in a while, walls get decorated, upholstery cleaned, carpets shampooed.'

'You took pity on me; was that it?'

Looking even more uncomfortable, she said, 'Well, yes, I suppose I did.'

'I thought it was because I'd asked you to marry me; because I'd told you I loved you.'

She was blushing now. 'Please don't look at me like that. I really don't deserve such reproachful looks.'

'Maybe you'd be interested if I was a doctor or a lawyer? Someone cultured; someone with an education?'

Tossing the napkin down, she snapped, 'Don't start that again. We've been over this before, but you never listen. I'm happy the way I am. I've got a nice home that's paid for. I've worked up a business I'm proud of: I could sell it tomorrow and retire. My life's ordered. I'm in control of it. I only have myself to please. I don't want marriage. I don't want relationships. I certainly don't want a man who works all hours, who spends weeks in hospital after criminals have given him a beating, who's never going to be there for me, who might not get up again after the next beating.'

'You seemed quite moved when I told you I loved you.'

'Because I knew what it had cost you to say it: you'd rather chew your own eyeballs than tell a woman you love her. And you'd been injured, and it was Christmas, and you were on your own.'

I gazed up at her for a while, then said softly, 'You're telling me there's no chance we'll ever get together?' I hated myself for sounding so pathetic, but I had to ask the question.

Melody let out an exasperated sigh. 'Stop looking at me like that. If you make me cry, if you make me smudge my mascara, I'll—'

'There's no chance?' I demanded.

'No chance, Paul. For the umpteenth time, *no chance*. Our jokey, flirty friendship's fine, but that's as far as it goes.' She forced her mouth into a bright little smile, then turned and headed for the landing. The suit jacket was short, the skirt tight, the sway of her hips captivating. But looking at her didn't give me pleasure any more; it just intensified the pain, reinforced the sense of loss.

She suddenly stopped and turned. 'I almost forgot. Someone at the Magistrates Court phoned, about an hour ago. Said he'd been told to give you a message from the Chairman of the Bench. Pearson: Mrs Emma Pearson. She's invited you to a cocktail party at her home. Glenwood on Milethorne Road. Starts at three.' Melody smiled. 'I'd stick to soft drinks if I were you. She hands out floggings to drink-drivers.'

'And benefit cheats,' I muttered.

When Melody's footsteps had faded down the stairs, I picked up the sandwich, stared at it, then tossed it back on the plate. It was humiliation I was feeling, not hunger. If I hadn't been so captivated by the hair, the face, the husky voice, the shapes under the clothes, I'd have read the signs years ago. Melody hadn't been playing games. She'd really meant it when she'd kept on saying no. And if I hadn't been so pathetically grateful when she asked me to spend Christmas at her place, I might have spared myself a lot of wounded pride. I hadn't begun to get the message until she bunked me down in the spare room and handed me my own soap and towel.

I checked the time. It was almost half-past two. I was tempted to give the cocktail party a miss, drive over to Birmingham and begin the search for Jason. But the formidable Mrs Pearson had recommended me to the Brodys, and her invitation intrigued me. For good reason, she'd distanced herself from me when I'd done a job for her a year earlier. I knew her darkest secrets. I figured I'd be the last person she'd invite to a cocktail party. Curiosity won. I decided to stop off for an hour before heading south to Birmingham.

* * *

A dozen cars were parked outside Glenwood. I slowed and glanced through a gap in a high beech hedge. The driveway was clogged with six or seven more. Cruising on to the end of the line of cars, I eased the Jaguar half on to the grass verge, then strolled back to Mrs Pearson's home. Like I said, her invitation intrigued me. When she'd hired me to get an incriminating video of her husband with his nubile young lover, she'd been careful not to leave any trace of her involvement with me. She'd sent the video to the girl's father. Hours later I'd found her architect husband dead in his office. 'Don't get mad, get even,' she'd said, during one of our clandestine meetings. Mrs Pearson had certainly got even.

I turned through the gap in the hedge and strode up the car-lined driveway. The big front garden was just lawn enclosed by high hedges, no flower beds, no shrubs. The house was large, detached, undistinguished, almost ugly: plain red-brick walls, plastic window frames, a red tiled roof and an arch over the entrance porch. The door opened as I was reaching for the bell.

Mrs Pearson must have been watching me approach up the drive.

She hadn't changed. Maybe she seemed a little more relaxed, her tan a little deeper. Tall and slender, she was looking very smart in a green woollen dress, and her silvery-blonde hair had been drawn tightly back and secured by a broad green ribbon.

'Mr Lomax! It was awfully short notice, and I'm so glad you could come.' She gestured for me to enter.

I gave my shoes a thorough wiping on a mat, then stepped on to soft, beige-coloured carpet. The carpet may have been boringly plain but she'd let herself go with the wallpaper: big yellow flowers on a background of blue leaves. Refined voices and restrained laughter were floating out of an open door. When I glanced towards it I could see a crowd of Barfield's movers and shakers; solid, mostly grey-haired citizens, crammed into a long sitting room that ran from the front to the back of the house. A plump, tired-looking woman in a maid's outfit emerged from another doorway along the hall. She was carrying a silver tray laden with canapés. When I turned, intending to head for the long room, I felt Mrs Pearson slide her arm in mine and hold me back. She led me into a small chintzy reception room on the other side of the hall, shut the door, then came close and looked up at me. She was just as I remembered. Her grey eyes were cold, her skin tight, her brownish-pink lipstick was still leaching into the fine lines around her mouth.

'Before I take you through to the others, I want to thank you, Mr Lomax.'

I raised an eyebrow.

'For your discretion. I read the police reports; those men who killed Andrew almost killed you, too, but you didn't say a word about my engaging you, or about the video. I was so vulnerable, and a person in my position, a magistrate, can't afford to be touched by scandal. I'm very grateful.' Her voice was unusually soft. It didn't have that harsh, penetrating tone she used for harassing court officials and cowing witnesses in the dock.

'You paid me to do a job, Mrs Pearson. Absolute discretion was part of the service.'

'I didn't pay you to be almost beaten to death. I really am very grateful.' Glad she'd got her little talk over, she showed me her teeth in a smile that didn't quite reach her eyes, then said brightly, 'Let's join the others.'

We crossed over to the crowded sitting room. With her arm still linked in mine, she began to introduce me to her chattering guests. I recognized a couple of lawyers, the architect who'd taken over her husband's practice and a surgeon who'd worked on me at the hospital. The others were business and professional people I'd never seen before. They were displaying the feigned affability of men and woman drawn together by self-interest and a sense of shared status. Everyone was talking, no one was listening, so no one looked bored. Mrs Pearson just gave them my Christian name. She made no mention of how I earned a living. They responded with curt nods and tight little smiles. Somehow they seemed to know I wasn't networking material.

When we'd made our way to some French windows that over-looked a long back garden, she turned me towards a youth with a very spotty face. His white cotton gloves were clean, but his black bow tie needed tweaking. He held out a tray of glasses. Recalling Melody's advice, I took a flute of orange juice.

'Has the dark-haired lady rejoined the party, Simon?' Mrs Pearson's voice had taken on its normal cutting tone.

'Not yet, Mrs Pearson.' He glanced through the French windows. 'She's still by the summerhouse.'

Crow's feet spread from the corners of Mrs Pearson's eyes as they narrowed in a myopic stare. 'So she is.' Mrs Pearson beamed up at me. 'Marlena's a smoker, Mr Lomax. She's gone into the garden so she can indulge the habit. I feel awfully guilty letting her go out there on her own but her cigarettes would make the house smell for days. Would you be awfully kind and take a drink and some canapés out to her; introduce yourself and keep her company for me?'

Shrugging, I smiled and said, 'Sure. Why not?' Talking to just one of Mrs Pearson's guests would be less hassle than trying to work the crowd in her big sitting room.

Emma Pearson glanced around, caught the maid's eye and beckoned her over. 'Put some things on a plate, Janet. Mr Lomax is going to take them out to the lady in the garden.' She turned towards the youth with the bow tie. 'Get the whisky decanter from the sideboard and pour a good measure into a tumbler. And pour a little water into a jug.'

I felt Mrs Pearson's arm sliding back into mine. She continued the introductions, breezily interrupting the chatter. Minutes later, the grey-haired maid returned with a tray laden with a tiny cut-glass water jug, a tumbler of whisky and things from the buffet on a fancy green and gold plate. I found a space for my flute of orange juice and took the tray from the maid. Mrs Pearson pushed open the French windows and I stepped down on to the patio.

'Would you escort her back for me, Mr Lomax, when she's finished her cigarette?'

I began to wonder if Mrs Pearson had invited me over just to do a little fetching and carrying. 'Sure,' I called back, then stepped off the paved area and headed out across the grass.

The summerhouse was an exotic affair: white painted barley-sugar columns, powder-blue lattice panels and a shingle roof. Facing down the garden, away from the house, it stood on a low timber platform that was enclosed by a handrail on a fretted balustrade. I climbed a couple of steps and walked round to the front. She was standing, her hands on the rail, gazing down the long garden. Fairly tall, very shapely; her dress had a grey velvet top with long tight sleeves and a skirt made of layers of filmy material that spilled over her hips and floated around her thighs and legs like a column of grey smoke. Dark-brown hair fell in waves below her shoulders. She turned when she heard my feet on the decking.

'Marlena?'

She smiled at me, but her huge dark eyes were remote, perhaps a little sad.

'Lomax: Paul Lomax. Mrs Pearson asked me to bring you a drink.'

The big eyes held mine and her smile widened. A pale complexion made her vermilion lipstick and dark eye-shadow seem almost theatrical. 'That's awfully sweet of you.' Her voice was low, not husky like Melody's, just soft and low. Her German accent was pronounced. 'Is it the orange juice?'

'The whisky. The orange juice is mine.'

Long lashes swept up. 'You don't look like an orange-juice drinker.' She stepped over to a bench that curved around the inside of the summerhouse and sat down.

I joined her and settled the tray on the bench between us.

Marlena clicked open a grey snakeskin clutch bag that matched her delicate little snakeskin shoes and grey stockings, and took out a black box. *Sobranie Black Russian* was embossed in gold on its lid. Pale slender fingers with vividly red nails flicked it open and took out a black cigarette. Sliding the box back into her bag, she rummaged around, found a stubby ivory holder, pushed the gold tip of the cigarette into it and placed it between her lips. Her fingers dipped into the bag again and emerged with a lighter. She pressed the igniter a couple of times, then said, 'This thing's hope-less. I can never get it to—'

31

'May I?'

'Please.' She passed it to me. It was chunky, fashioned in the Art Deco style, and closely set diamonds spelled out *Marlena* along its gold side. I eased the gas release lever over and when I pressed the button flame stabbed out. With her hand over the low square bodice of her dress, holding it against her breasts, she leaned towards the flame and lit her cigarette. I handed her the lighter. She dropped it into her bag. 'Thanks,' she said. The smoke she blew from her nose was sweet-smelling and aromatic. 'You don't mind me smoking?'

'I find it pleasant.'

'Mrs Pearson asks smokers to go outside. She has rather strong views about smokers.'

'She has strong views about most things.'

Marlena laughed, picked up the tumbler and sipped at her whisky. She was taking it neat; she hadn't bothered with the water. She wasn't bothering with the canapés, either. 'So, Mr Lomax,' she said, 'what are you captain of, or president of, or chairman of?'

I gave her a questioning look.

'Golf club, or Rotary, or Police Committee, or Chamber of Commerce?'

Laughing softly, I said, 'They'd black-ball me, Marlena. They wouldn't let me through the door.'

Huge dark eyes ranged over me. She took another pull at the cigarette, blew smoke into the air, then said, 'I think they'd welcome you in the Inner Wheel.'

'Inner Wheel?'

'Ladies Rotary.' She ran her eyes over me again. 'I think they'd make you very welcome.'

'Would I have to wear a frock and slingbacks?'

She laughed. 'I think they'd prefer you just the way you are.' She gazed at me from under lashes that were so long and dark and curly they had to be false, then blew smoke from her nose and said, 'You've worked down a mine.'

'And how do you know that?' I figured she ought to be doing my job.

'The blue marks on your cheek, on the back of your hands: coal dust in old wounds. I come from an East German mining town. I am accustomed to the injuries of miners.'

'I worked down a mine in Rossthorpe, a village about five miles west of Barfield. My wife persuaded me to leave the job when we got married.'

'You're married?'

'Widower.'

'Any children?' She sipped at her whisky. Her voice was matter-of-fact. She wasn't ladling out phoney sympathy.

'A daughter. She died with my wife. Juvenile joy-rider; head-on collision.'

'Was it long ago?'

'Seven years. My daughter would have been fourteen this year.'

She drew on the short ivory holder, inhaled the smoke, then tilted her head back and blew it into the air. 'And what do you do now, Mr Lomax, now you no longer work down a mine?' Making herself more comfortable on the bench, she crossed her legs. The swish of silk on silk was electrifying. Her big eyes were gazing at me thoughtfully.

Swallowing hard, I said, 'When I left the colliery I got a job with an insurance company; trained as a claims investigator and loss adjuster. I launched out on my own after my wife died.' I didn't say private investigator. Mrs Pearson wouldn't want her guests to know she'd been involved with a private investigator. Trying to jump the conversation on to fresh tracks, I said, 'You ask a lot of questions, Marlena.'

She laughed. 'Just curious about a guest who's not been a

captain of the golf club or a president of Rotary. Are you a member of anything?'

I shook my head. I was trying to guess her age. Her pale skin was unlined, her eyes clear and luminous, her dark hair gleamed; she'd never be more beautiful than she was now. She was a woman in full bloom, perfect, at her very best; immaculately groomed, expensively dressed. I guessed she'd be about thirty-five, but I could have been out by five years either way. The smoke from her black cigarette was drifting over to me, almost masking the fragrance of the perfume she was wearing.

'And you don't play golf?' she said.

'Couldn't handle the excitement. And I don't think I could spare the time.'

Marlena took another pull at her cigarette and sipped her whisky. Lipstick, red as blood, had stained the ivory holder and the rim of her glass. She was displaying a lot of shadowy cleavage; her voluptuous breasts rose and fell as she took in a breath then exhaled a cloud of smoke. 'My husband is a clever man, Mr Lomax. His shrewdness has made him rich. He once said to me, "Be courteous to those who count themselves amongst the great and the good, but don't befriend them or they'll exasperate you with their vain pomposity, then bore you to death with their banality." I think you have things in common with my husband.'

I smiled across the tray at her while I tried to make some sense of what she'd just said. Looking at her wasn't a chore. She wasn't quite the most beautiful woman I'd ever seen, but she smouldered with a kind of elemental sexuality that probably made her the most attractive.

She returned my smile, then turned her head and looked down the long garden. I followed her gaze, saw a tall, muscular man, wearing jeans and a tight cotton vest. His long blond hair was tied back and he was digging up shrubs and tossing them on to a pile.

His movements were controlled and effortless. Marlena puffed at her cigarette, then said, 'Jack the gardener. Do you think he keeps a pump by the bed so he can inflate himself every morning?'

'Steroids,' I said. 'Steroids and the gym. He didn't get a body like that digging up bushes.' And then I recognized him: he was the man in the photograph Daniel Brody had given me. I asked, 'Does he cultivate your garden?'

She laughed softly. 'I think one has to be a member of the Inner Wheel to qualify for Jack's services. Anyway, my husband employs a full-time gardener.' She pulled the butt of her cigarette from the holder, crushed it on the sole of her shoe, then dropped it through a gap in the decking. 'I'd better get back inside. My husband wouldn't want me to neglect the great and the good.'

When I rose, I reached for the tray.

'Leave it,' she said sharply. 'We're guests, not tray carriers. Mrs Pearson can send someone out for it.'

I led her around to the houseward side of the gazebo and offered her my hand while she negotiated the steps. She took it. She seemed to like being helped. When we headed across the grass to the house I felt her slide her hand around my arm.

'I hope you don't mind, Mr Lomax, but it's not easy to walk on spongy grass in high heels.' She laughed softly, tossed her long dark hair and came closer. 'And Barfield's great and good are watching us through the French windows; watching me walk from the summerhouse on the arm of a tall, dark, handsome man.' She laughed again, and her German accent became guttural as she said, 'The ladies of the Inner Wheel might never stop talking about it.'

THREE

When I left her, Marlena was mingling with the crowd in the long sitting room, charming wives, ignoring their husbands' admiring glances. I told Mrs Pearson I had a meeting in Birmingham and took my leave. When she saw me out, she thanked me again for being discreet and I walked off down the drive still wondering why she'd bothered to put me on the guest list. Ten minutes later, I was on the motorway, heading south.

Junction 28 was signposted up ahead. I turned off the M1, skirted Derby, then headed for Birmingham along the A38. It took me through the heart of the city, past the university campus. When the Chamberlain clock tower was in the rear-view mirror, I left the crush of evening commuters behind and plunged into an old residential area where row after row of small terrace houses ran off the main road. I was looking for Shinley Street and the house where Maria Brody thought her son was living. After cruising past a newsagent's, a hairdresser's, an off-licence and a corner shop, I saw the nameplate, mounted high up on grimy old brickwork. Braking hard, I swung the Jaguar down a roadway narrowed by parked cars and began looking for number 78. The houses were built up to the back of the pavements. Here and there glass sparkled, plastic front doors gleamed and net curtains were snow white, but they were mostly uncared-for scruffy-looking places, where students slept off hangovers and cooked the occasional meal.

Someone had painted a big 78 on the brickwork beside a front door. I found a space for the car and walked back. Brown curtains were drawn across a ground-floor bay window and the grating was missing from a coal chute beside the front step. I gave the faded green paint a pounding then glanced around while I waited. The light was beginning to fade and a cold wind was making litter rustle along the pavement. From an open attic window in a house on the opposite side of the street, I could hear the sound of chords being struck. Someone was practising the base guitar. An old car rattled past, heading towards the main road. Turning back to the door, I gave it another pounding and a woman's voice called, 'Coming; I'm coming.' Seconds later, it opened a couple of inches and a pair of blue eyes flashed at me around the edge. A towel was wrapped around her hair and I could just see a pink bathrobe. 'I was in the bath,' she snapped reprovingly.

'Sorry,' I said, and smiled. 'I'm looking for Jason Brody. I understand he lives here.'

'He did, but he found another place. He went there at the start of the new term.'

'Do you have his address?'

'Who's asking?'

I took a card from my wallet and handed it to her. 'Lomax: Paul Lomax. His mother's asked me to locate him. She's not been able to contact him for some time and she's worried.'

The girl sniffed. 'Mothers!' She handed back the card. 'You'd better come inside.' She opened the door wider and I stepped into a narrow passage. The door slammed and I followed her into what appeared to be a communal sitting room. It was shabby, but clean and tidy. The small television, sagging sofa and tired-looking armchair reminded me of home. A gas fire, hissing in an old tiled fireplace, was making the room pleasantly warm. She crossed over to it and began to sift through papers and envelopes heaped on the mantelpiece.

'His new address is here somewhere. He gave it to Samantha.'

'Who's Samantha?'

'We shared the house: Samantha, Jason and me. I'm Julie. Rent's a bit of a bind now Jason's gone, splitting it two ways instead of three, but it's not easy to find someone else, mid-year; not someone you'd be prepared to share with.' She moved on to the second pile of papers.

'Place looks comfortable. Why did he leave?'

She turned and frowned at me. 'You ask a lot of questions.'

'It's what I do for a living.' I gave her a big smile. Four more years and it could have been my daughter standing there in the pink bathrobe.

The girl turned back to the piles of letters. 'He said he wanted somewhere quieter, but I'm not sure that was the reason.' She laughed. 'Can't imagine anywhere quieter than this. It's like a graveyard. He used to write a lot. Mostly poetry. He's had quite a few poems published. His tutor warned him about it.'

'Why should he warn him?'

'Getting published too soon; exposing immature work.'

'If he didn't leave because he wanted somewhere quieter, why do you think he left?'

'Probably his girlfriend. Samantha came back one afternoon and heard voices in his room. Well, not so much voices as noises.'

'Noises?'

She turned. A blush was touching her cheeks and she was frowning irritably. 'You really do ask the most obvious questions. Lovemaking noises. Throes-of-passion noises.'

'Ah.' I smiled my understanding and watched her blush deepen. She turned back to the mantelpiece and began to work through the last pile.

'Thing was, Samantha was in here when they came down the stairs. His girlfriend was wearing a hijab and one of those ankle-length black dress things. She was Asian. Samantha said she had a beautiful face. The girl was shocked when she saw Samantha; scared almost. She just turned and ran out of the front door. Jason ran after her calling "Halima, Halima." I think he found a new place because she wouldn't come here again after Samantha had seen her … Got it!' She turned and began to read an address someone had scribbled on the back of an envelope. 'Harroven Road, number 34.' She glanced up. 'It overlooks a park.'

I noted the address down. 'Why wouldn't she come here again?'

Another stupid question. Julie rolled her eyes to show her exasperation. 'She was a Muslim girl. She wouldn't want to be seen with a non-Muslim white boy. And she'd be ruined if it got out that she'd been alone with a man in his room.'

'Have you bumped into Jason since he left?'

'Once or twice.'

'Did he seem OK?'

Julie shrugged. 'I suppose so. He's rather shy; better at writing than talking. Always a bit tense and nervous.'

'When was the last time you saw him?'

'Mmm … about ten days ago. Students' Union meeting. Not to talk to; he was on the other side of the room, but he looked OK. He's reading English, I'm doing maths, so we wouldn't normally meet one another.'

Tapping my notebook, I said, 'Thanks for the address, Julie. I'm very grateful.'

As she took me down the narrow passageway that led to the front door, she said, 'What's his mother like?'

'Pleasant, cultured; she's a musician.'

'Nice house, plenty of money?'

'You could say that.'

'Thought so.' She tugged open the sticking front door. 'Jason told me he'd been to public school. There's a lot of them at Birmingham.'

'A lot of them?'

'Public school types. He was different, though. They're usually so confident, so self-assured, but he was shy and withdrawn. Sweet, really. Samantha fancied him like mad. She was gutted when the beautiful Asian girl came on the scene. You won't tell him that, will you?'

I shook my head. 'Do you know where Harroven Road is?'

'Go back up the street and turn left. Keep on for about a quarter of a mile then turn left again, into a road that runs alongside a park. That's Harroven Road.'

Street lamps were flickering on when I began to motor past the park. The houses here were bigger, semi-detached, set back from the road behind privet hedges and small front gardens that were mostly well kept. There were hardly any numbers on gates or house doors, so I pulled over on the park side of the road and counted back from the one number I could see. A young Asian man, wearing a red quilted jacket and red baseball cap and carrying a red pizza box was hurrying along the far side of the street. He pushed at a gate and strode towards a front door. I checked the house numbers again. He was calling at number 34.

He rested his finger on the bell. A moment later a light came on in the upstairs bay window and a fair-haired young man with a longish, bespectacled face appeared. When the guy in the baseball cap held up the pizza box the young man shook his head and waved his hands from side to side in a not-at-this-address gesture. The delivery guy responded by brandishing the box and pointing at it aggressively. The young man I'd taken to be Jason Brody disappeared. A few seconds later, the door opened.

I caught a sudden flurry of movement in the rear view mirror.

Four Asian men were spilling out of a white Mercedes. They dashed across the road, jostling one another as they pushed through the gate and ran down the path. Jason was trying to close the door, but the pizza delivery guy had his shoulder against it. The door suddenly swung open and he almost fell inside. Jason Brody had let it go and retreated into the house.

Reaching between the seats, I grabbed my pick-axe handle, stepped out of the car, and ran towards the house. I could hear the shouting before I reached the garden gate: a chorus of voices, all yelling abuse and accusations. 'Depraved dog: you dishonoured my cousin. You violated her. You brought shame on our family. You're going to pay, you bloody white bastard—'

When I stepped through the doorway I saw a terrified Jason, half-way up the stairs, kicking out at a couple of men who were trying to drag him down. A bearded guy, wielding a butcher's knife, climbed on to a telephone table, grabbed the balusters and heaved himself up. He was level with Jason now. When he lunged with the knife, Jason flung himself against the wall, then slipped. Clutching hands grabbed his ankles.

I brought the pick-axe handle thudding down on the pizza man's baseball cap. He dropped without a sound and I strode past him into the hall. A tall, hard-muscled guy in a flower-pattern shirt suddenly noticed me. Wild-eyed, mouth ugly with hate, he lunged towards me, his hand wrapped around the handle of a long knife. He made a slashing motion, I stepped aside and swung the makeshift cudgel. He ducked, then came at me, screaming. The next swing caught him full in the face. I felt bone give and angry screams turned into moans as he sagged back against the wall.

One of the men trying to drag Jason down the stairs released his legs and glared across at me. I closed in. When I hoisted up the cudgel something shattered and the light went out. We circled one another in the gloom, crunching over broken glass. After making a few threatening movements, I brought it down. He jerked aside, it missed his head, smashed into his shoulder, and he dropped the knife and started howling.

Jason kicked his legs free, scrambled up to the landing on his hands and knees and disappeared into the darkness. I heard a door slam. The guy who'd been holding him was crouching on the stairs; the bearded man with the knife was still clinging to the balusters. They were eying me warily. I tightened my grip on the pick-axe handle. Fear and exertion and the adrenalin rush were making my breathing loud and harsh. We glared at one another, then the bearded man dropped down from the balusters, snatched up the flimsy telephone table and held it in front of him while he edged towards me, stabbing at the air with the butcher's knife. Maybe he tripped over a body, maybe his feet tangled in the telephone cord; suddenly he stumbled and I swung the pick-axe handle as if I were hitting a ball. It caught him full on the side of the head and sent him reeling. He dropped the knife and table and fell to his knees. The man on the stairs held his hands up, palms outwards, in a gesture of submission.

When I'd got my breathing under control I snarled, 'Why are you harassing Jason Brody?'

'The dirty bastard violated my cousin. He stole her innocence, raped her, brought shame on me and my family.'

'Raped her?'

'He must have taken her by force. Halima would never have allowed a dirty kafir near her.' The man was almost sobbing with rage.

'Your cousin told you that, did she?'

'The pig raped her.' He screamed the words at me. 'She is defiled and my family is dishonoured.'

'If you think Halima's been raped you should go to the police.'

'And bring more shame on us? Do you think we want the whole

bloody country to know some white bastard violated one of our women, lose all respect in the community? We deal with this our way.'

'Not this time,' I growled. 'Go to the police if you think he forced himself on her.' I pressed my back against the wall and hoisted up the pick-axe handle. 'Get your family out of here, and don't touch any knives.' He eyed me from the stairs, but didn't move. 'Out!' I yelled. 'Get out.'

He edged around me warily, muttered something to the guy who could still stand, then together they helped the others to their feet. The pizza man had to be almost carried down the path. I followed them to the gate, watched them limp across the road and pile into the car. Hands shaking, I found my pocket book and noted down the registration number as they were driving off.

With the front door closed and locked, I returned along the unlit hall and climbed into the darkness at the top of the stairs. I pressed a switch. A fluorescent light flickered on. Pale-green walls, dark-green cord carpet, a red fire extinguisher: the place was cleaner and neater than the usual run of student accommodation. Cylinder locks secured doors at either end of the landing. Through an open door at the top of the stairs I could see white tiles.

I called out, 'Jason?' then heard a click as the light went out. It was on a timer. I pushed the switch again and knocked on the nearest door. 'Your mother hired me to find you, Jason. She's worried about you.' I listened to my own heavy breathing for a few seconds, then headed along the landing and tapped on the door at the end. 'Those guys have gone, Jason. You're safe now. Your mother sent me to—'

A chain rattled, the door swung open and a tall figure with untidy hair blinked out at me through steel-rimmed glasses. There was a faint click and the place was plunged into darkness. 'Switch your light on, Jason. You're safe, they've gone.'

His hand brushed down the wall and an unshaded bulb glared behind him. When I advanced into the room he kept backing away from me until his legs hit the bed, then he sat down, his body shaking. He was wearing an open-necked shirt and an old-fashioned sleeveless blue pullover. His grey trousers were neatly pressed, his boat-like trainers clean and new-looking. 'You said my mother sent you. Why did she send you?' He spoke in a precise, clipped way that made him sound a little pompous. Shock was making his voice waver; shrill then deep, like an adolescent's.

'She's worried about you. When you didn't answer her calls she thought something might have happened.' I found my mobile, keyed in 999, then smiled at him. 'Seems she had good reason to be.'

'What are you doing?'

'Calling the police.'

'I've spoken to the police. They're not interested.'

'You've been attacked before?'

He shook his head. 'I was worried about someone.'

'Someone?'

'A friend: a girlfriend.'

Phone pressed to my ear, I glanced around the room while I waited for the operator. Single bed, wardrobe, chest of drawers, all old and drab; a cheap self-assembly desk, and some more green cord carpet. Jason's frightened eyes blinked at me through big lenses as I crossed over to the bay window. The park was in darkness now. Beyond grass and trees, swings and climbing frames, lights were gleaming in the windows of distant houses.

A female voice said, 'Which service?' I told her the police, then looked at Jason and asked, 'Why were you worried about a girlfriend?'

A lock of hair had fallen over his eyes. He was hugging his shoulders and rocking to and fro; trying to get his trembling under control. 'She's not been to lectures. I've not seen her for almost two weeks. The police said they'd look into it, but I could tell they weren't interested.'

Another female voice, this one with a strong Birmingham accent, asked my name and took the address. When she asked what the problem was, I said, 'Forced entry and attempted assault. Five Asian guys. Drove off in a white Mercedes, registration FD51UHO.'

* * *

The white cotton blouse with its long sleeves and plain turned-down collar looked clean and freshly ironed, the light-brown hair was a little tousled, the small hands that held the statement had carefully manicured nails. A plastic nameboard on the desk said she was Detective Chief Inspector Helen Houlihan. She glanced up and eyed me steadily while her mouth slowly shaped itself into a smile. 'A pick-axe handle, Mr Lomax: do you always carry one in your car?'

I shook my head. 'Replacement. I've got to dig up a soakaway. Bought it at a builders' merchants about a week ago. Put it in the back of the car and forgot it.'

'You've got a receipt?'

'It wasn't for the business, so I didn't keep the receipt.'

'Business ...' Her eyes dropped down to the typed sheet. 'You're a private investigator. Offices on the top floor of number 15, St John's Walk, Barfield.'

I nodded.

She laid the sheet on the desk and picked up another. 'And you were hired to find Jason Brody of Tanglewood House near Stanhope.' She glanced up. 'Where's Stanhope?'

'Small village to the south of Barfield,' Jason muttered. DCI

Houlihan smiled again. I'd no idea what she was smiling at, but the smile made her mouth look very kissable.

'Don't you think you've been rather unwise, Mr Brody, becoming involved with a young Muslim girl?'

'We're in love,' he retorted, as if that vindicated everything. His deep voice was steady now; he was getting over his fright.

She glanced down at the statement. 'And you opened the door for the pizza delivery man?'

'He was getting angry; insisting that I'd ordered it.'

'Did you?'

'Did I what?'

'Order it?'

'No. It was just a ruse to get me to open the door. When I'd opened it he leaned against it until the others came and pushed their way into the house. I've repeated this about a dozen times to the man who took the statement,' Jason muttered irritably.

'When they got inside, did they actually hurt you?'

'They were coming after me with knives, trying to grab me on the stairs. They—'

'I've read all that, Mr Brody. Did they hurt you?'

'No,' he muttered grudgingly. 'Mr Lomax came in and scared them off.'

DCI Houlihan's brown eyes rested on me. The smile on the kissable lips widened. 'Scared them off! You were fortunate your mother hired him. Even more fortunate he was waiting outside the house when they came to get you.' A frown chased away the smile. 'Did you know they were coming, Mr Lomax? Were you lying in wait with your pick-axe handle?'

It was my turn to smile. 'Four healthy young guys, armed with knives? If I'd known they were going to turn up, I'd have given your boys a call.'

There was a respectful tapping on the door and a young

policeman came in with a note. He walked over to the desk. 'Tracy took this down a couple of minutes ago, ma'am. I thought you might want to read it.'

Smiling up at him, she said, 'Thanks, Stanley,' then glanced at the slip of paper. After he'd left the room, she read, 'Four Asian men went into accident and emergency at the Ringway hospital about two hours ago. They're being attended to now: fractured jaw, fractured skull, concussion, broken arm, dislocated shoulder. They said they'd been assaulted by a large gang of drunken white males. Surprise attack. Said they wouldn't be able to recognize any of them. They arrived at the hospital in a white Mercedes. No one's checked the registration number, but we could get it from the surveillance cameras in the car-park.' She glanced at Jason. 'Do you want to press charges?'

'Would it do any good?'

'Maybe we should leave that decision until you've had a word with your parents,' I said, then glanced at DCI Houlihan. 'He doesn't have to decide now, does he?'

She shook her head. 'No, but he's got to make his mind up quickly. Hours not days.'

'It could be bad for Halima,' Jason muttered.

'Bad for Halima?' DCI Houlihan frowned at him, then relaxed back in her chair, stretched her legs under the desk and crossed them at the ankles. The hem of her black skirt just covered her knees, opaque black stockings were tight over plump calves, black shoes were laced around tiny feet.

'If I press charges God knows what they'll do to her. I phoned the police a couple of days ago and told someone she wasn't attending lectures; that she'd disappeared. They said they'd look into it, but I could tell they weren't interested. Someone must have told her family about us and they're keeping her away from university.'

'Do you have her address?'

Jason shook his head. 'Her home's in Leeds. She lives at her uncle's house in Birmingham during term time. She wouldn't give me her address. She has to be careful because they watch her all the time; her cousin, Ghinwa, travels with her to the campus and meets her when she leaves.'

'She was chaperoned! How did you two manage to see one another?'

'In the dining hall at first, and at lectures; we're both reading English.' He looked down at his hands and his voice was almost inaudible as he said, 'We sometimes went to my flat in the afternoons.'

'Sometimes?' DCI Houlihan was trying hard not to smile.

'Pretty often this term. I found a better flat away from the usual student accommodation. Halima was always edgy about being seen by someone who knew her.'

'What's Halima's surname?'

'Fahim.'

Houlihan noted it on the slip of paper. 'After what's happened, I'll have her situation checked out. If we can't get her term-time address from the university, we'll contact her parents in Leeds.'

'You'll do it tonight?' Jason was begging her.

'Tomorrow. Phone this number after eleven.' She scribbled on a pad, tore off the sheet and slid it across the desk. 'Ask to speak to Detective Inspector Anderson. He'll be able to give you any information we have.'

Suppressing a yawn, I mumbled, 'If there's nothing else—'

DCI Houlihan looked at me and shook her head. I rose to my feet, dog tired and dreading the drive home. Jason reached over and picked up the slip of paper, then we headed for a door in a glazed partition. Beyond it, I could see men and women, mostly uniformed, working at desks, filling out forms, taking calls, making calls.

'Mr Brody—'

We glanced back from the doorway.

'When you call tomorrow, tell Detective Inspector Anderson whether or not you're pressing charges. I don't want to leave it any later than that if we're going to carry out an investigation.'

* * *

It was almost 3 a.m. when I turned off the motorway and headed for the tiny village to the south of Barfield. Jason had fallen asleep. He wasn't much of a talker, so I didn't miss the conversation. Maybe if I'd been able to discuss Larkin and Auden, or Nabokov's novels, he'd have been more companionable.

A signpost flared in the headlamp beams. I turned right and headed on down a winding, misty-dark lane bordered by over-grown hedges. Minutes later I was driving through Stanhope. The car's lights washed over a row of cottages, a pub, a village shop; they touched a lych gate, but they didn't reach the old stone church lurking in the darkness beyond the graveyard. After cruising past a clutter of modern bungalows we emerged into open countryside. Another mile and I saw Tanglewood; its gleaming lights made it seem like a distant ship floating on a sea of mist. Before leaving Birmingham I'd called Maria Brody on her mobile, just as she'd asked, and told her I was bringing her son home. I hadn't told her about his little adventure.

Braking gently, I turned through the gateway, heard gravel peppering the underside of the car as I swept up the drive. The front door opened before the car had rolled to a stop. Maria, dressed in black ski pants and a baggy grey sweater, hurried over. I climbed out, went round to the passenger side and opened the door for her. She bent over her sleeping son, murmured his name and shook him until he woke. He unfolded his lanky frame from the car and stood beside her. She wrapped her arms around him and pressed her cheek against his chest. He just stood there, still dazed with sleep, his long arms hanging loosely by his sides. She pushed herself away and looked up at him. 'Are you all right, Jason?'

'I'm OK, Mum. I'm just tired … so tired.'

'Why not let him go up to bed, Mrs Brody. We need a few minutes together before I leave, and Jason can talk to you in the morning.'

'Of course.' She wrapped her arm around him and steered him into the house. I followed.

'Your father's asleep,' she whispered, as they crossed the hall. 'He doesn't know you're home. Your bed's made and the heating's been on in your room.' At the foot of the stairs she released him. I heard a mumbled, 'Thanks, Mum,' and we watched him shuffle up the stairs.

Turning towards me, Maria said, 'Coffee?'

'I'd kill for a cup.'

We went into the room she called the library; the room where a grand piano stood in one of the huge bay windows. She sat on the long sofa, I took one of the armchairs. An insulated coffee jug and three cups were arranged on the table between us. 'I was expecting you a couple of hours ago,' she said. 'Milk and sugar?'

'Black, two sugars. I had to involve the police. We had to make statements.'

'Police! You told me he was all right when you phoned.'

'He is all right, Mrs Brody. Exhausted and a little shaken up, maybe, but he's unharmed.' And then I watched her face become pale and still beneath the bottle-tan as I recounted the events of the evening.

'You say four men were attacking him?'

'Five with the pizza delivery guy.'

She stared at me, eyes wide and uncomprehending. 'Why on earth would anyone want to hurt Jason?'

'The note you found in the book, from the girl called Halima: she's Asian, a Muslim. The family must have found out she was involved with Jason. They'd be pretty upset about it.'

She cupped her hands over her knees and leaned towards me. 'They might not like it, Mr Lomax, but this is England. They can't go around assaulting people.'

I gulped at the hot coffee. 'They're intensely protective towards their womenfolk, Mrs Brody. Especially unmarried daughters and sisters. Girls aren't supposed to be in the company of men they're not related to. Halima's involvement with your son would have aroused strong feelings.'

'What about the girl? Where is she?'

'Jason thinks she might still be in Birmingham; living with her uncle. The police said they'd check and gave him a number to ring later today.' I drank some more of the coffee. 'Or she could have gone home. I understand her parents live in Leeds.'

'What if she doesn't want to return home? What if she wants to continue her education; to be with Jason? That's a terrible abuse of her rights.'

'Traditions, Mrs Brody. It's cultural.' I drained the cup, slid it on to the table and rose to my feet. 'The police asked if Jason wanted to press charges. I said that decision was best left until he'd spoken to you and his father, but they want your answer today.'

'Daniel doesn't know he's home. God, I'm dreading breakfast. He's going to be so nasty and unpleasant. I simply can't bear it when he's like that.'

I began to head out. 'If you'll excuse me, Mrs Brody. It's late and I—'

'Of course.' She rose, followed me from the room, then led me across the hall. 'I'm so sorry, Mr Lomax, I forgot to thank you. But it's been quite overwhelming, and I'm sure you know how grateful I am.' She opened the heavy oak door. 'What do you think Jason should do?'

'Concentrate on his studies. Try to forget the whole thing. And before he goes back to Birmingham he ought to talk to the student welfare people, tell them what's happened and ask for accommodation on the campus. He shouldn't go back to the flat in Harroven Road.'

'But he probably loves the girl. How can he just *forget the whole thing*?' I didn't speak, just stepped out into the cold darkness of the early morning and looked back at her. Her lips were trembling and her voice was low and tearful as she added, 'It's so easy to become lost in the country of love, Mr Lomax. There are no charts to guide us. One can lose one's soul as well as one's heart.'

FOUR

My mobile woke me. I reached out from under the duvet and groped for it on the bedside table.

'Where the devil are you?' It was Melody. 'Your phone's never stopped ringing. Everyone wants you.'

'Everyone?' I rolled on to my back, yawned and scratched my chest.

'Maria Brody phoned just after eight, her husband phoned a few minutes ago, and Abraham Feinburg's butler's called twice in between.'

'Abraham Feinburg? Who's Abraham Feinburg? And you're kidding me; only the aristocracy have butlers.'

'Abraham Feinburg has one, too, and Abraham wants you to pay him a call. His butler said eleven o'clock would be convenient. I said I'd try and reach you. Do you want me to call back and cancel?'

I groped for my watch on the bedside table. It showed a couple of minutes before ten. 'Is he local?'

'The Old Vicarage at Brenton.'

'Where's Brenton?'

'The butler said head out of town on the Retford Road and turn right at the roundabout after Hollingford. Brenton's three miles on from there.'

'Don't cancel.' I swung my feet to the floor. 'I'll make it.'

'Where are you?'

'I was in bed.'

'Bed!'

'Didn't get back from Birmingham until four.'

'And what were you doing in Birmingham until four?'

'Searching for Jason Brody.'

An exasperated sigh came down the line. 'Did you find him?'

'Found him and took him home to mother.'

* * *

The Old Vicarage at Brenton was big enough for a bishop. Its crenellated parapet hid most of the roof and ivy hid a good deal of the stonework. Windows on the ground floor were tall, and a pediment and pilasters framed an ornate fanlight and panelled front door. White paintwork gleamed, but the old stonework was powdery and crumbling. A brass bell pull was let into one of the pilasters. When I gave it a tug I heard a distant jangling. Seconds later, the red front door opened and a short white-haired guy in a black jacket and pinstripes was giving me a steady look. 'Lomax,' I said. 'I understand Mr Abraham Feinburg is expecting me.'

'Thank you for calling, sir.' He spoke slowly, in a deep velvety voice that made him sound like a hypnotist inducing a trance. 'Mr Feinburg instructed me to take you to him the moment you arrived. Would you step inside and follow me?' He led me, at a dignified pace, across a hall big enough to need a fireplace, then we turned down a wide corridor. I glanced into rooms through the occasional open door. Carpets were thick, curtains were heavy and held back by silk ropes, ceilings were ornate and wedding-cake white, and walls were papered in an elegantly restrained way. Flowers were everywhere: in front of gilded mirrors, on little mahogany tables, in recesses. Strong sunlight was blazing in through the tall front windows. Helped along by the central heating, it was making the house uncomfortably warm.

The butler tapped gently on a pedimented door at the end of the corridor and led me inside without waiting to be called. 'Mr Lomax is here to see you, sir.'

The man in the high-backed wing chair was wearing a white cravat and a black silk dressing-gown with quilted lapels. A red tartan rug had been tucked around his legs. He smiled at me and held out a hand. I crossed over and shook it. It was cold and soft and clammy. Glancing past me, he said, 'Thanks, Havers. Could you make sure no one disturbs us.'

'Of course, sir.' The butler faded from the room, closing the door softly behind him.

Abraham Feinburg nodded towards another high-backed chair. After I'd sat down he looked at me for a while without speaking. It was the thoughtful gaze of a man too tired and ill to be concerned about embarrassing me by staring. Presently, he took a breath and asked, 'Have you been in business long, Mr Lomax?'

'About seven years.'

'Is it going well?'

Smiling, I said, 'It's a living.'

He took his eyes from me and looked out through a tall window over the sunlit garden at the front of the house. I followed his gaze. He was studying my car, the ice-blue Jaguar XJ8; getting tired now, grimy after the rainswept run to Birmingham, mud splattered after that morning's dash along wet country lanes. He looked back at me. 'I'd like to engage you, Mr Lomax.'

'Why would you like to engage me, Mr Feinburg?'

'To watch over my wife; to protect her.'

'What would I be protecting her from?'

He took a deep breath. I guessed he'd be moving into his

seventies, but illness could have aged him. Dark flesh, puffy and jaundiced, ringed eyes that were haunted by pain. His abundant black hair was white at the roots. Slightly built, maybe five-ten tall, he'd been a handsome man. He let out the breath in a sigh. 'I don't have long to live, Mr Lomax. My doctor says six months, so I'm guessing I've got six weeks. I'm wealthy. I have many business interests. My wife's an astute and clever woman, and I've involved her as much as she cared to be involved, but her wealth will make her vulnerable when I die and my affairs have to be put in order.'

'You have accountants, lawyers?'

'Of course.'

'You don't trust them?'

He shrugged. 'They're very competent, they've always served me well, so I've no reason not to. But would they always do what's best for my wife, or would they persuade her to do what's easiest and most profitable for them?'

'I'm not a lawyer or an accountant, Mr Feinburg, and I don't know a thing about high finance.'

'My wife won't need someone who understands the law or finance, Mr Lomax. She's going to need someone who's accustomed to dealing with the shabbiness of mankind; someone who can cope with unpleasantness.'

'Why me?'

'You've been very highly recommended by Mrs Pearson, the magistrate. Her former husband's architectural practice used to do work for me. You're the only man I've ever heard her speak of in a complimentary way. She's usually quite contemptuous.' Illness had weakened him. He spoke softly and his smile was tired. I sensed he wasn't English, but there was no accent to help me guess his origins. He continued smiling at me in his tired way while I gazed at him over a vase of daffodils on a black lacquered table. 'I'd like to hire you for a period of six months,' he went on, 'starting on the day of my death; on call, around the clock, seven days a week. Presumably you'd be able to wind up anything you're working on in the time I have left. If my wife wanted to extend the period, that would be between you and her.' He took a leather-bound diary from the table, drew a slip of paper from between the pages, and handed it to me. 'Payment in advance. You'd claim expenses from my wife.'

The slip of paper was a cheque. I glanced down at it, then had to take a second look. It amounted to more than I usually made in a good year. 'Your wife might not like this, Mr Feinburg. Maybe she'll want to deal with things herself; make her own arrangements.'

'I've discussed it at length with my wife. We've no children and neither of us has any close family, so she'll be quite alone. She's more than happy with the arrangement. In fact, she's much comforted by it.'

'But she doesn't know me. She might—'

He interrupted me with his tired smile. 'Mr Lomax, what I'm doing has my wife's complete approval.'

'And you want me to watch over her; try and warn her if I think she's being short-changed?'

'More or less. I'm a very wealthy man; the short-change could amount to millions.'

His 'more or less' made me uneasy. 'Surely you need someone who understands high finance, Mr Feinburg.' I tapped the cheque. 'You could be wasting your money.'

'I want someone I can trust to watch over my wife. She'll have to deal with clever and unscrupulous men, and she needs someone who understands the darker side of human nature, who's experienced its wickedness; someone with physical presence; someone without ties or distractions.'

We sat in silence while an ornate gilt clock on an even more ornate marble mantelpiece tinkled out the half-hour. I was wondering how he knew I didn't have any ties or distractions. Presently he said, 'I'm dying, Mr Lomax.' His whispery voice was suddenly weaker. 'I need the comfort of knowing my wife's going to be watched over and protected. Say you'll do this for me, and cash the cheque.'

I didn't like it. There were things I needed to know before I accepted. There had to be more to this than indifferent accountants and lawyers, possibly men on the make, men on the take. But it was a generous payment at a time when my one steady earner had ended. It would be sensible to put the cheque in a drawer until he'd told me what his problems were. And those dark, dying-man's eyes were imploring me. 'I'll need briefing,' I said. 'The people I'm likely to meet, your thoughts about them, any particular worries you have.'

'My wife knows the people and she knows the business. I've gone over the assets with her many times.'

'It's your thoughts I want, Mr Feinburg. I want to know what's worrying you; why you're so concerned for your wife.'

He stirred in his chair, then frowned. The movement seemed to have caused him pain. Coughing, he said, 'You're right, Mr Lomax. We ought to spend a couple of hours together, and there is something that's—'

There was a gentle tapping on the door and the butler entered. 'The doctor has arrived, sir. I told him you were in a meeting, but he insisted on you being told he's here.'

'Thanks, Havers. Has Mrs Feinburg left for Barfield yet?'

'She left with Miss Macfarlane about ten minutes ago, sir.'

'Could you put him in the breakfast room, then come back and show Mr Lomax out?'

'Very good, sir.'

When the door had closed Abraham Feinburg smiled his tired smile and said, 'My doctor, Mr Lomax. He calls every day about this time, injects me with drugs that rob me of what little energy I have left on the promise of prolonging, for just a little while longer, a life that seems less and less worth living.'

'May I ask what the problem is?'

'Cancer. Been operated on twice, but that's not an option any more.'

I began to think the six weeks he was giving himself might be optimistic. 'When can we meet again?' I asked.

Sighing, he looked down at his hands. They were pallid, almost waxen, against the red tartan blanket. 'I'm going to have to talk to you about something I deeply regret, Mr Lomax, something I've begun to feel ashamed of, so it's got to be during the morning, before I have my injection. And it's got to be on a day when I don't feel too tired and ill. If Havers gives you a ring tomorrow or the day after, could you come straight over?'

Remembering the amount he'd entered on the cheque, I said, 'I'll be here within the hour.' I found my notebook, scribbled down a number and tore out the sheet. 'Tell him to call me on my mobile, not the office phone.' As I leaned forward to lay the note on the table, I heard a gentle tapping on the door. The butler had returned to show me out.

* * *

There was a chair and a music stand in the semicircular bay window, and a violin and its bow were lying on a square of purple velvet that had been unfolded on the lid of the grand piano. Maria Brody gestured towards an armchair and said, 'Sit down, Mr Lomax,' then crossed over to the long sofa and sat down herself. She was wearing a green woollen jumper that had long sleeves and a deep and almost off-the-shoulder-wide V neck. Her black skirt was long and full; her low-heeled black shoes had big gold buckles.

'How's Jason?' I opened.

'Distraught. His father was even more vile than I expected. He just ranted at the boy. I had to warn him he'd chase him away if he wasn't careful.'

'Is Jason pressing charges?'

She shook her head. 'He doesn't want to. He's afraid it could make things worse for the girl. That's mainly what the argument with his father was about.' She studied my face for a moment, then said, 'Jason told us you had to fight the men off; that some of them were badly injured. I didn't realize last night how much we're in your debt, Mr Lomax. Jason probably owes you his life.'

'Just luck,' I said. 'Being in the right place at the right time.' Jason's decision suited me. Assault with a pick-axe handle: a half-decent barrister could give me a very hard time in court. 'Has he decided to put the whole thing behind him?'

'You mean forget the girl?'

I gave her a steady look.

'He can't, Mr Lomax. He's completely infatuated. He loves her. That's why I called you. We'd like you to locate her.'

'And what happens when I've located her?'

Maria shrugged. 'I suppose he'll make contact.'

'He could get them both killed.'

She flashed me a condescending smile. 'Surely not, Mr Lomax. This is England. People are protected by the law.'

'Not when they're living with relatives who feel they've been stripped of their standing in the community.'

'You're trying to frighten me.'

'You don't need me to frighten you, Mrs Brody. Jason won't press charges because he's afraid it will make things worse for Halima. It's sensible to be fearful about the situation. Has Jason phoned the police in Birmingham?'

'A few minutes before you arrived. They told him they'd interviewed the girl at her uncle's home and she'd assured them she was all right. It seems she's leaving Birmingham; she's not going back to university.'

'She's returning to her home in Leeds?'

'Jason's afraid they'll send her to Pakistan.'

'To be married?'

Maria Brody shrugged.

'Why not leave things as they are, Mrs Brody?'

'Give in, you mean? Just walk away? I don't think so, Mr Lomax. I want to find her, not just for Jason, but for the girl's sake, too. I can't bear the thought of her being made to do something so life-changing against her will.' Her shoulders had stiffened and her small breasts were noticeable beneath the green jumper.

'She might be willing,' I said.

'And she might not. I think Jason's the best judge of that.'

'Is Jason here?'

'He's in his room. He went there to get away from his father's ranting.'

'Perhaps I could see him on his own?'

'And why would you want to see him on his own?'

'He might tell me things he wouldn't want his mother to hear.'

Maria bristled. Her breasts were thrusting hard against the green wool now. 'Jason and I are very close, Mr Lomax. I'm quite sure there's nothing he wouldn't want me to know. And he's extremely sensitive and very distressed about the girl. On top of that, his brute of a father's just traumatized him. I don't want him upset any more.'

'I don't intend to upset your son, Mrs Brody, I just want to talk to him before I start searching.'

She rose to her feet, hazel eyes flashing. 'But not on his own,' she snapped. 'I'll take you up.'

I could hear the faint hum of a lathe, the whine of a cutting tool, before we reached the top of the stairs. Daniel Brody was in the attic, working off his anger. Maria knocked on Jason's door, waited for the muffled, 'Who is it?' then said, 'It's Mother, Jason. And Mr Lomax.' The door opened, Jason stood aside and I followed Maria in. Jason took the chair from his desk and held it while his mother sat down. I propped myself against the window sill; he sat on the bed, his fingers linked around a raised knee.

Looking across at Jason, I said, 'You want me to find Halima?'

He nodded.

'Finding her could be dangerous: for her and for you.'

'I don't care. I'm desperately worried about her. I have to be certain she's all right.'

'Your mother tells me the police have checked and they've confirmed Halima's OK.'

'They said they'd called at her uncle's house and talked to her, but I don't trust them. They didn't seem all that interested. And if her uncle was in the room she'd have to say what he wanted the police to hear.'

'Why do you think she stayed away from university?'

'Her family must have found out about us and they kept her away.'

'But you were so careful. You even rented a flat well away from the usual student places.'

'Someone must have seen us together and told her uncle. She never talked about her life with the family. She just said things were difficult and she found it suffocating.' Sunlight suddenly gleamed on the lenses of his glasses, obscuring his eyes, and I couldn't read his expression, but his mouth was drooping and his body had sagged in a tired and dejected way.

'Perhaps she wants to end the relationship,' I said. 'Could that be why she's staying away?'

'We're very close and very open with one another about our

thoughts and feelings. I know it couldn't be anything like that. She'd have told me.'

'Were you intimate?'

'Intimate? I don't know what—'

'Really, Mr Lomax, is this necessary?' Maria Brody protested. 'I rather think that's my son's business.'

Ignoring her, I said, 'Sexually intimate.'

Jason took his hands from around his knee and lowered his foot to the floor. 'We were lovers,' he said softly, then pushed his glasses up to the bridge of his nose and stared at me defiantly.

I listened to the distant cawing of the rooks, the faint whine of Daniel Brody's lathe, while I allowed my thoughts to drift back to the previous night and the things his attackers had yelled. On a sudden impulse, I asked, 'How long has she been pregnant?'

He jerked his back straight and stared at me with shocked eyes. 'How did you—'

Maria Brody moaned, 'Oh, Jason!' then rose from her chair, sat beside him on the bed and wrapped her arms around him.

Jason gazed down at the rug. 'She told me about three weeks ago. She stopped coming to lectures a week later.'

'Did the police give you her uncle's address?'

'I asked several times, I begged them for it, but they wouldn't tell me. The man called Anderson kept going on and on about her being OK, and insisting that I should leave it alone. It was almost as if he was warning me not to cause trouble.'

'Would the university have the address?'

'They'd have her home address, her Leeds address, on the files. The police probably phoned her home to get her uncle's address in Birmingham.'

'If the police have seen her and talked to her, if they've assured you she's OK, surely you—'

'It's not good enough. Her uncle would have made her say she's all right. You're just like Father. You don't understand. I love her so desperately and I'm being driven mad with worry.' His face crumpled. 'I can't bear the thought of them sending her to Pakistan to marry someone she's never seen, someone she doesn't want. It's tearing me apart.'

'You think they'll be able to arrange for her to marry someone if she's pregnant?'

'They probably don't know. She'd be too scared to tell them. She was thinking about having a termination.'

Maria Brody moaned, 'Dear God, Jason. No!'

Then Jason went on, 'I begged her to come and live with me. I said we'd get married if that's what she wanted, but she was too scared and upset to think about it. And she was scared about having to take Ghinwa into her confidence if she had a termination.'

'Her cousin Ghinwa?'

He nodded.

'Could she have confided in Ghinwa, and then Ghinwa told her parents?'

'Possibly, but I don't think so. Halima was too scared to talk about it.'

'Have you tried phoning?'

'She asked me not to call her on her mobile but I did a couple of days after she went missing. There was no answer.'

'What about the phone in the house?'

'I couldn't search the directory because I don't know her uncle's name; he's her mother's brother.'

'What about the buses she travelled on?'

'Halima always made me leave her before Ghinwa collected her. I watched once or twice, but they just walked off. I didn't see them catching a bus or climbing into a car.'

'And she never said what part of the city she lived in?'

'Not that I recall. As I said, she didn't seem to want to talk about family things. It was an area of her life that oppressed her.'

'No address, no phone number, just a name. Do we have a photograph?'

He freed himself from his mother's arms, crossed over to the desk and picked up a wallet that was resting on a pile of books. He took out a small square of card and handed it to me. It was a passport photograph. The girl's hijab had been thrown back, exposing black hair around a beautiful face. The sudden flash of light in the booth had startled her and her eyes were wide, her lips parted. Long filigree ear-rings brushed her slender neck. I glanced up at him. 'Can I keep this?'

'Of course, but I must have it back. It's all I have.' His cheeks were wet now and his lips and chin were trembling.

'And you want me to find her?'

'We *both* want you to find her,' Maria Brody insisted. Jason just nodded. His eyes were very bright behind the lenses of his glasses. I guessed he couldn't trust himself to speak.

Suddenly remembering something from the night before, I said, 'The phone number DCI Houlihan gave you; do you still have it?'

Jason dipped into his wallet again, plucked out a piece of paper, and handed it to me.

Unfolding it, I said, 'I'll just note it down.'

'Keep it,' he said bitterly. 'I won't be phoning them any more. They're not interested. They're worse than useless.'

I pushed myself off the window sill and made for the door. 'Give me a couple of days. I'll try to get back to you before the end of the week.'

Maria Brody walked along the landing with me. When we reached the foot of the stairs she leaned against the ceiling-high newel post, closed her eyes and pressed the back of her hand against her brow in a rather theatrical way. 'I can hardly believe what I've just heard,' she moaned. 'I've got a concert on Friday evening. How am I going to practise? How am I going to concentrate on the music?' She opened her eyes and looked at me. 'A young girl's carrying my grandchild, Mr Lomax. My first grandchild!' She pushed herself off the newel post, swept across the hall and tugged the big outer door open. 'You've got to find her for me. I want you to find her and bring her back here. We'll care for her and keep her safe.'

The door slammed shut as soon as I'd stepped under the porch. Maria was probably dashing back up the stairs to have a more private talk with her son. I crunched over the gravel to the Jaguar and was about to slide behind the wheel when a voice called my name. Glancing round, I saw Daniel Brody standing down the side of the house. He was wearing an oil-stained engineer's smock over his khaki pullover and corduroys. I went over, he held out a hand, and when I took it his grip was firm, the shaking vigorous.

'Thanks for what you did for Jason. You probably saved the silly beggar's life. Have they asked you to find the girl?'

I nodded.

'They're stupid; absolutely stupid. Best to let sleeping dogs lie. Tried to tell 'em, but they wouldn't listen.' He sniffed through his moustache. 'Don't suppose you've started checking out Maria?'

'Not yet, Mr Brody. I'll try to find the girl, then I'll get on to it. Somehow, I think you're worrying about nothing.'

'Things are pretty chilly in the old marriage bed,' he muttered. 'No intimacy, no tenderness; can't even say there's any companionship.'

'I'm no expert, Mr Brody, but I think this situation's pretty common. It doesn't mean your wife's affections have gone elsewhere. Maybe your son leaving home troubled her more deeply than you realized.'

'Think so, Lomax?'

'Like I said, I'm no expert.'

I crunched my way back to the car, climbed inside and headed off down the drive. As I passed the end of the house, I caught a glimpse of a dejected Daniel Brody striding back to his workshop.

FIVE

igeons, roosting in the gutters, took flight on a flurry of
beating wings when I pushed open the dormer windows.
The office had that stale dusty smell that fills locked-up
rooms in old buildings; it was gasping for a change of air.

Melody hadn't left any little pink notes on the blotter; there
hadn't been any calls; there was nothing in the mail. Business was
quieter than a snore at a papal conclave. Abraham Feinburg's
cheque was hidden away in the bottom drawer of the desk. I still
had to meet him and find out why he wanted someone to watch
over his wife, but if what was worrying him didn't amount to too
much hassle, I'd take the job and cash his cheque.

I'd spent the previous evening watching Maria Brody for her
husband, Daniel. The Reverend Canon Dr Nathan Potter had
enthralled the Barfield Theological Society, a group of earnest-
looking individuals, with a talk entitled *St John's Gospel and the
Gnostic Heresy*. Maria arrived on her own, sat on her own, and was
on her own when I followed her back to Tanglewood. It made me
even more convinced her husband was wasting his money having
me check her out.

While the Reverend Doctor's nasal ramblings had been echoing
around the church hall, I'd reflected on the Jason and Halima
romance. The situation was difficult. My search for the girl would

have to be covert or I could put her in danger, and if I was going to find her, the sooner I began to look the better. But I'd no address; I didn't even know her uncle's surname. I could probably use some trick to get her home address, her Leeds address, from the university, but it was the house where she was staying in Birmingham that I had to locate.

The sound of cooing and rustling feathers began to mingle with the faint rumble of distant traffic, the murmur of voices and tread of feet along the paved area in front of the offices; the pigeons had returned to their roosts behind the parapet. I flicked through my notebook, found the slip of paper Jason Brody had given me, then reached for the phone and dialled the police station we'd attended a couple of nights earlier. When the switchboard girl answered, I got her to put me through to DCI Houlihan.

'Pick-axe man!' A warm little chuckle came down the line. 'You can't have it, Lomax. You've already caused too much mayhem in Birmingham.'

'Can't have what?'

'The address where Halima Fahim's living. I was expecting you to phone. DI Anderson got a real ear-bending from Jason Brody when he wouldn't tell him where she lodges.'

'Who said anything about an address? I was thinking about dinner.'

'Dinner?'

'You and me. I was hoping we could have a meal together.'

'Really?' She sounded intrigued. I heard surprised laughter, then she said, 'When?'

'Tonight.'

There was more laughter. 'Hell, why not? What did you have in mind?'

'Somewhere decent. Good food, good service, soft lighting,

plenty of space around the tables, maybe a little music. You know Birmingham; you choose.'

'Mmm ... Bertoli's is good. It's in Greek Street. And there's customer parking around the back.'

'I'll book a table. Where do I collect you, and what time?'

'I'm on days, but I'll have to change. The place has a bar. What if I meet you in the bar at 7.30.'

'See you in the bar.'

'We'd better exchange mobile numbers, just in case something crops up and I can't make it,' she said.

The operator at directory enquiries put me through to Bertoli's and I left a booking request on their answering machine; asked them to phone back and confirm when they opened. Dining with DCI Houlihan would lose me a day, but the chance of getting Halima's uncle's address, or even his surname, was worth it.

The desk phone began to ring. 'You're in! I thought you might be in bed. Mrs Feinburg's here to see you.' Melody's tone was decidedly frosty.

'Mrs Feinburg? Is her husband with her?'

'No, but her chauffeur's waiting outside. He's driven her big black limousine all the way up the pedestrianized area. The girls are looking at him through the window; quite an eyeful in his peaked cap and grey uniform. He's giving the windscreen a polish.'

Even allowing for illness, Abraham Feinburg had looked old and frail. His wife would be elderly, too. 'Can she manage the stairs?' I asked. 'Should I come down to her?'

'Manage the stairs?' A puzzled irritation had crept into Melody's voice.

'Stairs,' I repeated. 'Three flights. She can't be young and the last one's steep.'

'She can manage stairs, Paul. She might trip in her high heels, and she'll be as mad as hell if the flaky plaster in the attic rubs off on her Ungaro suit, but she can climb stairs.' Melody was decidedly tetchy now.

'Ungaro?'

'The size twelve black suit she's squeezed her size fourteen figure into. Emanuel Ungaro is the designer's name. I've seen it in Vogue: pencil skirt that's so tight it's ready to split and a tiny black jacket she couldn't button up if she tried.' Tetchy had become scathing. 'Shall I send her up?'

'Sure, send her up.' I braced myself. Abraham Feinburg had seemed a little too sure of himself when he'd said his wife had given the arrangement the OK. Some formidable matron could be about to put matters right and I'd never get to cash his cheque. It had all seemed too good to be true.

Footsteps tapped up the stairs, approached along the landing, then became muffled as they crossed the carpet in the waiting room. A shape moved behind the rippled glass panel of the inner door and there was a gentle tapping. I called out, 'Come on in.'

The door swung open and she approached the desk, hips swaying in a refined and very elegant kind of way. Stunned, I rose and gestured towards the visitor's chair. 'Mrs Feinburg?'

She lowered herself into it gracefully. Melody had been lying. Her skirt wasn't tight; it was a perfect fit. And it would have been a crime to button up the tiny jacket and hide the white silk blouse. Melody puzzled me. One day she tells me I'm a no-hoper; the next my female clients are upsetting her.

'Please,' – the voice was soft and low, the German accent strong – 'don't call me Mrs Feinburg. It makes me feel so old. Call me Marlena, and I shall call you Paul.' She rested a little black clutch bag on her lap and tugged off her gloves. Her dark eyes took in the battered filing cabinets, the paper-strewn desk, the faded decorations, then settled on me. I groped for my chair and sat down. She managed a bleak little smile.

I suddenly realized why I'd been invited to Mrs Pearson's drinks party: Marlena had been giving me the once-over while we made small talk in the summerhouse. Mrs Pearson had contrived the meeting for the Feinburgs. Still surprised, I said, 'I'd no idea you're Abraham Feinburg's wife.'

Marlena's rather full bottom lip began to quiver. 'Abraham's widow. My husband died, just after four this morning.'

'I'm sorry,' I said. 'I'm very sorry.'

'I had to come into Barfield, so I thought I'd stop off and give you the news.'

'He expected to live a little longer.'

She turned the corners of her mouth down. 'I was prepared for it, but it was shockingly sudden at the end. Not much more than an hour. He died in my arms.' Her voice was desolate. Sad eyes gazed at me for a while, then she said, 'My husband was Jewish, but he never went inside a synagogue. Should I arrange a Jewish funeral?'

'With a name like Abraham Feinburg, he deserves a Jewish funeral, Marlena.'

'But he'd absolutely no interest in his faith. Would he want a Jewish funeral?'

'Did you ever talk about it?'

She shook her head. 'When I knew how ill he was, it seemed rather indelicate.'

'Does it matter?' I said softly. 'If Abraham's faded into the dark, he'll never know; if he's waiting to be ferried across the Styx, a rabbi's prayers could calm the waters. Have the Jewish funeral, Marlena.'

She nodded. She'd not bothered with the false eyelashes, but she'd been busy with the eyeshadow and her lipstick was as red as rowan berries against the creamy whiteness of her skin. 'Puckatch and Gruber,' she said. 'I've driven in to look them over but they don't open their office until nine. Do you know if they're decent undertakers; someone who'll deal with things in a dignified way?'

'They specialize in Jewish funerals, Marlena. I'm sure they'll be OK. You know Jewish custom requires a quick burial?'

She shook her head. 'I didn't, but it shouldn't be a problem. I've got the death certificate. His doctor was with him when he died.'

Marlena winced. Deafeningly loud through the open windows, the church clock had begun to chime out the hour. When the clanging stopped, I said, 'Your husband was going to talk to me about some problems that worried him.'

She lowered her eyes. Slender fingers began to toy with the catch on her bag. 'I'm more than worried, Paul; I'm frightened. Perhaps we could discuss things after the funeral. Would you come to the funeral?'

'If you want me to.'

'I do. There won't be many people there. There's no family and Abraham had no close friends, so it'll just be household staff and one or two others.'

'What have they been told about me?'

'That you've been engaged to oversee the transfer of his estate to me. Everyone's been told: Reed and Russell, Abraham's solicitors; Nichols and Jordan, the accountants; the household staff.'

'He's taken us by surprise,' I said. 'I was expecting a little time to clear on-going cases.'

'I don't see any problems. I'm sure they can be fitted in.' She rose to her feet, tall in high heels.

I pushed my chair back and followed her to the door. Her haunches were swaying below the flared hem of her tiny jacket, and the close-fitting calf-length skirt made her legs seem even longer. 'Would it help if I came with you to the undertakers?'

'Thank you, but I'll be fine, Paul. Alice is with me. She's waiting in the car.'

'Alice?'

'Alice Macfarlane. She's my personal maid; well, more of a secretary and companion, really.'

We were standing quite close in the outer doorway. Her face was completely unlined; her sad eyes huge and dark; her full lips glistening. The warmth of her body was driving off waves of some elusive fragrance. I guessed she'd be closer to thirty than forty. She'd been the young bride of a much older man. 'I'd better give you my mobile number,' I said.

'I have it. It was on a slip of paper in my husband's diary.'

'I've business in Birmingham later today, but you can reach me on that number. If one of the staff could let me know the time and place of the funeral—'

'Of course.' She moved out on to the landing.

'I'm sorry,' I called after her, in the helpless tone everyone adopts when confronted by the newly bereaved. 'Deeply sorry.'

She glanced back. 'Thank you, Paul. But it wasn't unexpected, and for the rest of us life must go on.'

* * *

Detective Chief Inspector Houlihan didn't keep me waiting long. The bar and the seating area around it were elevated above the entrance, and I was able to watch her come in from the street. When she'd been helped out of her belted camel-hair coat I could see her dress. It was made from some silky, saffron-yellow material. The skirt was short and full; the bodice held in place by a choker collar, leaving her arms and shoulders bare.

The coat disappeared into the cloakroom, and a guy in a red waistcoat picked up a couple of menus and escorted her over. I rose and helped her into one of the gilded cane chairs.

'Hope I've not kept you waiting long?' She smiled up at me. She was wearing hardly any make-up, just a trace of pink lipstick. Shortish light-brown hair curled down behind her ears.

'A couple of minutes. Can I get you a drink?'

'That would be nice. What are you drinking?'

'Tonic water.'

She grimaced.

'How about a cocktail?'

'I'd prefer a gin and bitter lemon.'

The waiter handed out the menus and strode over to the bar.

'Beautiful dress.'

She looked up from the menu, smiled, and said, 'Thanks. And you've had your suit cleaned.'

'Is it that obvious.'

'It was pretty dusty and crumpled after the affray with the Asian men.'

The waiter slid her drink on to the table and asked if we were ready to order.

'Five minutes,' I said. He ambled off. The restaurant area was filling up. A pianist could be heard over the happy chatter. It was a popular place.

'Why did you ask me out to dinner?'

I shrugged. 'Just thought it would be pleasant.'

'And you've driven all the way from Barfield?'

'I'd have driven all the way from Edinburgh to see you in that dress.'

She laughed, poured bitter lemon into her glass, then said, 'I don't get invited out to dinner all that often.' She took a sip at her drink. 'Men seem to be intimidated by detective chief inspectors.'

'What about the boys back at the station? I'd have thought they'd have been queuing up.'

'Hardly. Anyway, I never get involved with brother officers.'

'Never?'

'Never. It's the canteen culture. The morning after every man on the force thinks he knows the colour of your underwear and tales of what happened are unbelievably inventive.'

'Do I call you ma'am or Miss Houlihan?'

She laughed. 'Helen will do. And I know you're called Paul. I hope there's no Mrs Lomax?'

I shook my head.

'Divorced.' She sipped her drink. 'I thought you might be.'

'Why did you think I might be?'

'The job. You'd have to have a very understanding wife or partner.'

'Widower,' I said.

'Ouch! Sorry.' She flashed me an apologetic smile. 'Any children?'

I shook my head again, and then the waiter was standing over us with his notepad. I said, 'We ought to decide what we're having.'

'Mmm … think I'll have a fillet steak with peppercorn sauce,' she said. 'Well done. And the soup.'

'I'll have the same. Are you driving?'

'Came in a cab.'

Opening the wine list, I glanced up at the waiter. 'What's your best Merlot?'

'Number twenty-seven is rather special, sir.'

I glanced at the list. I could have dined out for a week in Barfield for the price of Bertoli's bottle of Merlot. I smiled up at him. 'Then it's got to be number twenty-seven.'

The service was deferential, the meal as pleasant as the company. Helen Houlihan drank most of the bottle of wine, a glass of desert wine and a couple of brandies. I wouldn't have known. In the best traditions of the force, it didn't even bring a glow to her cheeks.

'I'm told you're called the Barfield Bounty Hunter.' She was rummaging around in her handbag, taking stuff out and putting it on the table.

'You've been checking up on me.'

'A girl's got to be careful, especially when the guy carries a pick-axe handle. DCI Hogan at Barfield CID said you're the dog's bollocks.'

'I thought Hogan was a detective inspector.'

'Chief inspector now. He said things you handed over helped with the promotion: murder and corruption case.' She was still searching in her handbag. 'You haven't told me why Barfield CID call you the Bounty Hunter.'

'I had a contract with the Department of Social Security: spot fee for every benefit cheat convicted and a daily rate for a court attendance.'

'Had?'

'They've called it a day. No more prosecutions.'

Without glancing up, she said, 'A victim of your own success.' She slid the lipstick, comb, compact and purse back into her bag and clicked it shut. 'Got to go to the powder room. Don't pay until I get back. I insist we share.'

I watched her walk away between the tables, the high heels of her strappy gold sandals rock steady, the skirt of her dress short enough to let everyone know her legs were plump, but shapely. I caught the waiter's eye, settled the bill, then reached for the black, official-looking notebook she'd left beside the flowers on the table. Rather like a shorthand pad, it was held shut by a thick rubber band. I snapped it off, lifted the cover and flicked through to the last entries. Her handwriting was small and neat. I read:

Mohtaran Cheema (Brit Cit), 96 Burbank Avenue, Birmingham: uncle of Halima Fahim. Nawaz Fahim (Brit Cit), Jaranwala, Kirkstall Road, Leeds: Halima's father. DI Anderson interviewed Mr and Mrs Cheema and Halima Fahim at 96 Burbank Avenue at 8.36 on 10 March. Halima nervous but OK; family cooperative. Halima said she'd decided not to complete her university course and returning to her parents in Leeds sometime next week. Involvement with J Brody not mentioned. Mohtaran Cheema said, as far as he was aware, no member of family had been the recent victim of an assault. DI Anderson made telephone check with father, Nawaz Fahim, who confirmed that his daughter would be coming home over the space of the next few days. DI Anderson advised Halima to let university know she is abandoning her course.

Glancing around to make sure no one was looking, I tore a sheet out of the desert menu, scribbled the names and addresses on the back, then folded it and tucked it in my wallet. That done, I snapped the rubber band back over the notebook and replaced it in the same spot on the table. Seconds later, Helen Houlihan was making her way towards me across the crowded dining area.

* * *

'I like the car.' She ran her fingers over the cream leather armrest. We were cruising along brightly lit and almost deserted streets, heading for her flat.

'It's comfortable,' I said, 'and it still looks OK, but it guzzles gas and it's getting tired.'

'You shouldn't have paid for the meal.'

'I wanted to see you again. I don't mind paying for the meal.'

'I thought you just wanted Halima Fahim's Birmingham address.'

'Why should I want Halima's address? Anyway, son Brody had it. He found it on a note she'd sent him.' It was only half a lie.

Spending the evening with Helen Houlihan had been worth the drive over.

'He didn't have it when DI Anderson asked. We had to get it from her father.'

'Who is the father?'

'Nawaz Fahim. Leeds business man. Property, wholesale foods, food processing, restaurants; big contributor to political parties. Been selected to stand as an MP.'

'One of the great and the good.'

She laughed. 'You're a cynical sod.'

'Occupational hazard.'

'Turn left here.'

I swung the Jaguar into a low-rise flat development. Red brick and Portland stone, Regency-style windows, ornamental street lamps, plenty of shrubs and plants: the place looked tasteful and exclusive. 'Nice estate.'

'I'm mortgaged up to the eyeballs. Turn right here, down the side of this little park, then drive under the archway.' We emerged into a service area graced by some more islands of shrubbery. 'Park next to that little building. It's the space reserved for visitors.'

I did as she asked, then went round and helped her out of the car. DCI Houlihan wasn't accustomed to being helped out of cars. She led me over to a door, punched numbers into a key pad, then we stepped inside on to the kind of hard-wearing carpet they sometimes lay in offices. A flight of stairs took us up to a landing. She unlocked her door and we entered the scented warmth of a long and narrow hallway. I helped her out of her coat and laid it over her bag on a tiny, glass-topped table. Her dress was cut low at the back; her bare arms and shoulders were silky-smooth and flawless. She glanced at me over her shoulder. 'Coffee?'

'Coffee would be fine.'

I was following her down the hall when she slowed and faced me. 'The Brodys want you to check out the girl, don't they?'

I smiled and nodded. There was no reason why she shouldn't know.

'And did you really have Halima Fahim's address?'

'Jason Brody found it for me. I told his mother the job would be too much hassle, cost her too much, if they didn't come up with the address. I'm going to book into a hotel and check it out tomorrow.'

She frowned up at me. 'Don't know why you're bothering. DI Anderson talked to the girl and made sure she was OK. Jason Brody knows that.'

'Jason's madly in love,' I said. 'He can't believe she'd just ditch him. He's worried; he wants more reassurance.'

'Leave your pick-axe handle in the car. There's enough trouble in the manor as it is.' She took another couple of paces, then stopped and turned again. 'And you really did drive over here just to take me out to dinner?'

'I'd have flown in from New York to take you out to dinner.'

'It was a drive down from Edinburgh last time.'

'It's the little yellow dress,' I said. 'It captivates me, and the more I look at it, the more captivating it seems.'

She began to laugh. 'You're a smarmy bugger, Paul Lomax.' Her hair was a nondescript light-brown, but it was thick and silky and stylishly cut. Her brown eyes were clear and bright, her teeth cared for, her mouth generous and well shaped. She'd never win the Miss World contest, but she radiated good health and energy and a fragrant cleanliness. 'How do you like your coffee?' She was walking down the hall again.

'Black; three sugars.'

She stopped once more, turned and frowned up at me. 'You really did just want to take me out to dinner?'

'I just wanted to take you out to dinner.' I studied her face. Detective Chief Inspector she might be, but she seemed low on personal self-esteem. Her brown eyes were searching mine; her lips were parted. Resting my hands on the swell of her hips, I lowered my head and kissed her very gently.

'And you really do like my dress?'

'I like looking at *you* in the dress.' She let me kiss her again; longer this time.

Her hand groped for mine, then she pushed at a door and led me through. 'You'd better help me take it off.'

SIX

Massively built semi-detached houses, four storeys high, glowered at one another across a strip of grass and shrubs and mature trees that divided the sunlit avenue. I found a parking space close to the Cheema residence and looked around. Some of the houses had become bed-and-breakfast places, one had been converted into a home for the elderly, a few were dingy and neglected. Before climbing out of the car, I slipped on some heavy horn-rimmed glasses I wear in court. They lend a certain gravitas, impart an official look, and if any of the guys I'd whacked with the pick-axe handle were lurking inside number 96 Burbank Avenue, they'd find it not quite so easy to recognize me.

An ornate iron gate, a flagged path and six or seven broad steps led up to a porch. I made it to the top and rapped on a glass panel that had a leaf design etched into it. From up here I could see through the side light of a big bay window. The room beyond had a high ceiling with deep cornices and blue and gold wallpaper. A big blue armchair almost filled the bay. Turning back to the door, I rapped on the glass again, harder this time.

'Coming! I'm coming!' Irritation sounded in a woman's voice. The door opened a few inches and a dark face, framed by a black hijab, frowned at me through the gap.

'Mrs Cheema?'

She nodded. The frown became a scowl.

'University of Birmingham Welfare Department. We've been asked to call and enquire about ...' I flicked through my notebook and peered over the glasses at a page, 'a Miss Halima Fahim. She's missed several lectures and her personal tutor's—'

'Wait,' she snapped. 'You must talk with my husband. I will see if he's home.' She slammed the door and her blurred shape faded away behind the etched glass.

The photograph Jason Brody had given me was tucked inside the notebook. I studied the small, rather indistinct image of a beautiful young girl and tried to memorize what I could see of her features. Suddenly the door was wrenched open and a stocky, heavily built man with greying hair and a pock-marked face was glaring out at me. 'Mr Cheema?' He nodded, and I went through the spiel about university welfare again.

'I'm bloody sick of this. Police yesterday, you today. Why are you wasting my time?' His lilting Pakistani accent heightened the agitation in his voice.

'Students who miss three lectures are reported to the welfare team, Mr Cheema. They're mostly young people, living away from home, and they could be ill, they could be in difficulties. We're legally obliged to check that they're OK.' It was just patter. Halima's personal tutor probably had no idea who she was, and he'd care even less about where she was.

'Of course she's OK. And she's not living away from home. I'm her uncle. We are family. My home is her home.'

I gave him a genial smile. 'Her personal tutor ...' I peered over my glasses at the notebook then tossed out a fictitious name, '... Doctor Digby, is concerned, Mr Cheema. This is her final year. He's waiting for the draft of her dissertation. He's already extended the deadline twice.'

'Deadline? What do I care about deadlines? My niece is leaving the university.'

'Leaving?' I pushed the glasses up to the bridge of my nose and stared at him. 'A few months before her finals? Seems rather a waste, Mr Cheema.'

'The waste is our business. And there are more important things in a young girl's life than books.'

Scribbling a note in my pad, I said, 'Could I just see Halima before I leave, Mr Cheema?'

'See her? Why do you want to see her?'

'I'll have to report back to the governing committee; tell them she's abandoning her course. They'll expect me to mention her reasons in my report.'

'The reasons are her business; her father's business.'

'At the very least I've got to be able to report she's not abandoned the course because she's ill or having difficulties. As a member of the welfare team I have that responsibility, and if I don't report having actually seen her they'll arrange for someone to visit you again.' I gave him another genial smile. He stared back at me, suspicious and irritated. He was wearing a blue check shirt with a button-down collar. His blue tie was spotted with food stains and his black trousers were baggy and creased. Glancing over his shoulder I noticed a movement, in the shadows, half-way up a wide flight of stairs. He turned to see what I was looking at.

'I told you to stay in your room.' Cheema's voice was stern and reproving.

'Asifa said I had to come down for coffee.'

'You'd better come over here first. The university is asking about you, Halima. Come and tell Mr—'

'Fanshaw, Welfare Department,' I trotted out.

'Come and tell this man what you told the police.'

The girl began to descend the stairs. A shapeless black chiffon over-dress covered her arms and wafted around her ankles; a black hijab concealed her hair. She floated out of the shadows like a spectre, her huge dark eyes nervous, almost frightened. She paused at the foot of the stairs and rested her hand on a swirl of gleaming mahogany.

'Tell him,' her uncle snapped. 'Tell him what you told the police.'

'I've decided to leave the university. I won't be finishing the course.'

'Is something about the course not right for you? Is something causing difficulties?'

She shook her head. 'Nothing like that. I've decided it's not what I want. I'm going back to my father's house in Leeds. I'm going to be married.'

'Seems a pity,' I said, 'when you're so close to your degree. Your personal tutor, Dr Digby, is confident you'll get a first.'

'Dr Digby is very kind, but it's no longer what I want. The degree is no longer important to me.'

Halima probably had the same personal tutor as Jason, a Professor Vincent Price-Maynard, but the girl hadn't corrected me when I'd said Digby. I glanced down at my notebook, flicked through to the photograph, and took a covert look. It was small and not easy to compare with the beautiful face of the girl at the foot of the stairs.

'Is it illness that's preventing you attending?'

'No, I'm perfectly well.'

Mohtaran Cheema turned from the girl and scowled at me. 'Satisfied?'

'Sorry to have disturbed you, Mr Cheema.' I flashed him another genial smile. 'But when young people suddenly stop attending … I'm sure you understand.'

The girl came and stood beside the grey-haired man. I studied her features, then glanced down at her hands. She was wearing a ring decorated with a blue stone, and there were some tiny patches of unpigmented skin. 'Would you thank Dr Digby for me,' she said. 'He's been very kind. Tell him I'm sorry if I've disappointed him.'

'Of course.' I could hear a hoover droning to and fro at the back of the house. A door slammed and the sound suddenly faded. Smiling at the grey-haired man with the pock-marked face, I said, 'Thanks again, Mr Cheema. Sorry to have troubled you,' then turned and descended the steps, strode down the short path and through the gate. Sensing he was watching me, I walked on, past the Jaguar, then crossed over to the strip of vegetation that divided the road. I heard the front door slam. When I'd passed through the bushes and trees, I looked back. He came to the bay window, stared down the street for a few moments, then disappeared from view. I crossed over to the car and climbed inside.

Hunched down in the seat, I found my mobile and called Mrs Brody. It rang for some time. When she answered, I said, 'Is Jason at home?'

'Mr Lomax! Do you want to speak with him?'

'Please. Could you take your phone to him? I might not be able to talk for long.'

'Of course.' I heard a door opening, the sound of running feet, then a breathless voice was saying, 'Is everything all right, Mr Lomax?'

'The investigation's going fine, Mrs Brody. I just need some information from Jason.'

I heard muffled voices, then Jason was saying, 'Hullo?'

'You and Halima, Jason; you're on the same course. Your personal tutor would be her personal tutor?'

'That's right. Vincent Price-Maynard.'

'And does she have small patches of lighter skin on her right hand?'

'Don't think so. Her skin's perfect. Why are you asking?'

'Just checking,' I said. 'I thought I might have seen her, but it seems I was wrong.'

'Have you found the place where she's been staying?'

'Just been talking to her uncle.'

'Halima: is she there?'

'If she is I didn't get to talk to her.' The door of the house opened, Mohtaran Cheema and his wife emerged, trotted down the steps and out of the gate, then climbed into an old white Mercedes that was parked outside. I heard the starter whine. 'Got to go, Jason. Talk to you later.' I tossed the phone on to the passenger seat and keyed the ignition as the Mercedes was pulling out. It accelerated up to the junction with the main road, then turned left. I followed.

Traffic was light and I'd no difficulty keeping the white car in view. We crossed over Shinley Road then headed into narrow streets of small terrace houses where the dome of a red-brick mosque rose, like a huge yellow balloon, over the rooftops.

After a good deal of twisting and turning, Cheema slowed and parked. I swept past and eased the Jaguar into a space further down the road. Watching through the rear-view mirrors, I saw him push through the front door of a house without bothering to knock. About five minutes later he hurried out, followed by two women in black hijabs and the all-enveloping black robes. The women were carrying bright metal buckets, yard brushes and what looked like cleaning materials. Cheema slid behind the wheel, the women climbed into the back of the car, then it pulled out and accelerated past me. I followed as they circled the mosque then plunged deeper into the labyrinth of narrow streets.

Eventually Cheema turned down a hill that sloped towards an area of rubble-strewn ground, dismal and desolate despite the spring sunshine. As we approached the bottom of the hill, I could see a few of the houses had been boarded up and some were no more than derelict shells. He slowed, then parked in front of a narrow gap between the terraces. I swung into a space higher up the rise and watched as the women clambered out of the car with their brushes and bright new buckets. They waddled after Cheema and his wife who'd already disappeared into the opening.

After a couple of minutes, the stocky Mr Cheema returned to the car carrying a pair of blue plastic sacks, one under each arm. He lifted the boot lid, dropped them inside, then took a quick look around the deserted street before heading back down the passageway.

He returned with his wife who was helping him carry another blue plastic sack that was bulkier than the first two. They lowered it into the boot then he disappeared around the back of the house while she climbed into the front passenger seat. He brought out two more sacks; one large, one small. After laying them in the boot, he slammed down the lid, climbed into the car, and drove off, turning right almost immediately.

I followed them along a short connecting road that linked two of the endless rows of terrace houses, then we turned right again, motored back up the hill, and headed in the general direction of the city centre. On Golden Hillock Road I had to jump a couple of red lights to avoid losing them. Then we crossed over Walford Road and began to drive past small shops, a doctor's surgery, a public house. Without signalling, he suddenly turned into a minor road. A restaurant stood on one corner; a branch of Barclay's Bank on the other. *Finest Indian Cuisine* was written in yellow letters along the restaurant's red fascia.

He parked across the access to the rear yard, unlocked high gates, then lifted the boot lid and began to carry the blue sacks inside. I pulled into a space at the side of the bank. A stiff breeze blew one of the gates open while his wife was helping him with the last and largest sack, and I saw a bulk refuse container, its lid up and resting against a wall. They heaved the sack inside, he dropped the lid, then they both remained in the yard while he closed and locked the gates. I guessed they'd be going into the restaurant by a rear door.

Something told me to go back and take another look at the house near the wasteland. Leaving the Cheemas, I found Golden Hillock Road, drove along it for a few hundred yards, then turned off and got lost in the maze of streets. I was cruising around, trying to get my bearings, when I suddenly saw boarded-up houses, the area of rubble-strewn waste ground and the hill beyond. I motored over, parked half-way up the rise, and walked back to the tiny house.

The front door was locked and curtains were drawn across the windows. Moving between high walls, I headed down the narrow gap and found myself in an alleyway that ran along the backs of the houses. When I worked the latch on the rear gate and pushed, it opened. The tiny yard was concreted over and criss-crossed with clothes lines. A woman emerged from the back door, the sleeves of her long black dress pushed up to her elbows; her face, framed by a black hijab, gleaming with exertion. She poured dirty water into a grate, then waddled back inside. She hadn't noticed me peering around the edge of the opening. I heard her refilling the bucket from a tap and calling to her companion in a language I didn't understand, then the sound of her voice faded as she moved to another part of the house.

Crossing the yard, I pushed at the half-open back door and stepped into a tiny kitchen. The bucket was standing on the hob of an old cooker, gas flames licking around it, heating the water inside. Moving into a room at the back of the house, I saw a couple of threadbare armchairs on a square of cheap carpet. Cardboard boxes had been stacked against the inner wall, and a portable television set was resting on a wooden crate.

A metal bucket clattered as it was dragged across an upstairs room; brushes swished water over boards: the women were scrubbing the floor. A door in the far wall was open. I walked through, found myself in an internal lobby no bigger than a telephone booth. On my left, stairs rose to the first floor. Straight ahead, another doorway led to a room at the front of the house. Curtains shut out most of the light, but when I peered into the shadows I could make out more cardboard boxes, stacked waist-high, all over the floor. I stepped inside and read some labels. The boxes held canned food and restaurant supplies.

The sound of brushes on boards, the clatter of buckets and chattering voices, was louder in here. The women were in the room directly above. I glanced up. A beam of light from a parting at the top of the curtains illuminated a crack in the old lath and plaster ceiling. It seemed to be widening and creeping across the flaking surface. Something gleamed in it; something dark and viscous. The women were still chattering, still scrubbing. Hearing a faint thud, I looked down. Fluid had dripped from the crack and splashed on to one of the boxes. There was suddenly something more pungent, something sour and salty and animal, riding over the damp musty smell of the old house.

Glancing up again, I saw the crack was still widening; the plaster beginning to sag. The drips were pattering down like rain on to the cartons now, making big red blotches. I heard a bucket handle rattle, water splash, and the drips began to turn pink, then became almost clear, as they rained down faster. The sagging patch of ceiling suddenly fell with a crash, scattering dust and plaster around the room. Laths, like white bones, still bridged the gap. They were stained red where they'd crossed the line of the crack.

Feet clattered down the uncarpeted stairs and the two black-robed women appeared in the doorway, blocking my escape. Flicking dust from my suit, I said, 'Birmingham City Council,' then dipped my fingers into my breast pocket, plucked out a card and waved it at them. 'This house is included in the next phase of the demolitions. Is Mr Cheema here? I have to make arrangements for services to be cut off and all this stuff cleared out.' I gestured towards the debris covered boxes.

One of the women stepped into the room. 'Demolition? This house not owned by Council. House my brother's. You not pull down my brother's house.' The other woman gazed over the first woman's shoulder at the mess. The smell of sour blood and bleach, damp wood and plaster, was overpowering now.

Maintaining the pretence, I took out my notebook and flicked it open. 'This is 48 Steelyard Street?'

'48 Faxby Road. I don't know Steelyard Street. No Steelyard Street round here.'

'Sorry.' I smiled apologetically. 'I've come to the wrong address.' I nodded towards the blood-splattered boxes. 'Looks as if you've got a leak. I'll leave you to clear up the mess.' Smiling, I squeezed past the women, slipped out of the house, and hurried down the passageway. Seconds later I was in the car, driving towards the main road.

Mr and Mrs Cheema had stayed on at the restaurant. If they were still there, the girl I'd seen in the big semi-detached house could be at home alone. It took me about ten minutes to find my way back to the avenue divided by the line of bushes and trees. There was no sign of a white Mercedes, so I parked on the far side of the vegetation, walked over and hammered on the door. After a long wait a shadow moved behind the patterned glass and a frightened little voice said, 'Who is it?'

'The man from the university. Can we talk for a few seconds?'

'I've said all I have to say.'

'Just a few words. I won't keep you long.'

'It is not possible right now. If it is important, you must come back when my parents are at home.'

She'd said parents, not uncle or relatives. Certain now that I was talking to Ghinwa, Halima's cousin, I took a card from my breast pocket, scribbled my mobile number on the back then crouched down and pushed up the flap of the letter box. Holding the card in the narrow opening, I said, 'Don't worry, I'm going to go. But if you're upset about anything, if anyone scares you, if you need help, or if you just want to talk, call this number.' Slender brown fingers suddenly appeared and took the card.

'It says Paul Lomax, Private Investigator. You said you were from the university.' Her voice, faint beyond the door, was reproachful.

'I'm searching for Halima. Friends are worried sick about her.'

'I am Halima and no one needs to worry about me.'

I was becoming concerned about the Cheemas returning and finding me there, so I said, 'If you want to talk, call the mobile number I've written on the back of the card, day or night. OK?' I let the letter flap clatter down, then trotted back to the car and climbed inside. I was sliding the ignition key into its slot when my mobile bleeped.

I flicked it on and muttered, 'Lomax.'

'It's Havers, sir.'

'Havers?'

'Mr … Mrs Feinburg's butler, sir. She's instructed me to tell you that the funeral will be held at Rosemount Cemetery at 12.30, in the section reserved for Jewish burials. I gather the gates are about fifty yards on from the main entrance. The service will be at the graveside and the mourners are invited to return to the Old Vicarage for refreshments after the interment. Rabbi Bernstein will be officiating.'

'Thanks, Havers. Tell Mrs Feinburg I'm in Birmingham right now, but I'll do my best to get there. And Havers?' I was holding him on the line.

'Yes, sir?'

'Do you have a Christian name?'

'It's Edward, sir.'

'May I call you Edward?'

'Havers would be more usual, sir, but I don't mind if you prefer it.'

'Thanks, Edward.'

Dark windows glowered back at me when I took a last look at the Cheema residence. As I moved off, the white Mercedes turned into the road and approached along the opposite carriageway. Through a gap in the vegetation, I checked its registration number. It matched the number of the car that had whisked Jason's attackers away from the flat overlooking the park.

SEVEN

B lack hair, fiercely intelligent black eyes, neatly trimmed black beard; Rabbi Isaac Bernstein was young and tall, and had the calm and dignified air that befits a man about to conduct a funeral service. His single-breasted suit was black, his tasselled prayer shawl white, his skull cap a blue so deep it was almost black. He'd come from Barfield's Boswel Road Reformed Synagogue, and his black shoes gleamed in the plastic grass they'd laid around the grave.

Marlena was wearing the black suit she'd worn when she'd visited the office the day before: the one Melody had called an Ungaro. Her face was composed; her dark, heavily made-up eyes remote. Glistening scarlet lipstick made her mouth seem like a ripe and succulent fruit. She'd pinned up her dark hair, a torn black ribbon fluttered on her lapel, and her hands were sheathed in tight black gloves that buttoned above the wrist.

A sandy-haired woman of perhaps thirty, her pale face dusted with freckles, was standing next to her. I guessed she was Miss Macfarlane: personal maid, companion and secretary. Closer to Marlena, with a comforting arm around her waist, was Mrs Brody; we'd exchanged surprised glances when we'd first seen one another. Edward Havers, the butler, was standing beside his plump little wife. Next to them was the handsome grey-uniformed chauffeur and a pretty blonde woman wearing a dark-blue trouser suit. An older man, who I took to be another employee, was hunched under a heavy brown overcoat. I was standing with four smartly dressed men I couldn't place on the other side of the grave.

The funeral director had handed out black skull caps to the men and we'd donned them before walking with the coffin from hearse to grave. There was an atmosphere of money and class and a determination to do things the way they should be done.

Rabbi Bernstein adjusted his shawl, looked everyone in the eye, then opened his book and in a voice that was deep and sonorous began to recite the Shema. 'Hear, Israel, the Lord is our God, the Lord is One. Blessed be the name of His glorious kingdom ...'

Miss Macfarlane began to sob. Havers took his wife's hand in his when she joined in. Marlena, suddenly realizing her maid was distressed, stepped away from Mrs Brody, put her arm around her and drew her close. Mrs Brody gave them a long look, then dabbed at her nose with a tiny handkerchief and stared down at the coffin, a plain wooden box, in the Jewish manner. Bring nothing in, take nothing out. Abraham was certainly leaving plenty behind for the beautiful Marlena.

My mind kept returning to the events of the morning. Before I left Birmingham, I tried to contact DCI Houlihan, but she was embroiled in a murder investigation so I had to make do with DI Anderson, the guy who was supposed to have checked out Halima. He wasn't friendly. It wasn't until I'd got round to talking about blue plastic sacks and floor scrubbing and trapped blood raining down from a crack in the ceiling that he got interested. He demanded to know where I was; insisted I come to the station and make a statement. Abraham Feinburg had paid me well and I felt honour-bound to drive north to Barfield for the funeral. Not wanting to be hauled off the road by the police, I told a protesting DI Anderson I was heading south for a meeting in London, and I'd be in touch.

Four men in pinstripes and black jackets stepped forward and took hold of straps that passed beneath the coffin. Another pulled aside timbers that had been supporting it, then Rabbi Bernstein began to read the Twenty-third Psalm as it was lowered into the grave. Miss Macfarlane's sobbing became uncontrollable. Marlena wrapped both arms around her and held her like a child. Mrs Brody gave them another look.

The funeral director took a shallow brass bowl, scooped loose earth from a pile beside the grave, and crossed over to Marlena. She released the sobbing Miss Macfarlane, took a handful and scattered it over the coffin. One by one, the rest of us followed suit.

Rabbi Bernstein wound up the proceedings with prayers in Hebrew, then the group began to drift back to the cars. Feeling a hand on my arm, I turned and saw Marlena, still holding her blotchy-faced maid. 'I've invited Rabbi Bernstein to travel with me, Mr Lomax. Would you bring Miss Macfarlane back to the house?'

'Be glad to.'

Marlena looked at her maid. The sobbing had stopped and she was dragging in shuddering breaths. 'This is Mr Lomax, Alice. You don't mind driving back with him?'

She shook her head and I offered my arm. She slid her hand over it and I helped her across the sheets of plastic grass that hid the disturbed earth around the grave. We walked out of the Jewish cemetery, then followed Marlena and the rabbi along a path to the car park. I held the door of the Jaguar while Alice climbed inside, then we watched the chauffeur help Mrs Brody, the rabbi and Marlena into her big Daimler. Havers and his wife, the blonde woman, and the elderly man I learned later was Stanley, the gardener, were accommodated in one of the undertaker's limousines. The rest of the mourners climbed into their own cars.

'You OK?' I glanced at Alice Macfarlane, neat, almost prim, in her black winter coat.

She nodded. 'I'm sorry about Mr Feinburg, but the service was reminding me of my father's funeral. I was only fourteen when he died and it took me ages to get over it. When the rabbi started saying prayers, it brought it all back.' Alice's Scottish accent was strong; she was really rolling her r's.

We were gazing through the windscreen, across the car park, watching the funeral cortège get itself together. 'Have you worked for Mrs Feinburg long?'

'About six years.'

'Enjoy it?'

'It's like being part of a nice family.'

I took that as a yes. Mrs Feinburg's car pulled away, the undertaker's limousine followed, then the rest of us tailed along.

Alice began to chatter. 'I don't think Mr and Mrs Feinburg have any family. They seem to have made a family of the people they employ: Edward the butler and his wife Ethel; Alan the chauffeur and his wife Margaret; Stanley the gardener. Working for Mrs Feinburg's been very pleasant.' She glanced at me. 'We've all been told you've been brought in to deal with the transfer of the estate.'

The job description was beginning to sound daunting. I didn't say a word, just concentrated on following the black limousines.

'Is it going to be difficult, transferring the estate?'

'There could be problems,' I said vaguely. I'd really no idea. I needed the conversation with Marlena that I should have had with her husband before I accepted the job, but I wanted Alice to go on talking.

'It's the Chinaman, isn't it?' she said.

'He could be difficult.'

'And the rich Indian gentleman?'

'Possibly. I'll know better when I've had a chance to go through the papers.'

'Things were never quite the same after that business with the

Chinaman. I shouldn't call him a Chinaman, but I can't remember his name, and I could never pronounce it.'

We were circling Barfield on the ring road. Traffic was light, Marlena's chauffeur was cruising at an appropriately dignified pace, and I was having no difficulty staying in the convoy. I risked a glance at Alice. 'What made you say things were never the same?'

'I don't know, really.' She stretched her legs out and settled back into the leather. She seemed to be recovering from her experience at the graveside. 'Living together, in the house, you pick up the atmosphere, but you never know precisely what's happening. I'm pretty sure it started with the dress.'

The cortège slowed and stopped at a red light. 'Started with the dress?'

'Mr Feinburg was supposed to be taking Mrs Feinburg to London for the final fitting of a dress he'd bought her, but he couldn't go so she took me instead.' Alice sighed. 'We had a perfect day: nice lunch in an expensive restaurant, tea at a big hotel, and Alan drove us round the city for ages so we could see the sights. Mrs Feinburg tried the dress on in the morning, at a shop in one of the streets behind Harrods – I think it was called Yves Saint Laurent. The dress was ...' She held her breath, groping for the right word, then said, 'wonderful, absolutely wonderful. It had a tiny gold bodice, and the skirt was layers and layers of purple chiffon, right down to her ankles. A seamstress worked on it through the day: it was strapless and very low, so the top had to be a perfect fit. When Mrs Feinburg tried it on again in the afternoon it took your breath away. It was absolutely stunning. The skirt fell from the bodice, it wasn't gathered at the waist, and when she moved the chiffon sort of swirled and flowed around her like purple water. My mother would have been disgusted by it.'

Alice clicked open a tiny handbag and took out a neatly folded handkerchief.

'Your mother would have been disgusted?' I said, trying to keep her talking.

'It was very low cut and Mrs Feinburg has such an emphatic figure. And when she stood against the light you could see her through it, all misty and indistinct. My mother's a staunch Presbyterian, Mr Lomax, a devout Christian woman. She'd have said it was shockingly provocative.'

After dabbing her nose, Alice went on, 'I think Mr Feinburg bought it for her to wear when the Chinaman came. He used to visit the house about once a month to play cards; Chinese men are fond of gambling, aren't they? They started playing more often and I overheard Edward telling Ethel that Mr Feinburg was losing a lot of money. Edward use to wait on them, take in sandwiches and drinks, then Mrs Feinburg began to do it herself. And on the Chinaman's last visit, she wore the dress.'

'The last visit?' I negotiated a roundabout and accelerated after the line of cars. We were heading out of town now, towards Brenton and the Old Vicarage.

'After the night of the dress, the Chinaman never came again. Edward said there was a good deal of unpleasantness, and Mr Zhang Shensu – there, I've remembered his name – flung a bundle of papers at Mr Feinburg and stormed out. Mrs Feinburg came up to my room. It was quite late: I was asleep and she had to wake me. She was crying and she asked me to go into her dressing room and help her unfasten the dress. When she stepped out of it she kicked it across the room and told me to take it away and burn it.'

'Did you?'

Alice laughed. 'Heavens, no! It must have cost a fortune. It's hanging at the back of one of her wardrobes in a plastic cover. Anyway,' she went on, 'we made a bed up for her on a couch she has in her dressing room. That's where she slept. I could hear Mr Feinburg knocking on the door and calling to her for ages.

She slept in her dressing room for two or three nights after that.'

'And you've no idea what had gone wrong?'

'Not really. Like I said, you pick up the atmosphere, but you don't really know anything. Edward couldn't tell what Mr Feinburg and the Chinaman were saying: they spoke French and a bit of what sounded like Chinese. We guessed the Chinaman had gambled away more than he could afford. He never came to the house again after that, but Edward said he made some abusive telephone calls. And then the rich Indian man started to be abusive when he called.'

'How did you know he was rich?'

'He came in a chauffeur-driven Rolls Royce. He was very dignified and quite handsome, but he wasn't a gentleman like Mr Feinburg. Mr Feinburg seemed edgy when he called, and when he became ill he refused to see him any more. Once the Indian man drove all the way up from London and Mr Feinburg told Edward to tell him he wasn't at home. The Indian got very angry and unpleasant, started saying Mr Feinburg didn't realize who he was disrespecting. Ethel ran and fetched Alan over, just in case he became violent.'

'This Indian man; do you know his name?'

'No, but Edward would. He had to deal with him.'

We were motoring along tree-lined country lanes now, moving faster, and I was wondering what sort of a crazy mess I'd got myself into.

Alice sighed and, in her broad Scottish voice, said, 'Mrs Feinburg looked stunning in the dress: better than a film star. Shameless: that's what my mother would have called it. Absolutely shameless!'

I flashed Alice a smile. 'But you liked it?'

She laughed. 'I adored it. It was a dream of a dress.'

'And you're feeling better now?'

'I think so. I'm very sad about Mr Feinburg. A little bit fright-ened, too. It's as if the house is suddenly unguarded; as if we're all alone and unprotected.'

When I'd parked in the road outside the gates of the Old Vicarage, she unfastened her seat belt, then turned and looked at me. 'I'm glad Mr Feinburg engaged you, Mr Lomax. We're all glad. Someone's got to sort things out for Mrs Feinburg.'

* * *

Mrs Feinburg, or, to be precise, Mrs Feinburg's cook and house-keeper, Ethel Havers, could teach Mrs Pearson a thing or two about laying on a buffet. And Edward could handle a tray of drinks with more decorum than the spotty youth who'd been working the room for Mrs Pearson that afternoon I'd met Marlena in the summerhouse.

I was sitting on a fragile-looking chair, sampling the smoked salmon and cucumber sandwiches, sipping at a glass of very decent wine. Mrs Feinburg was being charming and attentive to Rabbi Bernstein, helping him select kosher things from the buffet. The four well-dressed, middle-aged men who'd stood near me at the graveside were in a huddle by the fireplace, toasting their backsides.

Edward Havers had just returned with more drinks when Mrs Brody entered the room. She'd got rid of her grey coat and was showing off a severely elegant black dress that was, for her, surpris-ingly short. Her hazel eyes were discreetly made up, she'd applied a touch of lipstick, and high-heeled shoes were making the best of her rather fine legs. Dressed that way she looked younger and very feminine, despite the shortness of her greying hair. When she took a glass of sherry from Havers's tray I caught her eye and followed her over to the window.

'I didn't realize you knew the Feinburgs.' She sipped at her drink.

'I was working on something for Mr Feinburg,' I said evasively.

'How's the search for Halima going? I gather from Jason you've located her uncle's house in Birmingham.'

'Found the house, but I don't think I met Halima.'

She raised her eyebrows and sipped at the sherry.

'I'm pretty sure they were passing off her cousin, Ghinwa, as Halima. I think they did that when the police called.'

'Why on earth would they—'

'I'm pretty sure Halima's dead, Mrs Brody.'

'Dead?' Shocked eyes searched my face. 'How can she be dead?'

'We ought not to go into the details here. I've reported what I've found to the police in Birmingham. They're investigating it now.'

'She was carrying my grandchild, Mr Lomax.' Her voice was little more than a whisper. 'And Jason's going to go crazy. What am I going to say to him?'

'Say nothing. It's not certain until the police have found her body. Tell him I'm still working on it.'

She stared blindly out of the window. We were standing very close and I could smell her perfume. It was tangy, almost astringent. She closed her eyes for a few seconds, as if trying to compose herself, then she looked at me and forced a smile. 'How's the Wee Lassie?'

'Wee Lassie?'

'Marlena's maid. I can't think why she had to make such a holy show of herself at the graveside.'

'The prayers were reminding her of her father's death. She was OK by the time we arrived here.'

'You found Halima's house very quickly. Did the police give you the address?'

'They'd never release information like that, Mrs Brody. I've got a system that usually works.'

'Tricks of the trade?' She sipped at her sherry.

I smiled. 'Tricks of the trade.'

'Dead,' she whispered to herself. Her eyes were very bright and her lips were trembling. 'What am I going to tell Jason?'

'Nothing for the time being,' I said.

'Time!' She glanced at her watch. 'I've got to go.' She swallowed the rest of her sherry.

'Got to go?'

'I take a little group at church, Wednesday afternoons. Tiny Tots: we sing songs about Jesus, do a little craft work, then have refreshments. The children are very sweet. We all enjoy it. If I don't hurry, they'll be waiting for me.' She moved away from the window, then glanced back at me. 'What's going to happen about Halima now?'

'I've got to make a statement to the police. I expect they'll keep me informed. I'll pass on what they tell me.'

'Thanks, Mr Lomax. You've been very efficient and very kind.' She strode over to Marlena who was introducing Rabbi Bernstein to the men standing by the marble fireplace. The two women exchanged a few words, a kiss and an embrace, then Mrs Brody rushed out of the room. I turned and watched through the window. A minute later her silver Vauxhall was reversing past the other cars parked on the drive.

I had to talk to Marlena, discover what problems she'd inherited from her husband, find out what sort of a mess I was involved in. She was still being charming to Rabbi Bernstein. It would be some time before we could talk privately, and tonight she might be too exhausted to talk about distressing things. Maria Brody was on her way to St Edmund's Church. I could follow her, go through the motions of checking her out for her husband. And while I was doing that, I could put a call through to the police in Birmingham and see how the Halima situation was developing.

Sliding my glass on to the window sill, I began to take my leave of the other mourners. When I was shaking hands with one of the men in the group by the fireplace, he said, 'You're Lomax, aren't you? The man appointed to oversee the transfer of the estate to the widow?'

'Something like that.' I watched him exchange a knowing smile with his companions.

'I'm John Reed, and this is my partner, Patrick Russell: Reed and Russell, were Mrs Feinburg's solicitors. And this is Frank Nichols and his partner Max Jordan, They're Mrs Feinburg's accountants.' Their smiles and handshakes were friendly. That surprised me. I'd been expecting them to regard me as a trespasser on their turf and be very aloof. John Reed glanced around to include the others, then said, 'We advised Abraham to engage someone months ago. He should have done it sooner, but he wasn't to know. The mess would have been cleared up by now and Marlena would have been spared the bother of it.' Looking me in the eye, he patted my arm. 'Still, you're on board now, Lomax. That's all that matters.'

I was intrigued. I was more than intrigued, I was deeply worried. What kind of problems did Marlena have that solicitors and accountants couldn't handle?

'When will you be getting started, old man?'

'As soon as I've had a chance to talk things through with Mrs Feinburg.'

'Sooner the better.' Reed looked at Nichols. 'We don't really want to push ahead with probate until you've sorted out the mess. Taxation's going to be steep enough as it is without overvaluing the estate.' He smiled at me. 'Don't suppose you want to tell us too much.' He laughed. 'Can't say we want to know too much, but if we can help in any legitimate way, don't hesitate to call on us.' The other three were nodding.

I managed to return his smile. 'Thanks, I appreciate that. If you'll excuse me, I've got to move on.'

Crossing over to Marlena, I touched her arm and said, 'I've got to leave, but we must talk. Can I meet you tomorrow?'

'Of course,' she said. 'Come here at nine.'

I shook the rabbi's hand then escaped into the hall and out of the house. Minutes later I was meandering along country lanes kissed by that first pale-green of spring, the low afternoon sun blazing through the windscreen.

An ice-blue Jaguar is eye-catching. If Mrs Brody saw it, she'd know I'd followed her. So I parked outside the general store, between a van and a pick-up truck, and walked the remaining hundred yards to St Edmund's Church. Mrs Brody's Astra and a couple of other cars were parked in a haphazard way on a grassed area beside the lych gate.

The sound of children singing was suddenly loud as I stepped inside the church and made my way between the pews. Rounding a pillar, I saw them through a glazed screen: a dozen small children sitting, cross-legged, on the floor of a meeting hall. Mrs Brody was at the piano with her back to me. A younger woman was conducting the group, telling them when to wave and clap. It was that kind of song. When I moved closer to the glass screen I saw two more women, standing at a table beside the far wall, pouring orange juice into paper cups and piling biscuits on to plates.

I left the church, walked back down the village street and climbed into the car. Maria Brody would drive the other way if she headed home and I'd see her leave from the spot where I'd parked. I dialled Birmingham's Danville Road police station and asked for DCI Houlihan. This time she was at her desk and they put me through.

'Paul!' She sounded pleased.

'How's the murder investigation going?'

'Closed. Pulled a couple of youths in, one's confessed, the other's still denying it. They kicked an old vagrant to death in a park.' I heard an angry sigh. 'Courts are jammed, jails are over-flowing; we'll be lucky if they get an asbo. Arrests are hardly worth the paperwork.' Her voice brightened. 'How about dinner?'

'That's the second best thing I've heard all week.'

She began to laugh. 'What's the first best?'

'Help me take off this dress.'

'You were a bit out of practice.' She was still laughing.

'I thought I got the dress off OK.'

'I'm not talking about unfastening dresses.'

'It's been a long time.'

'That's pretty hard to believe.' She was silent for a few seconds, then said, 'Well, how about it?'

'How about what?'

'Dinner. My shout this time.'

'Tomorrow night?'

'Sounds good. Pick me up at the flat. Shall we say about seven. If anything crops up, I'll give you a ring.'

'How's DI Anderson?'

'Not pleased. The bulk refuse container at the back of the restaurant had been emptied and the stuff taken to a tip: it was the morning for the collection. The house in Faxby Road was on fire when the squad arrived.'

'On fire?'

'Can you think of a better way to get rid of evidence? It's ashes, Paul. The forensics people are going over it, but there's not much hope of finding anything.'

'What's Cheema's story?'

'Said some boxes of cooking fat must have caught fire. When

they talked to him about blood, he said he'd been doing some halal slaughtering for his restaurants: he owns four. It's illicit, but it's not murder. And there's no evidence now, so we couldn't charge him.'

'Nothing's ever simple,' I muttered.

'The chief's authorized a search and Anderson's had the rubbish tip shut down. Council's Environmental Health Officer went ballistic, said the city can't afford to lose the facility, so lights have been rigged up and a team are going to work through the night, see if they can find any body parts in blue plastic sacks. DI Anderson wants you to make a statement.'

'No problems. I'll call at the station before I come to the flat.'

'I wouldn't do that, Paul. Anderson's not pleased, the men who are going to search the tip aren't pleased, the chief's livid about the cost of the overtime. They could keep you at the station quite a while.' She laughed. 'They're all so pissed off you might never get out. Come straight to the flat and go in the morning after.'

It seemed the Jason and Halima romance was going to continue haunting me. And I'd yet to discover what delights Marlena had in store. 'Tomorrow night,' I said. 'I'll be there at seven.'

A throaty chuckle rustled in the earpiece. 'I'm looking forward to it.'

I switched off the phone and glanced down the village street. Cars and some four-by-fours had begun to line up outside the church and mothers were congregating in little groups, chattering while they waited. Minutes later, Mrs Brody's Tiny Tots were dashing though the lych gate, waving bits of coloured paper they'd glued together. While they were being helped into cars and driven away, Maria Brody emerged from the church and headed down the path. The younger and the two older women followed her. No men, not even a vicar.

Trying to make sure she didn't see me, I kept well back when I followed her home. When she eventually turned into Tanglewood, her car was no more than a silver speck in the distance. I'd checked her out. I'd done what her husband had asked me to do. I reversed the Jaguar in a field gateway and motored back to town.

EIGHT

Edward Havers unlocked the door and entered the darkened room. 'If you could just remain in the corridor a moment, sir, I'll open the curtains.' He disappeared into the shadows, still talking. 'This was Mr Feinburg's study, sir. When he became ill he gradually stopped using it. It's been shut up like this for several months.' Curtains rustled along rails and sunlight flooded the large square room. I followed him in. 'Mrs Feinburg instructed me to offer you breakfast, sir. Would you care for breakfast? Mrs Havers could soon prepare some for you.'

'Kind of you, Edward, but I'll give it a miss this time.' The unaccustomed luxury would have been pleasant, but I didn't want anything to intrude into my talk with Marlena.

'Very good, sir. But you'll have coffee? I'll bring some in as soon as Mrs Feinburg joins you. She asked me to tell you she won't be long.' He was tying back red velvet curtains with silk ropes.

I sat in a low-backed brown leather chair, facing a large mahogany desk, and glanced around the room. There was a brown leather sofa and a matching wing chair. Two more of the low-backed leather chairs were arranged on either side of a mahogany gaming table, and shelves in a recess behind the desk were crammed with books that looked as if they'd been read. The titles on the spines were in French, German, Russian and English:

Abraham Feinburg had been quite a linguist. Table lamps, with black and gold shades, were spread around the room. I heard the soft click of a latch. When I glanced over my shoulder, Edward Havers had gone.

Two tall windows overlooked a cobbled yard enclosed by outhouses and stables that had been converted into neat little cottages for Mrs Feinburg's family of domestics. Alan, the chauffeur, was in his shirtsleeves, working a vacuum cleaner over the interior of the Daimler.

The door opened and Marlena swept in wearing a black woollen dress. 'Sorry to keep you waiting, Paul.' I rose and watched her move over to the sofa. When she'd settled herself into it, she explained, 'I overslept and Ethel's breakfasts aren't things to be rushed.'

Crockery rattled, then Havers appeared carrying a silver tray. He laid it on a low table in front of the sofa. 'Shall I pour the coffee, ma'am?'

'I'll do it, Havers. Could you make sure we're not disturbed?'

'Of course, ma'am.'

Marlena gestured towards the wing chair. 'Please, Paul, come and sit closer to me.'

I did as she asked, turning the chair to face the sofa. She'd pushed the sleeves of her dress up to her elbows, exposing pale arms and a clutch of gold bracelets. She was still being generous with the eye-shadow and her lips and nails were a sultry red. The black dress was no more than a gesture; she hadn't plunged headlong into mourning for Abraham.

'How do you like your coffee?'

'Black, three sugars.'

She handed me a cup, left me to spoon in the sugar, then opened her little clutch bag and took out the black and gold box of Russian cigarettes. 'I gave these things up the night Abraham died, but coming in here—' She glanced around the room, shivered, then pressed a cigarette into the stubby ivory holder and fumbled with her lighter.

She wasn't getting anywhere, so I said, 'May I?' I took it from her and turned up the gas flow, pressed the igniter and held it towards her. She leaned forward, laid her hand on mine to steady herself, and drew the flame into the black cigarette. Her hand was soft and cool and dry, her breasts heavy against the black wool of her dress. 'Thanks,' she said, then blew smoke from the corner of her mouth.

'We need to talk about the problems with the transfer of the estate, Marlena.' I handed her the lighter; she dropped it in her bag, then sank back into the sofa and crossed her legs. Her dark hair was down today, tumbling around her shoulders in a mass of loose curls.

Eyes narrowed, she gazed at me through the cigarette smoke for a moment, then said softly, 'Before I can tell you about the problems, I have to tell you a little about my life and my marriage. If I do not do that, you will not understand.'

A quick run over the facts with me asking questions was what I wanted. But her voice was low and pleasant, and her German accent somehow made the mundane seem interesting. So I settled back in the chair and smiled to let her know I was ready to listen to what she had to say.

'I come from Brussendorf, an East German mining town,' she began. 'My mother abandoned me to my grandmother a week after I was born and went to Poland with a man. I don't recall ever having seen her again. It was my grandmother who had me baptized Marlena. She adored old black-and-white movies; I suppose I might just as easily have been called Greta. East Germany was bleak but disciplined under communism. Miners of coal were valued, the schools were excellent, and I had a good basic education. In my teens I was in the school orchestra: I played the cello. I wanted to go to university and study music, but—' She shrugged, sucked at the little ivory cigarette holder, then exhaled and gazed at me absently.

'You wanted to go to university,' I prompted.

'University … mmm, yes, university.' She sighed. 'There was no chance of that. My grandmother supported us by cleaning offices. When I was fifteen she began to take me with her. We started at five in the morning and finished at eight, then went to other premises in the evening until about ten. Abraham had offices in one of the buildings where we cleaned. I think he realized communism was about to come to an end and he'd established himself there so he could take advantage of the changes. He worked late and he used to tell us to clean around him. He was always pleasant. He made you feel as if you mattered, as if you were important. When you clean offices, the last thing you feel is important.

'When I was sixteen he asked my grandmother if he could take us both for a meal to celebrate my birthday. After that, he'd sometimes take me to places on my own. And when he learned of my love for music, he arranged for me to have cello lessons from someone quite distinguished. When I was almost seventeen, my grandmother asked me how I'd feel about marrying him. Abraham must have been talking to her about it. I was shocked. To me, he was like a father. I'd never thought of him in any other way, and his behaviour towards me had always been completely proper. My grandmother told me it would be advantageous for me. I'd become the wife of a wealthy man. I'd have status and he would care for me and protect me, and the drudgery of work would be over.'

Marlena tapped her cigarette over a tiny silver ashtray. 'I was barely seventeen, Paul. I'd never been kissed in a passionate way. What was I to make of it? My grandmother kept going on and on about what a good thing it would be for me, how easy my life would become. In the end, I agreed. A week later, Abraham took me to dinner and proposed. We were married in the town hall the following month. The only guests were my grandmother, her sister, and two people from Abraham's office who acted as witnesses. More coffee?'

I shook my head and watched while she poured herself another cup.

'I was so innocent, little more than a child. The only advice my grandmother gave me was: "Always be welcoming to him, Marlena; always show pleasure. Do that and he'll be good to you."' She laughed softly. 'I'd no idea what my grandmother was talking about. I thought she meant welcome him and be pleased to see him when he came home from the office.' She laughed again, then flicked ash from her cigarette. 'But he was a sensitive and culti-vated man; never coarse, always considerate. And he bought my grandmother a very nice flat, furnished it for her and gave her a generous allowance. At first everyone we met thought I was his daughter. That embarrassed him. He encouraged me to make up my face; made sure I dressed in the kind of smart clothes a wealthy mature woman would wear. After a while, the misunderstanding didn't happen so often.

'On the whole, things were fine. I thought he loved me and treasured me.' She paused, holding back tears, and I followed her gaze through the tall windows. The chauffeur was washing the Daimler's coachwork. When her eyes found mine again, they were bright and her chin was quivering. 'Women need to be loved completely,' she went on. 'Unconditionally; without measure. But men are not capable of loving like that. It is alien to their nature. If I'd disappointed Abraham, if I'd not always followed my grand-mother's advice, if I'd been unfaithful, he'd have set me aside. I was a possession, a trophy, a thing to be coveted.'

Leaning forward, I found a space on the tray for my cup then sank back into the chair again. This outpouring may have been cathartic for her, but it wasn't telling me anything about her problems. I watched her crush the stub of her cigarette in the ashtray, then fumble inside her little bag and fit another into the holder. She seemed to be marshalling her thoughts, trying to decide what to say. After I'd helped her light the cigarette, she began to talk again.

'My husband enjoyed playing cards: that and reading were his only relaxations. He had a business acquaintance, a Chinese man called Zhang Shensu, who speculated and imported silk and porcelain. Perhaps they felt they had things in common. They used to meet here and play' – she gestured with her cigarette – 'on that table over there. My husband began to lose money; serious money. He'd never done that before and he suspected Shensu was cheating him. But he had the gambler's compulsion to keep on trying to win it back and they began to play more often; once a week instead of once a month. Abraham told me to wait on them instead of Havers; serve them drinks and sandwiches, bring them cigarettes and cigars.

'I hated Zhang Shensu. I absolutely loathed him. Only a woman could understand what it felt like to be stared at in the depraved way he stared at me. He frightened me; made me feel dirty. Abraham should have protected me, not exposed me to a man who didn't bother to hide his lust for me. But Abraham delighted in it. He seemed to draw satisfaction from possessing something another man desired so intensely.

'I realized later that Abraham wanted me in the room for a reason. I was there to distract Shensu. He even bought me a special dress. Buying me a dress wasn't unusual; Abraham was always buying me clothes, but this dress was quite striking. He made me wear it on Zhang Shensu's last visit; told me on no account to leave the room while they were playing. They used to talk and joke with one another in a mixture of French and Mandarin. I couldn't understand much of what they were saying, but by the end of the evening I realized I was Abraham's stake in the game. Abraham was wagering sex with me for property owned by Shensu.

'I'd been in there for hours; fetching, carrying, lighting their cigars, displaying myself in the dress: I'm sure Zhang Shensu thought I was a willing party to the wager.' She puffed nervously at her cigarette. 'Dear God, I blush when I think about it! When I realized what was going on I left them, came upstairs and asked Alice to help me out of the dress then take it away and burn it. The next morning I learned that Abraham had got what he wanted. He'd won back the money he'd lost and some property Zhang Shensu owned in Leeds.'

Marlena looked down at her hands. Trembling fingers were stroking the diamonds that spelled out her name on the cigarette lighter. Suddenly, I realized she was weeping. I pulled the hand-kerchief from my breast pocket, reached over and laid it on her lap. She picked it up, dabbed at her eyes, then moaned, 'Dear God, I vowed I'd never cry about it again after that night. You see, Paul, my husband had revealed something I should have understood from the very beginning. My grandmother had traded with him: marriage to me in exchange for comfort and security in her old age. I'd spent years wearing fine clothes for him, hanging on his arm, always available, pretending to enjoy his wet kisses, his old-man's flabby body making love to me, forever trying to ignore his smell.' I must have looked surprised, because she added hastily, 'He bathed, Paul. He was very clean. It was just his personal smell. I never became accustomed to it.' She waved the black cigarette. 'That's why I began to smoke the most aromatic tobacco I could find. I had to dull my sense of smell.

'That night, the night of the dress, his behaviour told me I was no more than a possession to him; something he'd bought from my grandmother, a body that was his to use and offer to any man he chose. Zhang Shensu had understood that. Once, weeks later, I answered the phone when Abraham was out. It was Shensu. He said, "You strut around in your fine clothes, in your fine house, but I know you're just a cheap little whore he picked up in Germany, and if I don't get my property back you're going to …".' Marlena snuffled into the handkerchief. '… I simply can't repeat it,' she sobbed. 'God, I hate men. They're cold, heartless brutes who don't know the difference between lust and love.'

This wasn't getting me anywhere. She still hadn't spelled out what her problems were. I was becoming impatient, but I let her weep for a while, trying my best not to be one of the cold, heartless, selfish brutes she loathed so much. Her grandmother might have encouraged her to marry the man so she could get a flat and an allowance, but Marlena hadn't done badly out of the deal. OK, Abraham shouldn't have behaved the way he did, but he'd probably never had any intention of handing Marlena over to Shensu. Abraham had been a shrewd operator. He'd just laid on a distraction. And if Marlena in the dress had been half as eye-catching as Alice had described, there was no way Zhang Shensu could have concentrated on his cards. 'The property your husband won,' I said presently. 'What happened to it?'

'Abraham's solicitors had his ownership registered within days.' She rose, crossed over to the desk and searched amongst the papers. She came back and handed me a typewritten sheet before settling into the sofa again.

I ran my eye down a list of properties, all located in Leeds; just addresses that meant nothing to me with rough valuations pencilled in alongside. I glanced across at Marlena. 'Do you still own these places?'

'Abraham was going to keep them, but he suddenly changed his mind and put them on the market. He seemed anxious to get rid of them.'

'Have you considered reimbursing Zhang Shensu?'

'He wants his property back and it's no longer mine to return. He was becoming very aggressive and difficult before Abraham died. That's the main reason why Abraham engaged you.'

'The main reason?'

'I think there may be another problem. An Indian businessman used to call. He'd be locked in here with Abraham for ages. I've no idea what the meetings were about, but when Abraham became ill he refused to see him any more. Once the Indian kicked up quite a fuss, said Abraham didn't realize who he was disrespecting, and he kept phoning and making threats.'

'Threats?'

'He warned Abraham that if he wouldn't do some deal, he'd use his political connections to make life very unpleasant for us both.'

I raised an eyebrow.

'We don't have British nationality. I'm German; Abraham was Russian. He said he'd have our right to remain here challenged.'

'Do you know the man's name?'

'He's called Fahim. He has offices in Leeds and London. Charming until he's crossed. He's supposed to be very well connected, socially and politically.'

Helen Houlihan had told me Halima's father was a wealthy Leeds businessman with political connections. It was unlikely there'd be two property-owning Fahims in the city. 'Would this Fahim be Nawaz Fahim?'

'Possibly. Nawaz certainly sounds familiar.'

'And have you any idea what he wanted from your husband.'

She shook her head. 'None at all.'

'Why is Zhang Shensu suddenly demanding the properties

back? He passed the deeds to Abraham. He seemed to accept he'd lost them fair and square.'

'He's not suddenly demanding. Just days after he'd lost them he was asking for another game. Gamblers win, lose, then play on in the expectation of getting everything back. They think they understand the laws of chance. But Abraham wouldn't agree to another game; perhaps he wanted to quit while he was ahead as they say, or perhaps it was because his illness was beginning to make him very tired. It was when Shensu realized he wasn't going to be given the opportunity to win it back that he became so aggressive.'

'You want me to resolve the situation?'

'I want you to make Shensu stop harassing me, and if Fahim tries to contact me, find out what he wants and deal with it.'

'We're talking about serious money, Marlena, several million, and the men we're dealing with are smart operators, probably pretty ruthless, too.'

'I rather think that's why my husband engaged you, and paid you in advance.'

She'd very deftly put me in my place. Smiling at her, I said, 'What about recourse to the law?'

'My husband thought about talking to the police when Shensu became really unpleasant. John Reed said the police wouldn't be interested until he'd actually broken the law. That's when Abraham decided to engage you.' Her voice suddenly became brisk, 'Anyway, I'm not proud of my involvement in all of this, and the last thing I want is the police talking to a man who thinks I'm a whore he almost won in a game of cards.'

'Do you have addresses for Shensu and Fahim?'

'They'll be in one of my husband's notebooks or amongst the papers on the desk.'

'May I take a look?'

'Why not? It's just as he left it. Do what you want with it all.'

There was a gentle tapping on the door and Havers drifted in. 'Mrs Brody and the other ladies have arrived, ma'am. I've shown them into the sitting room. The chairs have been arranged and the music stands set up.'

'Thanks, Havers. I'm coming through now.'

'Shall I serve coffee, ma'am?'

'In an hour, Havers. We've a lot to get through.'

I heard the door closing, then Marlena said, 'We've a concert tonight; at The Town Hall. This is our last chance to run through everything.'

'Concert?'

'The Eressian String Quartet. I play the cello, Maria Brody plays first violin, Janet Smith second, and Clarise Cunliffe the viola. We've hardly been able to practise. I've had Abraham's illness and death to cope with, Maria's having problems with her son, and none of us is very familiar with two of the items on the programme.' She rose to her feet. 'Forgive me, Mr Lomax, but I must go through.' As she was heading for the door, she said, 'What do you propose to do?'

'Sift through the documents, think things over, then we might need another talk.'

After she'd gone I spent a couple of hours looking through Abraham Feinburg's papers, noting names and phone numbers, gathering related documents into folders and stashing them away. There were several unopened packs of playing cards, some boxes of good cigars and a couple of bottles of malt whisky in one of the drawers, but nothing that threw any light on the situation. What little information I found was in the papers and notebooks strewn over the red leather top of the desk.

Edward Havers brought lunch in for me on a fancy trolley; said Mrs Feinburg had instructed him to. Lamb stew with dumplings and all the trimmings, hot plum tarts and cream. It was probably the best meal I'd had since my wife died. While I was eating, faint sounds of music wafted into the sunlit study, and when I walked past the sitting room on my way out, the Eressian String Quartet were giving a bravura performance. I'd no idea what they were playing, but it sounded polished and professional.

Life at the Old Vicarage was cultured and refined: the cuisine, the music, the house and its gardens. It was a world away from my sad little bungalow with its tiny patch of lawn, my microwaved meals, the mindless triviality of a television set I occasionally switched on just to hear the sound of a human voice. Now Abraham was dead, Shensu and Fahim might try to move in and destroy it all, and I didn't have the faintest idea what to do.

* * *

Sitting behind the desk in my own office, I leafed through the mail. Melody had left two pink notes on the blotter. *Hazel Hooligan phoned. I have her message for you.* The other read: *Mr Zhang Shensu called. Very large and very unpleasant. Said he would call again around three.*

I picked up the desk phone and keyed in 04 for Melody.

'Not before time! You might have told me you weren't coming in.'

'Had a meeting with a client. Your note; you said Miss Houlihan left a message.'

'Found yourself a Brummie girlfriend, have you?' Melody's tone was icy. 'She seems to be on very intimate terms: tell Paul this, tell Paul that.'

Melody was a mystery to me. She'd rebuffed my advances, turned down marriage proposals, now she was bothered about Helen Houlihan. Maybe she wasn't really bothered at all. Maybe she was just playing silly mind games. Laughing, I said, 'And what did Detective Chief Inspector Houlihan ask you to tell me?'

'Detective Chief Inspector! She didn't sound like a detective chief inspector. She asked me to tell you that tonight's off, that they've not found anything on the rubbish tip, that there's no evidence left in the house, and that Detective Inspector Anderson wants you to call in and make a statement.'

The police hadn't found Halima's body. The Brody business was going to go on demanding attention when I needed to be done with it. 'Thanks,' I mumbled.

'Tonight's off!' Melody's tone was mocking. 'You sound heart-broken.'

'I was going to look through files; try to identify someone.' It was a lie, but Melody and I went back a long way and I didn't want to risk upsetting her. 'Did she say why it's off?'

'Hold-up in a travel agent's. A woman's been shot. And the way she spoke it didn't sound like searching through files. It sounded like … Oh my God, that dreadful man's back again. What's his name? Zhing? Zhang?

I heard her talking to someone, then she came back on the line. 'Watch out. He's coming up and he's very big and very angry.'

NINE

Tall for an oriental, and about seventy pounds overweight, Zhang Shensu didn't bother to knock; he just burst through the door and advanced towards the desk. 'You Lomax?' Barely repressed anger was making his voice shrill.

I nodded. 'Take a seat.'

'I'm Shensu.' He flopped down in the visitor's chair, his fat legs wide apart, his flabby torso straining against the waistcoat of a grey pinstriped suit. 'You managing Mrs Feinburg's business?'

'Who told you that?' I looked into his broad flat face. Eyes like splinters of black glass glittered back at me through slits in greasy putty-coloured flesh.

'Her solicitor, John Reed; Reed and Russell. He told me you the number-one man now Abraham dead.' He removed his grey homburg hat and rested it over his knee. His black hair had been trimmed down to a fuzz.

'How did you know Mr Feinburg had died?'

'That all you do, ask stupid questions? Been expecting it. Phone Read, phone Russell, every day.' His thick lips suddenly stretched in a humourless grin. 'Russell tell me Abraham dead. Now you're the man.'

I gazed at him over the piles of papers on the desk. He went on grinning. I sat there, waiting.

Presently he said, 'Marlena tell you about my property?'

'Mrs Feinburg mentioned that you'd transferred some commercial properties to her husband in settlement of a gambling debt.' We did some more eye-wrestling, then I added, 'They've all been sold on. She's no longer the owner.'

His grin faded. 'You, Reed, Russell; you all strum same fucking tune on your sanxians. Not a gambling debt. Abraham suckered me; won game by trickery.'

'You're saying he cheated you?'

The big man shook his head. 'Tricked me. Abraham very tricky-tricky. I was winning; been winning for weeks. Then he gets the beautiful Marlena of the pale and perfect face into room, bringing drinks, bringing food. Sometimes long dresses, sometimes short dresses; all breasts and legs and backside. "Can I bring you this, Mr Shensu? Can I bring you that?" Abraham knew how I felt about his wife. How many times did I tell him what a lucky devil he was? And with her in room I wasn't winning so much. He say we play again, give me chance to break even. I know Marlena will be there. He know how abscessed I am – that what you say, abscessed?'

'Obsessed.'

'Yeah, abscessed. I was abscessed. So we play every week. One night maybe I drink too much. Can't take my eyes off her. Hey! Can't take my eyes off her when I not drink. You've seen her. You man. You know how it is. I say, Sidings Lane properties: I wager all Sidings Lane properties. If I win game, you give me Marlena for six months. All time she in room, wafting around, making it fragrant. Abraham knew how I felt about her. Marlena knew. They took advantage of the way I felt.'

He must have noticed the questioning look on my face, because he leaned forward and wagged a big fat finger at me. 'You never been abscessed by a woman, Lomax? You never meet a woman you couldn't stop thinking about?'

'Sure,' I said. Melody had sprung to mind. 'I've been there, but when you know there's nothing on offer all you can do is move on and get over it.'

'I'll never get over Marlena, Lomax.' He slid his hand inside his jacket, tugged out a folder of six-by-fours, and leafed through it. He found the photos he wanted, then tossed them over the papers at the front of the desk.

I studied the first image: Marlena in a fitting room at the back of a dress shop, wearing a strapless purple gown with a glittering gold bodice that supported but didn't do much to conceal her breasts. Her hands were resting on her hips and she was looking over her shoulder at a seamstress who had a pincushion on her wrist. Alice Macfarlane, saucer in one hand, cup in the other, was sitting on a tiny carved chair. The second photograph showed Marlena stepping out of the gown, displaying black silk underwear, stockings, and a lot of pale, creamy skin. The images were sharp and clear. I glanced up. 'How did you get these?'

'Hired a woman private investigator to follow her, take photos, see where she went; told her Marlena was a mistress who was swindling me. Here,' he tossed the folder over, 'take a look.'

Obsession, infatuation, call it what you want, as I leafed through the photographs I realized Zhang Shensu was a pretty sad guy. There were a few more of Marlena in her underwear; Marlena wearing a fur coat over a black evening gown with Alan, her chauffeur, carrying her cello case; Marlena, still in the evening gown, embracing Mrs Brody who was wearing an off-the-shoulder green dress; and some of Marlena out shopping with Alice Macfarlane. I slid the glossy six-by-fours into the folder and handed them back to Zhang Shensu.

'No man could concentrate on his cards with her in room, Lomax. Abraham and his wife set out to trick me.'

'You passed over the deeds, you signed the papers transferring ownership.'

'Debt of honour,' he hissed. 'And I expected to play some more; be given chance to win property back, chance to win some fucky-fucky with Marlena. Fortune wax and wane like moon, Lomax. Abraham lost for months, then he began to win. I expected my chance to win again, my chance to have Marlena. But there were no more games. I invite him over to one of my clubs; very nice place, good food, pretty girls. I invite him many times, but always excuses. We never play again.'

'Mrs Feinburg didn't realize what was happening in that room, Mr Shensu. She was just acting the hostess, doing her husband's bidding. If you'd won, she'd never have gone along with it.'

He wagged a huge finger at me again. 'She knew. She see the way I look at her, she hear us talk.'

'French and Mandarin?'

'She much travelled woman, very cultured. She knew she was being offered to me. She didn't complain.'

'That's not how she told it to me.'

His mouth opened, revealing tiny wide-spaced teeth that were worn and uneven. He was laughing silently. 'You believe a woman, Lomax? You believe the daughter of a whore, a woman whose grandmother cleaned offices in a miserable little mining town? You more stupid than I thought.'

'Perhaps your obsession with my client made you get the wrong idea.'

'I don't get wrong idea, Lomax.' He was wagging his finger at me again. 'Abraham was offering her to me, and she knew it. They'd worked it out together: her in room, wearing that dress, leaning over me to put down glass so she could show me breasts, bending over to pick up tray so she could show backside; distracting me, making me horny as hell. She knew. She was willing.' He grinned. 'Abraham was old man, tired, becoming ill. Maybe Marlena hoped I'd win.'

'The property's been sold on, Mr Shensu.'

'You think I don't know it's been sold on? The rents I pay to new owners! Romanians, Albanians, Russians, Greeks: all grasping bastards. Did she tell you I phone her, tell her if I don't get my Sidings Lane places back she got to give me plenty fucky-fucky?'

'It's been sold, Mr Shensu. She can't give it back and there's nothing else on offer.'

'You the main man now, Lomax. Solicitors and accountants going to do what you say. You got to sort it. You got to get my places back.'

'You did the gambling. I think you've got to accept you lost the game, they've gone, and we can't get them back.'

'Big problem. Not mine to gamble with.'

'Not yours to—'

'Owned by business associate. Important man. Going to be Member of Parliament. Very sensitive about his pubic image.' He must have noticed my smile, because he said, 'Pubic image? That how you say it, pubic image?'

'Public, Mr Shensu. We say public.'

'Yeah, pubic. Anyway, he very devout man, deeply religious. He wanted Sidings Lane properties for long-term investment. He say to me, Zhang, you buy, register ownership in your name, I pay. You occupy rent-free for ten years, maybe a little less, then I sell.'

'Why did being devout and a public figure stop him owning the properties himself?'

'All massage parlours, sex shops, gambling clubs, rooms sublet to whores: he wouldn't want it known he owned places like that.'

'And does he know the property's been sold on?'

'Shit, no!' Shensu looked uncomfortable at the thought.

'If your associate's so smart, how come he let you register his property in your name? He took a risk and he's going to have to accept he's lost it.'

126

'We go back long time together. He trusted me. We're both honourable men, but I got a weakness for cards; got a very big weakness for Marlena. Are you stupid or something? I had to have the woman. That night, having her was all I could think about. Now I've got to recover property before associate finds out I lost it. I hire agents to talk to new owners, but they're grasping bastards; want much more than they paid.'

I gazed at him across the desk. His face was a mask. Only the eyes were alive: points of light shimmering out of moist black slits. Clearing my throat, I said, 'What is it you want me to do about all this, Mr Shensu?'

'You got to persuade Marlena to give me what Abraham made when he sold the property, plus maybe fifty per cent, so I can start negotiating to buy it back.'

'I couldn't advise her to agree to that. And why should she?'

'Abraham and Marlena put their heads together and tricked me. She must pay back.'

'Mrs Feinburg knew nothing about the wager. When she realized what was going on she became very distressed. You lost the game, Mr Shensu; Abraham's dead; it's all over and you've got to live with it.'

'When associate finds out, he won't let me live with it. I get properties back, or maybe I end up dead. Tell Marlena if she won't refund cash, I got to leave country, and if I leave country, she's coming with me. You tell her I treat her OK, handle her like Ming vase.' He settled his homburg at a jaunty angle, then rose to his feet. 'Seven days, Lomax. I come and see you again in seven days. You better have something for me.' He rose to his feet and his body began to sway from side to side as his short legs propelled his bulk towards the door.

'Your associate,' I called after him, 'the man you were holding the property for, would he be called Fahim: Nawaz Fahim?'

That stopped him dead in his tracks. He turned and looked back at me, his face and body perfectly still. 'How you know that. Supposed to be secret.'

Smiling, I said, 'Don't worry, Mr Shensu. I'm good at keeping secrets.'

He adjusted his hat, then turned and headed out on to the landing. I sat there for quite a while, thinking about what I'd just heard. It was obvious now why Abraham's solicitors couldn't deal with it. They'd done everything by the book and, like John Reed had said, the police wouldn't be interested until Zhang Shensu did something he could be charged with. And I could understand Marlena not wanting to be questioned about the part she'd played.

Guessing that Shensu's associate was Fahim hadn't been all that inspired. Marlena had told me a man called Fahim had visited her husband; that he was an influential Leeds-based businessman with political aspirations. Maybe Fahim knew more than Shensu realized; maybe that's why he got angry when Abraham refused to see him.

Melody, breezing in with the afternoon coffee, stopped me brooding about it. 'Desperate Dan's gone then?' She balanced the tray on the paper-strewn desk.

'Desperate Dan?'

'That's what he looked like: hat, big head, big body, little legs; the cowboy in the comics. A Chinese Desperate Dan. Has someone stolen his cow pie?'

'Bit more than a cow pie. And they didn't steal it, he lost it.'

'He didn't look any happier when he walked out.' She glanced up from pouring the coffee. 'And you're looking sorry for yourself.'

'I've finally decided to abandon the dream.' I gave her a wry smile.

'Don't, Paul. Don't start giving me those looks and putting pressure on me again.'

'Can't help it.' I let my eyes browse over the blonde hair brushing her shoulders, the kingfisher-blue dress that matched her eyes. The dress was too summery to be seasonal, but it looked very fetching. Suddenly realizing I'd been staring for too long without saying anything, I came out with, 'Fabulous dress. Suits you.'

'You've seen it before and you've never commented.' She reached over and put the cup on the blotter. 'I bet you notice what Myra Finkelburg's wearing.'

'Marlena Feinburg,' I corrected. 'She's not my type: too exotic, maybe a little too mature.'

Melody was trying hard not to laugh. 'Too exotic; too mature! What is your type then?'

'Younger women: blue-eyed blondes who wear blue summer dresses.'

Melody flashed me a grateful little smile. 'I bet I'm older than she is,' she said, then deftly changed the subject. 'I told Rachel not to bother getting you anything for lunch. You're never in these days.'

'Mrs Feinburg asked her cook to give me lunch.'

'Mrs Feinburg has a cook?'

'And a butler, and a companion-cum-secretary-cum-personal maid, and a gardener, and a chauffeur.'

'I've spoken to the butler and I've seen the chauffeur; very handsome. Mr Feinburg must be careless as well as wealthy.'

'Careless?'

'Wives shouldn't be driven around by men as handsome as that.'

'He's dead,' I said.

'The chauffeur's dead!'

'The husband, not the chauffeur.'

She sighed with relief. 'And what services are you offering the beautiful widow that the chauffeur can't provide?'

'Problems with the estate. There are one or two things that have to be sorted out.'

'Can't her solicitors do that?'

I took another sip at the coffee. 'Not those kind of problems.'

'Has Desperate Dan the Chinaman got anything to do with it?'

'Mmm … a little.'

'You're going to get hurt again. You might not recover this time.' Melody picked up the tray. 'What time will you be in tomorrow?'

'Could be mid morning. I've got to drive over to Birmingham this afternoon and I might stop over.'

'I'll tell Rachel to put you on the sandwich list.' The movement of her hips had just set the hem of her dress swaying when she stopped and looked back at me. 'Little Miss Hooligan lives in Birmingham.'

'Detective Chief Inspector Houlihan.'

'And you're stopping over?'

'Might do. I've got to check a few things out and give a statement to a cop called Anderson. It could get too late to travel back.'

'Is Miss Anderson a detective chief inspector, too?'

'It's a mister, about six-three, but he's having the hormone injections and next month he's going to Istanbul for the operation.'

'The operation?'

'Gender reassignment. He's looking for someone to teach him how to walk in high heels. How about it?'

She was still holding back the laughter. 'And why should I teach him … her, how to walk in high heels?'

'No one looks sexier than you when you're walking in high heels.'

Melody gave me her long-suffering look, then tossed her hair and strutted out on to the landing.

* * *

A harsh fluorescent light that left no shadows glared on metal desks and filing cabinets, made the shirts and blouses of the half-dozen men and women working in the big office seem vividly white. If Detective Inspector Anderson had been having hormone injections, they'd not been a success. Prematurely bald, his cheeks and chin were dark with evening stubble and he had that meaty look that comes from spending too much time driving around cities in squad cars. His shift had ended an hour ago. He probably had a wife and kids to go home to. Instead, he was trying to concentrate on my three-sheet statement. When he glanced up, tiredness and irritation were shaping his coarsely masculine features and his gruff voice was scathing. 'Blood began to drip from a crack in the plaster, then the ceiling collapsed?'

'The women were scrubbing the floor upstairs,' I explained. 'Using yard brushes and a lot of hot water. It must have poured through gaps in the old boards, started to wash blood from the voids between the joists, then brought the old ceiling down. It's all in the statement. Just read on.'

'How did you know it was blood?'

'It was red, sticky looking, had a sour, salty smell; what else could it have been?'

'You say here you could smell bleach.'

'After the blood had been washed out, after the build-up of water fetched the plaster down, you could smell the bleach the women had been using to clean the floor.'

'Cheema said he used the house for food storage and halal butchery; said it was the only way he could get decent meat for his restaurants.'

'Didn't see a fridge in the house. And he wouldn't make sheep and goats climb stairs to be slaughtered; he'd do it in the back kitchen. A girl could climb stairs, though. And it would have been more remote up there; a more secret place for a killing, for cutting up a body.'

DI Anderson frowned at me. He was clicking his pen against the edge of his metal desk. After a dozen clicks he looked down at the statement again. 'The two women who were doing the cleaning: Cheema collected them from a house in Gifford Road. Number—'

'Twenty-seven.'

'I can read, Lomax. And you say his wife was with him in the white Mercedes, reg FD51UHO, when he picked them up and took them to the house in Faxby Road. And shortly after they arrived in Faxby Road, Cheema and his wife carried blue plastic sacks from the house, loaded them into the car, then drove to a restaurant at the junction of Dencroft Street and Marbrook Road where Cheema transferred the sacks to a bulk refuse container. How many sacks?'

'Five,' I said. 'It's all in the statement. One sack heavier than the rest. His wife had to help him carry it out of the house, and she helped him carry it over to the bin behind the restaurant.'

DI Anderson stifled a yawn. 'When the squad arrived at the restaurant the container was empty. Cheema said the rubbish had been carted away.'

'Convenient,' I said, 'The council collecting it like that.'

'Not council. Council only does domestic refuse. Commercial waste collected by private firms. Businesses make their own arrangements.'

'Who did Cheema use?'

'Firm called Disposal Direct. They do a lot of Indian restaurants: non-recyclable waste that goes straight to land-fill.' Anderson glanced down at the statement again. Behind him, a phone began to ring on an unmanned desk. No one bothered to answer it. 'When you left the restaurant, you went back to the house in Faxby Road. Why?' His cold cop's eyes were searching mine.

I shrugged. 'Just curious. Women with new metal buckets, brushes and cleaning stuff go in; blue bags come out. I wanted to take a look.'

'Blue plastic bags are standard issue for commercial waste. What was so strange about blue plastic bags?'

'Five bags, one head-size, one torso-size and obviously heavier than the rest, a bag for both arms, and separate bags for the legs. Legs severed at the hip can be heavy.' The phone on the unmanned desk stopped ringing.

'Spare me the anatomy lesson, Lomax. So, you went into the house and heard the women scrubbing upstairs?'

I nodded. 'And saw a bucket of water being heated on the stove.'

'Illegal entry, Lomax.'

'Back door was open. I went inside to talk to the occupier. Nothing illegal about that.'

He glanced down at the statement. 'And when the ceiling collapsed the women came down and found you standing there?'

'That's how it was.'

'Great hulking guy in their sitting room; they must have been scared to death.'

'Store room,' I corrected. 'Cardboard boxes were piled all over the floor. I told them I was from the council, checking properties scheduled for demolition. Houses are being pulled down further along the street.'

'Impersonating an official.' He tapped the typewritten sheet. 'That's not in the statement.'

I said nothing, just grinned at him. My return visit to the big house in Burbank Avenue wasn't mentioned either.

'Houlihan give you Cheema's address?'

'Houlihan?'

'Don't slow-time me, Lomax. You know who DCI Houlihan is. She interviewed you after you'd assaulted five citizens with a pick-axe handle.'

'*That* was DCI Houlihan?' I feigned surprise.

'Yeah. You get Cheema's address from her?'

'From the Brodys.'

'Jason Brody didn't have it when we talked to him. Said the girl was too scared of her relatives to tell him where she lived. We had to contact her father in Leeds. He wasn't pleased.'

I raised an eyebrow.

'Wealthy businessman, big contributor to political parties, pillar of the Asian community and currently running for Parliament. Said his daughter was OK; living with his brother in Birmingham. When we said she'd been reported missing by a fellow student he got seriously angry. He gave us the address but he said he was going to complain.'

'Complain about what?'

'Started talking about intrusion into his family's privacy, racially motivated harassment, that sort of crap.' DI Anderson stared at me across the desk for a while, did some more tapping with his pen, then said, 'Houlihan gave you the address, didn't she?'

'Mrs Brody found it for me. Halima had scribbled it on a note she'd sent Jason. He'd used the note as a bookmark.'

Anderson gave me a knowing look. 'You got something going with Houlihan, Lomax?'

'Didn't remember who she was until you reminded me.'

'She seems sweet on you.'

I met his gaze, remained silent.

Anderson said, 'I wanted to contact Barfield CID, have them arrest you.'

'On what charge?'

'Plenty to go on: perverting the course of justice, refusing to attend the station and give a statement, wasting police time. Houlihan wouldn't hear of it. Told me to cool off. Said you'd come in.'

'And here I am.' I smiled. The phone on the unmanned desk started ringing again.

Anderson turned to a young woman peering at a computer screen. 'Get that call, will you, Monica? And tell the switchboard Pete's out.' He looked back at me. 'Don't get the wrong idea about DCI Houlihan, Lomax. She's a vicious little ball-breaker. No woman makes DCI at her age without being a hard-nosed bitch.'

I put on the puzzled look again. 'She just interviewed Jason Brody and me after the Asian guys attacked him. I hardly remember the woman.'

He leafed back to the start of the statement. 'What made you follow Cheema and his wife to the house where they collected the two women?'

'I was pretty sure Cheema was passing off his own daughter as Halima.'

'And what gave you that idea?'

'I invented a name for her personal tutor; concocted some tale about her dissertation being late. The girl didn't correct me; she went along with it all. And there were tiny marks on the back of her right hand; patches where there was no pigment. I checked with Jason. He said Halima's skin was perfect.'

Anderson scowled. He was clicking his pen on the edge of the desk again. 'When we visited we got them all in the sitting room, talked to Halima, got Cheema to fetch her birth certificate, her passport, stuff like that. The girl in the room looked like the girl in the passport photograph, just a bit older.'

I said, 'Halima and her cousin, Ghinwa, look very much alike. Jason Brody found me a recent photo of Halima. The girl they presented to me wasn't the girl in that photo.'

'And why didn't the Brody boy let *us* have the photo? Why didn't he give *us* the address?'

'Maybe he wasn't thinking straight. His girlfriend had gone missing; he'd been attacked by her relatives. And he's a very sensitive boy; writes poetry. He was deeply upset.'

Anderson was going to need surgery to get the curl out of his upper lip. 'A very sensitive boy? Writes poetry?' he sneered. 'You're messing me about again, Lomax.'

'You said you got them all in the sitting room; who was in there?' I asked.

'Cheema, his wife, and Halima.'

'His own daughter, Ghinwa, wasn't there?'

He shook his head and looked angry. 'Why should she be there? We were checking out Halima Fahim.'

'Halima was pregnant,' I said.

'So?'

'Made pregnant out of wedlock by a white boy, an unbeliever. Being involved with a white guy, a kafir, would have been bad enough; being made pregnant by one would have been devastating for the family.'

Anderson stared at me for a while, then let out a tired sigh and nodded towards a thick yellow folder at the front of his desk. 'See that lot, Lomax? Government circulars, internal guidance notes, seminar papers, all telling me how to deal with ethnic minorities, how to ensure their human rights are protected, how to avoid offending their religious and cultural sensitivities. The girl belonged to a particular culture. She knew what she was doing. If she was stupid enough to let a white youth knock her up she's got to—'

'The law is the law.'

'Don't mouth off at me about the law, Lomax. I made twenty men, Birmingham's finest, sort through a pile of rubbish bigger than a house. Rubbish tips stink worse than stewed dog shit, did you know that? The stench gets in your hair, on your hands, your skin. No matter how many showers you take, you can still smell it. An officer's wife left the marital home because of it; she'd had enough. And all they found in the hundreds of blue bags piled where Cheema's refuse would have been dumped were food scraps and animal remains: hoofs, offal, skin, bones. Nothing human. And the house where you say you saw the blood has been torched; it's just a blackened shell.'

'The case stinks worse than the tip,' I said.

He leaned towards me over the desk and stabbed the yellow folder with his pen. 'My hands are tied, Lomax. What more do you think I can do about it.'

'Have the girl they say is Halima tested?'

He let out an amazed laugh. 'Tested for what?'

'Pregnancy, DNA matches.'

'You're crazy, Lomax. If I dared to even suggest that I'd be kicked out of the force. And what would it prove? That the girl's an unsullied virgin, that her uncle's her father? She could still claim to be the girl known as Halima. Jesus, Lomax, if we started treating minorities like that the '80s Milford Hill riots would seem like a spat at a Women's Institute meeting.'

'WI meetings can get pretty rowdy.'

'This isn't funny, Lomax. I've had the bollocking of a lifetime from the chief for acting on crank calls—'

'Crank calls?'

'Yeah, they're calling you a crank, Lomax. A guy who makes stupid, unfounded accusations against respectable citizens.'

'I told you exactly what I saw. It wasn't embellished in any way. It was no crank call. We both know the girl's probably been murdered.'

'And her father, who should know his own daughter, says she's

OK; says she's going home to Leeds to be married.' He shuffled the typewritten sheets, stapled them together and slid them into a file. Then he leaned forward and lowered his voice as he said, 'You're ruffling some very fine feathers, Lomax; fine-feathered birds who have such a high perch they can shit all over us. Take my advice: leave it alone. And do me a favour: stay in Barfield. Don't bother coming back to Birmingham.'

TEN

Barfield is proud of its town hall. Built in the 1930s, it's an Art Deco evocation of the classical; the sort of thing Albert Speer might have cobbled together for Adolf Hitler after a night getting legless on schnapps. Pigeon droppings coat its cornices and window sills. Its white stone walls and columns are enclosed in a carapace of grime.

I'd arrived back in town a little before 10.00 p.m. and parked in a bay down the side of the high building. It was Friday night and the Eressian String Quartet was playing to a packed house. During the drive back from Birmingham I'd decided I may as well watch Maria Brody leave and follow her. Then I could report to Daniel Brody and close an investigation that had been a waste of my time and his money.

Rain, driven by a gusting wind, peppered the roof of the car; I had to set the wipers to give the screen an occasional flick so I could see the bronze doors at the top of a short flight of steps. A Daimler limousine, big and black, whispered past, then reversed into an empty bay and reappeared. Alan Lewis, Marlena Feinburg's grey-uniformed chauffeur, was at the wheel. He parked close to the steps, then killed the lights. Minutes later, people were scurrying down the street, hunched against the driving rain, heading for cars left down the side and around the back of the hall. The performance had ended.

When the crowd had gone, one of the bronze doors opened a crack and a man in an evening suit peered out. Lewis emerged from the Daimler, collected a huge black umbrella from the boot, then ran up the half-dozen steps. The door opened wider and a tiny, black-haired woman stepped out. Lewis took her violin case and held the umbrella over her while he helped her down the steps and into the Daimler. After stowing her violin in the boot, he escorted a bespectacled blonde to the car, then Mrs Brody, then Marlena Feinburg. Marlena had draped a long silver-fur coat over her bare shoulders and gems were sparkling above the bodice of her gown. She slid into the front seat, then the chauffeur deftly gathered the hem of her dress into the foot-well before closing the door. He made a few more trips up the steps to collect violin cases, Marlena's cello case, and some big bouquets of flowers, arranged them all in the boot, then got behind the wheel, his cap and jacket darkened by the rain. A starter whined and the big limousine moved off. I keyed the ignition and watched. He made a left at the junction with the main road. I pulled out and followed.

A few Friday-night revellers, braving the rain, hurried along wet pavements, but the roads were quiet and I'd no difficulty tailing the Daimler to the inner ring road. Lewis surprised me by turning off at the first junction. After following him for another mile I realized he was taking the party to Tanglewood, not the Old Vicarage at Brenton. When we'd driven through Stanhope, I pulled into a field gateway, the same gateway I'd used when I'd followed Maria Brody home from Tiny Tots, and watched the Daimler's tail lights blur, then fade, beyond the curtain of pouring rain. A minute or so later, headlamp beams swept over the façade of the house. Maria had been driven home.

My mobile began to bleep. I patted pockets until I found it, keyed it on and muttered, 'Lomax.'

'Where are you?' It was Detective Chief Inspector Houlihan.

'Parked in a field gateway.'

'I hope you're not snogging someone.'

'My snogging-in-field-gateway days are over.'

'Depends who you're with. I hope you'd give me a quick snog.'

'Give you a long snog if you were wearing the yellow dress.'

'What is it about that yellow dress?'

'It's the woman in the dress.'

Laughter came trilling down the line. 'You're a smarmy bugger. Where's the field gateway?'

'Down a country road about seven miles south of Barfield.'

'Thought you might still be in Birmingham.'

'I got your message about being on a case, so I gave Anderson the statement and drove straight back.'

'Woman who took the message sounded a bit frosty. Is she always like that?'

'Not usually.'

'She your receptionist?'

'Sort of.' I didn't want to explain Melody's role.

'Is she attractive?'

'Most guys would say so.'

'Do you say so?'

I was digging myself into a hole. It was time for a little evasion. 'Not really my type,' I lied.

'Why isn't she you're type?'

'Can't say why, she just isn't.'

'Why are you in a field gateway?'

'Questions, questions.'

'It's the job. It gets to be a habit. Why are you parked in a gateway?'

'Surveillance for a jealous husband.'

'And has the wife been two-timing?'

'I'm pretty sure she's not.'

'Only pretty sure? He'll want you to be certain.'

'You can only be certain when you catch them cheating. You can never be sure they're not. How's the murder investigation going?'

I heard a sigh and the laughter went out of her voice. 'Off-licence hold-up that went wrong. Sawn-off shotgun. Blew half the shop-assistant's face off. She was twenty-six. Two little kids. I've just left the house. Husband's traumatized.'

I wished I'd not asked. I closed my eyes, tried to shut out the still vivid memory of the police coming to the place where I'd worked, telling me my wife and little girl had been killed. 'Have you got the guy?'

'Not yet, but we know who he is: video camera in the shop produced a clear image for once and he's got a lot of form. A team's out, searching the likely places. We'll have him by morning.'

I listened to the silence for a while, still thinking about my wife and little girl. Presently I said, 'DI Anderson seems a bitter individual.'

'What makes you say that?'

'Kept on suggesting you gave me Halima Fahim's Birmingham address. I told him I got it from Jason Brody. I think you should be on your guard.'

'He's peeved,' Helen said, 'because he keeps asking and I keep saying no. And sending twenty guys to search a rubbish tip without a result won't help his promotion prospects. The chief's livid.'

'Anderson warned me off the case,' I said. 'Told me you're being leaned on pretty hard.'

'It's the girl's father, Nawaz Fahim. He insists he's seen his daughter and she's OK; says she's going home to Leeds to be married and he'll make a formal complaint if his family's harassed any more. We don't have a body, the house where you saw the blood's been burned down, and Uncle Cheema's got a plausible explanation for it all.'

'Which fire brigade attended the blaze?'

'Leave it alone, Paul. This is one we've all got to walk away from.'

'Just curious. Surely you can tell me which station.'

'Crosby Street responded to the call. The incident was in their sector. But you've got to forget it. Fahim can pull strings. If things went wrong and you pissed him off, you wouldn't get any help from us. And you've seriously upset DI Anderson. If he can finger you for anything, he will.'

'The rubbish smelt that bad, did it?'

She was laughing again. 'The crew almost mutinied. One guy's wife's left him over it.'

I peered through the windscreen. I could just make out the lights of Tanglewood, gleaming faintly across a mile of rainswept darkness. The big Daimler hadn't returned. Maybe they were having a post-performance celebration. I said, 'When am I going to see you again?'

'Mmm ... tomorrow's going to be hectic. Sunday could be diffi-cult. Monday I'm doing a late shift; how about Tuesday?' The voice with the Brummie accent had lowered in pitch, become more gentle. I sensed she was pleased I'd asked.

'Pick you up at the flat? Seven-thirty?'

'Sounds good.' Detective Chief Inspector Helen Houlihan laughed softly. 'I'm looking forward to it.'

* * *

The rooks were still busy nest-building at the tops of the tall trees. I thumbed the bell and before I could get too tired of the frantic cawing the door opened and Maria Brody was smiling out at me. She'd made-up her face, clipped pearl studs to her ears and fluffed her short hair up a little. 'Come on in.' She kept her voice low.

'Jason's working in his bedroom. He doesn't know you're here.' I stepped past her into the big hallway and she closed the door. 'I was having coffee in the kitchen. Do you mind if we talk in the kitchen?'

'Kitchen's fine,' I said, and followed her across the hall and along a short, oak-panelled passageway. Her pert little posterior and slender thighs were shaping some tight black trousers. Her tiny breasts were lost beneath a thick white sweater that had a roll neck. She pushed through a swing door and we moved into a kitchen that was full of hand-crafted fittings and grey granite worktops. A red Aga gleamed beneath a copper canopy. Two bar stools, with chrome legs and red leather seats, were arranged in front of an island worktop. She perched on one, I took the other and watched her pour coffee into a dark-blue mug decorated with daisies. She slid the matching sugar bowl and milk jug towards me.

'How did the concert go?' I was ladling sugar into the coffee.

'You remembered the concert!' She sounded pleased. She crossed long legs and wrapped the fingers of both hands around her coffee mug. Hazel eyes studied me over it while she took a sip, then she said, 'Everything went very well, considering.'

'Considering?'

'How little practice we managed to do.' She smiled at me. 'We all came back here afterwards and had a celebration. Daniel and Jason wore their dinner jackets and bow ties, and Daniel managed to be charming for once.' Her face suddenly became serious. 'How's the police investigation into Halima's disappearance going?'

'It's not going anywhere. They've closed the files.' I leaned an elbow on the worktop and took a first sip at the coffee. It was almost as good as Melody's. 'How much do you want me to tell you about this, Mrs Brody?'

'Is it that dreadful?'

I nodded; took another sip at the coffee.

'I think you'd better tell me everything. I can decide what I'm going to say to Jason. He's pining for the girl.'

I told her about my doorstep conversation with the Cheemas; about the house where blood, then water, had poured from a crack before the ceiling fell; about the plastic sacks I was pretty sure contained Halima's body.

'She was dismembered? The girl who was carrying my grand-child was dismembered?'

'I'm pretty sure of it.'

'Then how can the police just close their files?'

'Cheema had a plausible explanation for it all: halal slaughtering at the house for his restaurants. And when he realized I'd been inside and seen the blood, he set fire to the place. It was a burned-out shell by the time the police arrived. The evidence had gone. They didn't find any body parts at the council tip, Nawaz Fahim assured them his daughter was OK, and when they visited the Cheemas they interviewed a girl who said she was Halima.'

'Perhaps you're wrong, Mr Lomax. Perhaps the girl you saw was Halima.'

'There was a strong resemblance, but she wasn't the girl in the photograph Jason gave me. And there were small, irregular patches of pale skin on the back of her right hand. I checked with Jason. He confirmed her skin was perfect. I'm pretty sure it wasn't Halima, Mrs Brody.'

'Presumably you've told the police about the different girl; the girl with marks on her hand?'

I nodded. 'They didn't want to know. Halima's father says she's OK, they've interviewed a girl who claims to be Halima, they haven't found a body, so they're letting it go.'

'What if Jason were to visit the house with the police: he could tell them the girl wasn't Halima?'

'The girl would probably say he was crazy, that she hardly knew him, that he was fantasizing about a relationship. And Halima's father has influence. He's threatening the police with a complaint about harassment. They'd probably refuse to go.'

She closed her eyes and pinched the bridge of her nose. 'What am I going to tell Jason, Mr Lomax?'

'Why not tell him the police have checked it out; that Halima's father's assured them she's OK and she's going home to be married. That's the truth as far as it goes.'

'They were lovers. She was pregnant with his child. He won't accept that she's going home to marry someone else.'

'Then tell him the whole truth. Tell him I'm pretty sure she's been murdered, but the police don't have enough evidence to pursue it.'

Maria Brody frowned down at her coffee mug. 'I haven't the faintest idea what to do. She was his first real girlfriend. They probably lost their virginity to one another. She was carrying his child.' Maria glanced up at me. 'How would you feel if it had happened to you?'

'Sick with worry and rage.'

'Exactly, Mr Lomax. Sexual love is a powerful thing. It can overwhelm us; take us completely unawares. And we've no control over our feelings. Love can make the most sensible people do the craziest things.' She fell silent and gazed at me with eyes that weren't seeing me, her mind in another place. A tall refrigerator with double doors was humming softly. A wall clock with a slowly swinging pendulum was ticking away the seconds. My coffee mug clattering down on the worktop brought her back to me. After taking a deep breath, she said, 'Jason's very intuitive and sensitive. He'd love like a woman loves; he'd give himself completely to the girl. That's what's making it so difficult for him to bear.' Her eyes became distant again, and her voice was little more than a whisper as she added, 'Very few men are capable of loving in that way; they always hold a part of themselves back, they never love completely. Don't you agree, Mr Lomax?'

'Not really, Mrs Brody. In my experience, women usually offer love on a strictly conditional basis.' I met her gaze. She was pressing her lips together in an attempt to hide the smile that was shining in her eyes. I was trying to recall a comment she'd made, at an earlier meeting, about the nature of love, but I couldn't. It was a theme she kept returning to. Maybe she was trying to tell me something about the state of her marriage.

Her smile suddenly showed. 'Love can never be conditional, Mr Lomax. Women like that aren't really in love.' She laughed. 'I gather you carry your share of emotional scars?'

'Don't we all?' I drained the coffee. It was too good to leave. 'Do you want me with you when you talk to Jason?'

She shook her head. 'I'll tell him her father's told the police she's leaving university and going home and they've closed the files. I'll see how he responds before I tell him any more.'

'He ought to let it go,' I said. 'In her family's eyes he's seduced her, brought dishonour on them all.'

'This is England, Mr Lomax. What about the law?'

'People aren't compelled to respect the law, Mrs Brody.'

She slid from her stool. 'I'll go up to his room and get it over with. When will you send your bill?'

'After the end of the month.' I followed her out of the big bright kitchen, down the passage and across the hall. The monotonous cawing of the rooks invaded the house when she opened the front door. 'Phone me,' I said. 'And tell me how Jason reacts. But it really is time for him to let go.'

Sunlight was warm on my face as I crunched over the gravel towards the car. I strode on past it, went round the back of the house and stepped into the gloom of the garage. After circling

Maria's silver Astra and Daniel's black BMW, I climbed the rough wooden steps and the flight of stairs to the workshop and peered inside. Daniel Brody was sitting at a brightly lit bench, assembling parts on to the chassis of his latest locomotive. He was engrossed. He hadn't heard me open the door, but he glanced up when I began to cross the boards.

'Lomax! Drag a pew over.' He gestured towards a chair tucked beneath a drafting table that was piled with drawings. He was eying me apprehensively. 'You've got news for me?'

'Nothing bad, Mr Brody.' I lifted the chair over to the bench and sat facing him. 'I've checked your wife's visits to Tiny Tots, the Theological Society, her performance at the town hall with the string quartet; followed her home when she left her engagements. There's never been anything untoward; never been a man involved.'

He sniffed and twitched his moustache. 'You're assuring me she's not having an affair?'

'I can't do that, Mr Brody. I can only say that while she was going about her business, there was never any indication that she's involved with another man. Has she been to places other than the ones you mentioned?'

He began to shake his head, then muttered, 'She went to the Feinburgs' place to practise for the concert.'

'What about church yesterday? That's the only thing I haven't checked. Did your wife attend the Sunday service at St Edmund's?'

'She didn't go. Exhausted by the performance and the party. They all came here after the concert and they were talking and drinking into the early hours of Saturday morning. Darling this and sweetie that; telling one another how marvellously they'd played. Arty-farty nonsense. They even tried to persuade Jason to give a reading of some of his poems. Thank God he had the good sense to refuse.'

He frowned down at the workbench and a wistful note crept into his voice. 'Marlena Feinburg, woman who plays the cello, is very striking, Lomax. She's German; a Kraut: dark hair, skin like porcelain, emphatic figure; and she was drenched in perfume and spilling out of her dress. Seems to get along well with Maria. They were very chummy. Couldn't understand the woman myself. Very remote and dreamy. And she certainly wasn't interested in anything I had to say. Musicians! You've got to ground yourself in reality, Lomax. It's engineers that have shaped the world, eased man's burdens, improved his quality of life, not arty-farty musicians and poets and painters. Feinburg's chauffeur was a decent chap, though. Used to work for an engineering firm. Brought him up here to see the locos. He was fascinated, absolutely fascinated. He understood. He could appreciate fine engineering. And I was dammed glad to get away from all that lovey-dovey-sweetie-darling nonsense.'

Daniel Brody sniffed, wiggled his moustache, then his frown faded. Feeling better after his rant, he was bringing his attention back to the business in hand. 'So, you don't think my wife's having an affair?'

'I'm pretty sure she's not, Mr Brody.'

'What if I asked you to go on watching?'

'You'd have to contact me whenever she left the house so I could check her out. We'd fit a bug on the phone and connect it to a recorder; maybe fit a bug in her car. It would get expensive.' His watery blue eyes studied me for a while, then I said softly, 'You'd be wasting your money, Mr Brody. Over the past week, I've checked her out every time she left the house and there's nothing to report.'

'You didn't check her when she was supposed to be practising at Feinburgs' place.'

'I was there, Mr Brody. I heard them: four women playing

together in a room at the front of the house.' I didn't like revealing I had some contact with Marlena Feinburg, but mistrust and jealousy seemed to be eating him away and I wanted him to relax and forget it, for my sake as much as his.

He sniffed. 'What about Feinburg's chauffeur. He's a big handsome beggar. If I were Feinburg I wouldn't want him driving my wife around.'

'The chauffeur's married to a woman who works in the house.'

'I still think old Feinburg's being very naive.'

'Mr Feinburg died last week, Mr Brody. Your wife went to the funeral. She dashed off to attend Tiny Tots at St Edmund's. I followed her there, then followed her home. She didn't even speak to a man.'

Bushy eyebrows lifted. 'You've been thorough, Lomax. And I didn't realize Marlena had just been widowed.'

'You're worrying about nothing, Mr Brody.'

He turned back to the workbench, reached out and ran his thumb along the gleaming edge of the steel chassis. The big driving wheels were in place; the other parts were laid out on yellow dusters that lined a metal tray. Frowning again, he muttered, 'There's something, Lomax.' He flicked the wheels with a grimy finger and watched them spin. 'Don't know what it is, but there's something. Went out of my way to be pleasant when she had the party, but there was nothing doing afterwards. Flinches when I touch her. Can't seem to stand me being near her. Not interested in a thing I've got to say. It's just Jason, Jason, Jason, and that bloody string quartet.'

'It's men and women, Mr Brody. I don't think your situation's unique.'

His face cracked into a grin. 'You're probably right, Lomax. And you'd better tell me how much I owe you.'

I thought about it, added up the hours and the mileage, and told him the amount.

He seemed surprised. 'That's very reasonable.' He reached into his back pocket.

'Why don't I lose it in the bill I'm going to give your wife for the Jason and Halima business? That way you won't have made me a payment and you can just forget the whole thing.'

'Good idea.' He tapped the side of his nose and left an oily smudge. 'And if I want you to go on checking?'

'Just phone me, Mr Brody.' I groaned inwardly. 'But if the surveillance becomes more intensive it's going to become a lot more expensive. And you really would be wasting your money.' I rose and carried the chair back to the drafting table. The overhanging roof shaded the long window, kept out the sun, and the workshop was a gloomy place. A lathe, a metal bending machine, a pillar drill, tools in racks along the wall, gleamed where they reflected the bright lights above Daniel's bench.

He called after me, 'Did you find Jason's girl, Lomax?' The question sounded like an afterthought.

'Disappeared without a trace,' I said. 'I gave your wife all the details before I came up here. She's talking to Jason about it right now.'

As I drove back to Barfield I pondered on the Brodys and Marlena Feinburg. It had been good of Mrs Pearson to recommend me. Knowing the woman, I could even say it had been extremely flattering. But they were a couple of troublesome cases I'd never have taken if I'd still been hounding benefit cheats for the DSS. With any luck I was finished with the Brodys and I could begin to concentrate on Marlena's problems. I still had no idea what to do. It might come down to just maintaining a protective presence until the situation resolved itself.

ELEVEN

The rumble of distant traffic, the cooing of pigeons in the gutters behind the parapets, wafted in through the open dormer window. They were familiar sounds. I found them comforting. In some ways my attic office was more of a home than the tiny bungalow that became shabbier by the year. That morning's mail was mostly circulars; no cheques, no letters of instruction. At least I'd been working for the Brodys. Next week I'd send them their bill. And having been drawn into sorting out Marlena's problems, I could cash Abraham's cheque with a clear conscience. The desk phone began to ring. I picked it up.

'I've been calling your home since seven; calling your office for the past half-hour.'

'I was probably in the shower, Mrs Brody. And then I'd be driving in. How can I—'

'Jason's gone.'

'Gone?'

'Back to Birmingham. He must have left the house early and caught the bus at the Stanhope turn off. He left a note in his room; said he had to go into the university to see his tutor and then he was going to talk to the student accommodation people about a flat on campus.'

'That worries you?'

'Of course it worries me,' she snapped, rebuking me for being so stupid I'd had to ask. 'He's very distressed about the girl and he'll be all alone in a depressing little room in the house where he was attacked. And his state of mind's so fragile. Even Daniel's worried.'

'How much did you tell Jason when you spoke to him yesterday?'

'That the girl had gone back home to her father's house; that the family would probably arrange a marriage for her. I told him you'd checked with the police and they were satisfied she was all right. I didn't tell him you thought she was dead.'

'And how did he take it?'

'Badly. He never said a word, just listened to what I had to say, then put his head in his hands and started sobbing. I got him a brandy and stood over him while he drank it; tried to persuade him to come down and help me make lunch, but he wouldn't. I didn't involve Daniel. He's no help at all in situations like this. He'd have just got angry; told Jason to stop snivelling and snap out of it. He's never shown Jason any affection. Sometimes, I think he detests his son.'

'Have you tried calling Jason on his mobile?'

'He's left it in his bedroom. Anyway, he gave up answering his mobile weeks ago.'

Trying to hide my irritation, I asked, 'What is it you want me to do?'

'Go and find him again, make sure he's all right and try to persuade him to come home.'

'He's twenty-two, Mrs Brody.'

'And he's sensitive, creative, highly intelligent and utterly lacking in common sense. He's a complete innocent and the world's become such a wicked and violent place. He's dreadfully vulnerable.'

'He might listen to his mother's entreaties; he probably wouldn't listen to me. How about you and your husband driving over and—'

'No, Mr Lomax. I'm not prepared to wander down unfamiliar streets knocking on doors. I told you that when we engaged you. And even if I was, I couldn't tear Daniel away from his bloody toy train set.' Her voice became a tearful whimper as she went on, 'I'm so terribly upset by all this. My life's completely disordered. I can't attend to the house, I've no time for music or my friends, and just when I need some support, Daniel's so irritable and off-hand. Now you're refusing to help me.'

'I'll be glad to help you, Mrs Brody, I'm just trying to make sure you really know what you want, and I want you to be sure you're not wasting your money.'

'Money's not a problem. I've already told you that. And if you hadn't gone to Birmingham before, Jason would probably be dead. I daren't think what might be happening to him now.'

'Nothing's happening to him, Mrs Brody. He's travelling to Birmingham on the train. And my saving him from the men was pure luck. I just happened to be watching and waiting outside the house when they arrived.'

'When will you go?'

'If you're sure it's what you want I'll drive over this afternoon.'

'Why not this morning?'

'Because he'll probably go on the campus when he arrives. He won't head for his flat until later in the day.'

'Will you bring him home to me?'

'He might not let me.'

'God, I'm so worried. You simply don't understand how worried and upset I am. Daniel doesn't understand; no one understands. Will you phone me when you find him? Phone me on my mobile, like you did before?'

'Sure, I'll phone you.'

'Day or night?'

'Day or night, Mrs Brody. But don't panic if I don't call for a while. Like I said before, finding him could take a little time.' There was a click followed by a faint hum on the disconnected line. I cradled the phone. The Brody job was an ongoing distraction that refused to go away when I needed to give all my attention to Marlena Feinburg's problems.

Footsteps echoed faintly up the narrow stairwell, heels tapped along the landing, then Melody wandered through, carrying a tray. 'I don't suppose you've had breakfast?' Her husky voice was terse, almost chilly.

'Forgotten what it is.'

Her blonde hair had been pinned up, her red silk blouse had a Mao collar, the hem of her red skirt was cut just above the knee. 'I've done you some toast.' She lowered the tray on to the desk. 'I can't think why I bother.'

Smiling up at her, I reached for a slice while she poured coffee into a big breakfast cup. She was avoiding my gaze.

'Your lady friend phoned,' she said.

'Lady friend?' I bit into the toast.

'The one with the Brummie voice: Hazel Hooligan.'

'You mean DCI Helen Houlihan.'

'Whatever. She says she can't make it tonight. Something's cropped up and she'll call you later to explain. Dinner for two, was it?'

'Missing persons. I was hoping she'd give me a lead.' It wasn't a complete lie. I was expecting to find out if the police knew more than DI Anderson had told me.

Melody extricated a plate and a half-eaten sandwich from beneath the papers on the desk and stacked them on the tray. 'Cosy,' she said. 'Scourge of Barfield's benefit cheats and

Birmingham's best burglar chaser: a real crime-busters' confer-
ence. Attractive, is she?'

Shrugging, I said, 'Just a woman in a police uniform.'

'Some men have a thing about women in uniform.'

'I had a very big thing about you.'

'Had?' She flashed me a tight little smile.

'Had, have: last week you were telling me I was a complete no-
hoper.' I chewed, swallowed, then reached for another slice of
toast.

'Must you eat like that?'

'It's tasty and I'm hungry.'

'Butter's running down your chin. It's going to drip on your tie.'
Scowling, she held out a paper napkin then snatched up the tray.
'At Christmas you told me you loved me. And I never said you're
a no-hoper. I'd never say anything like that. You just make things
up. You—'

The ringing phone cut her short. I snatched it up and Melody
strutted out.

'Thank God!' Agitation was making Marlena Feinburg's accent
particularly guttural. 'The Indian businessman's just phoned me.
Havers is holding him on the house phone; I'm talking to you on
my mobile. He wants to see me. He said it's about a business
matter. I told him you were dealing with things, but he's insisting
on seeing me.'

'You mean Fahim: the guy who used to visit your husband?'

'That's the man. Abraham was always so upset and angry after
he'd been. I don't want to see him. I don't want to have anything
to do with him.'

'Let Fahim come to the house at eleven. I'll drive over and
Havers can show him in to me. I'll tell him you've been called
away.'

'Thanks, Paul.' I heard her instructing the butler, caught a faint,

'Very good, ma'am,' then she was talking to me again, 'You will be here, won't you?'

'I'll be there by ten-thirty at the latest, Marlena. We need to talk before Fahim arrives.'

* * *

I followed the driveway round to the back of the Old Vicarage, passed under an archway and hid the Jaguar in the enclosed rear yard. Mrs Feinburg's big black Daimler and a couple of smaller cars were lurking in a garage that had once been a coach house. Havers the butler must have seen me walking past the kitchen window with my attaché case because he was waiting by the open front door. 'Mrs Feinburg is in the small sitting room, sir. May I take you through?'

'Thanks, Edward.' As I stepped inside, I said, 'A man called Fahim, Nawaz Fahim, is going to pay her a visit.'

'So I understand, sir. At eleven.' He led me across the entrance hall.

'When he arrives, don't tell him Mrs Feinburg's out, just show him into the study. I'll be waiting for him.'

'Very good, sir.' He opened a door and led me into a sitting room at the front of the house. 'Mr Lomax, ma'am.'

Marlena turned from the window and gazed across at me. She looked very elegant in a dove-grey suit. Black piping edged the cuffs and lapels of the jacket, and wider bands of black silk ran around the hem of the skirt. I wondered if it was something the Ungaro guy, or maybe Yves Saint Laurent, had cut and stitched specially for her. She was holding a pair of long grey leather gloves in one hand while she repeatedly dragged them through the other. 'I've asked Lewis to drive me over to Maria Brody's. I presume you won't need me here when you talk to Fahim.'

'Might be best if you got clear of the house. Tell Lewis to take the country lanes for a while. You don't want to pass Fahim on his way in.'

She stepped forward, sat on a tiny Empire-style chair and arranged the hem of her skirt over her knees. 'You said we needed to talk.'

I perched on the arm of a sofa. 'Zhang Shensu called at my office. Said he was going to negotiate with the new owners; try to buy back the property he lost to your husband. He demanded money: what your husband sold it for plus fifty per cent to give him some negotiating room.'

'But that would be ...' She closed her eyes while she tried to total the figures.

'More than twenty million. I told Shensu your husband had won the wager fair and square; told him he'd willingly signed over the properties and there was no way I could advise you to agree to what he was demanding.'

'God, that wager!' She began to drag her gloves through her hand again. 'It haunts me. I blush when I think about it. And if I don't agree?'

I shrugged. 'We'd await developments and act accordingly.' This wasn't the time to tell her Shensu had threatened to carry her off if she didn't pay.

'The man who's calling, Nawaz Fahim; have you any idea what he wants?' she asked.

'Shensu was holding the property for Fahim, occupying some of it himself. It's mostly massage parlours, sex-trade places, prostitute houses. Fahim has big social and even bigger political aspirations, so he couldn't be seen to be the registered owner. Shensu told me Fahim has no idea he's lost it and he's panicking at the prospect of Fahim calling it in to recoup on the investment. Presumably that's why he's leaning on you for some buy-back cash. Perhaps Fahim's found out Shensu lost the property to your husband. Perhaps he wants to talk about it.'

Closing her eyes, she muttered, 'God, what a mess. Why on earth did Abraham make that stupid wager?'

'Let's see what Fahim has to say, Marlena. But I take it you don't want to buy them off?'

'Not for more than twenty million pounds Abraham's already paid tax on.'

'I had to check,' I said. 'I'd better go though to the study and get ready for Fahim.'

She returned my smile but a frown was creasing her brow and she was still dragging the long grey leather gloves through her hand. 'It's going to be all right, isn't it, Paul? The last thing I want to do is call in the police, I couldn't bear—'

'Everything's going to be OK, Marlena.'

She reached for a grey snakeskin bag that matched her high-heeled shoes. I picked up the attaché case, then opened the door and followed her out into the hall.

'Lewis is ready, ma'am.' Havers materialized out of the shadows beyond the stairs.

'Thank you, Havers.' Marlena turned towards the front door. Havers glided on ahead and opened it for her. She glanced back at me. 'How long do you think Fahim will be here?'

'Not more than an hour. Probably much less.'

She stepped out on to the sunlit drive, dark curls swirling around her shoulders. Alan Lewis, the chauffeur, was holding open the door of the Daimler.

When she'd driven away, I headed down the corridor that ran off the back of the hall and entered the late Abraham Feinburg's study. Laying the attaché case on the desk, I clicked it open and prised a tiny camera and video recorder from the protective foam. I should have recorded my conversation with Zhang Shensu, but he'd caught me unawares. There was a chance Nawaz Fahim would say incriminating things, and this time I intended to be prepared.

The high bookshelves behind the desk were the obvious choice. I dragged a chair over and stood on it while I hid the recorder and battery pack behind Tolstoy's *Resurrection* and Dostoevsky's *The Idiot*, two large volumes on the top shelf. The tiny camera was almost invisible in front of the dark leather bindings. Climbing down, I took a monitor from the case and switched it on. The camera was capturing a clear picture of most of the room, from the leather top of the desk to the windows that overlooked the rear yard, from the double entrance doors to the long leather sofa.

I pressed the monitor back in the foam, closed the attaché case, then relaxed in Abraham's chair. The rear yard was deserted; the rooms and passageways of the big old house enveloped in silence. Sunlight, slanting through the tall windows, gleamed on the mahogany gaming table, and the smell of cigar smoke still lingered in the room. It wasn't hard to picture Marlena, in her purple dress, serving drinks and sandwiches while Abraham and Shensu talked and played cards.

Fahim was punctual. After no more than five minutes the phone rang. 'Mr Fahim's car has just driven up to the front of the house, sir. I thought you might like me to warn you. Would you wish me to serve coffee?'

'Thanks, Edward, but no coffee. Just bring him in here.'

'Very good, sir.'

A car door slammed and the bell rang. After a discreet interval, the front door opened. The hall was too far away for me to hear what the voices were saying but, seconds later, I heard the soft tread of feet approaching along the carpeted corridor. There was a faint tapping, then the door swung open and Edward Havers was saying, 'Please follow me, sir.'

The man walking behind Havers was about five-ten tall, black-haired, dark-skinned and handsome. Probably in his fifties, his body had succumbed to the fleshy heaviness of middle age. Bushy black eyebrows, grey hair at the temples, and an erect bearing made him look quite distinguished. When Havers left and closed the door, Fahim turned towards me. His dark eyes widened. 'I understood I was meeting Mrs Feinburg.' He spoke English in the lilting way Asians do, and he wasn't bothering to hide his irritation.

'She's been called away unexpectedly. My name's Lomax. I was retained by Mr Feinburg before he died to resolve any outstanding issues with his estate.'

'Mrs Feinburg told her butler to suggest I deal with you when I telephoned. I made it quite clear it was a matter I wished to discuss with her and no one else.'

'Please, Mr Fahim.' I smiled and made my voice genial. 'You've travelled some distance. At least have a seat, and if you feel it's a matter you can't discuss with me then we'll fix another appointment with Mrs Feinburg.'

Struggling with his anger, he took a deep breath then advanced towards the desk and sat in one of the low-backed leather chairs. He laced his fingers; they were short and tufted with black hair. His light-blue suit was whispering Savile Row and the blue silk handkerchief bursting from his breast pocket matched his blue silk tie.

Relaxing back, I kept up the friendly smile and said, 'The problem is, it could prove difficult.'

'Difficult?' he snapped. 'What could prove difficult.'

'Arranging another appointment with Mrs Feinburg. You probably know she's *the* Marlena Feinburg, the famous cellist? Day after tomorrow she begins a European tour. That's caused the problem this morning: she's had to clear up some matters with the organizers.'

'I've been told Mrs Feinburg's strikingly beautiful. I had no idea she's so talented.'

'You haven't met?'

He shook his head. 'I've only had a few business meetings with her husband. When he became ill, I stopped pressing him.'

'Pressing him?'

Nawaz Fahim eyed me in silence for a while, then said, 'It was business. Purely business.'

Smiling again, I said, 'I've been retained to resolve all outstanding matters, Mr Fahim. If we're lucky enough to arrange another meeting with Mrs Feinburg, she'll discuss any issues with me before reaching a decision. You may as well—'

'How long will she be away?'

'Six months.' I plucked the figure out of the air. It seemed a long time for a string quartet to be on tour, but I was trying to persuade him to deal with me.

'Six months! I've already let things drift for a year while Abraham was ill.' He turned and frowned out of the windows. I followed his gaze. The chauffeur's blonde wife appeared from a doorway at the far end of the yard, dropped a basket she was carrying and began pegging sheets on to a clothes line. Fahim cleared his throat and returned his gaze to me. He seemed to have come to a decision. 'It concerns property,' he said. 'Close to the Central Station in Leeds.'

I braced myself for a tirade about Zhang Shensu's lost wager, but he surprised me.

'Property Abraham owns. I have a ...' He looked over my head at the bookcases behind the desk while he searched for the right word. 'An option on an island of properties enclosed by Sidings Lane, Tipside Street and Gresley Road, to the east of the station. It's run down, needs redeveloping for the good of the city. Abraham owns an office building at the corner of Tipside Street and Gresley Road. A radio station occupies the top floor; Rhythm and Talk 105. A local newspaper leases the ground and first floors. I've been trying for years to persuade him to sell it to me. He's never said no, but I couldn't get him to make a decision.'

'I take it that when you call in your option on the other properties, you'll control the redevelopment of the entire block if you have Abraham's office building?'

'That is correct.'

We eyed one another in silence for a while, then I reached down and tugged open a drawer. When I'd trawled through Abraham's papers a few days earlier I'd arranged them in some sort of order. I flicked through hanging pockets, lifted out a file, then opened it on the desk. Inside was Abraham's list of the properties he'd acquired from Zhang Shensu and a plan showing their location in the network of streets near Leeds Central Station. A corner plot had been coloured red on the plan and someone had printed *Plan Referred to* at the top of the sheet and drawn a north point. *Reed and Russell, Solicitors, Conway Place, Barfield,* had been rubber-stamped at the bottom. I closed the folder to hide Abraham's list, then handed Fahim the plan. 'That the site you're interested in?'

He took it and groped behind the handkerchief in his breast pocket for his spectacles. When they were resting on the end of his nose, he began to study it. 'That's the property: the one that's been coloured in. I have an option on the others.'

'Provided Mrs Feinburg's solicitors and accountants raise no objections, I see no reason why it shouldn't be sold.'

'I think that was Abraham's attitude,' Fahim said. 'It was just a question of agreeing a price. Towards the end he didn't seem to have the energy to deal with it.'

'Why don't I clear it with Mrs Feinburg, check with her solicitors, then instruct valuers to agree a price with your valuers?'

Fahim was nodding. He was warming to me. He'd got the

decision he wanted, but it was obvious he'd no idea his associate, Zhang Shensu, had gambled away his other places. The puzzling thing was, why did Abraham sell them on so quickly when he owned the entire site? Maybe, like Nawaz Fahim, he didn't want to be the owner of massage parlours and similar places. Or maybe he anticipated trouble when Fahim discovered what had happened.

Fahim smiled at me for the first time. 'I take it you'll be able to clear it with Mrs Feinburg before she goes on tour?'

Returning his smile, I said, 'I most certainly will.'

The phone began to ring. I gave Fahim an apologetic look, then picked it up. It was Edward Havers. 'I'm dreadfully sorry to disturb you, sir, but I have Mrs Feinburg on the line and she's extremely distressed. She's asking to talk to you.'

'Put Miss Macfarlane through.'

'I … very good, sir.'

The phone clicked and I heard rapid breathing. 'Fahim's still with you?' Marlena had got the message.

'For the present.'

'I've just had the most frightful experience. Zhang Shensu must have been watching the house when we left and followed us. When Lewis stopped at some traffic lights, Shensu opened my door, climbed into the back and started yelling at me. Said if I didn't give him money for the property he'd lost he'd take me. Then he shoved his hand up my skirt and fondled my thighs while he said filthy things. Lewis was pounding his back, trying to drag him away from me, but he's so huge. Lewis got him out in the end and pushed him away, then we drove off. God, I was so scared. I'm still shaking. If Lewis hadn't been with me I'm sure Shensu would have raped me. And Lewis heard all the vile things he said to me.'

'Where are you now?'

'In Stanhope, parked on a little green in front of the church where people can see us. Shensu might still be waiting somewhere: I'm too frightened to drive down that lonely road to Maria Brody's, or to drive home. And I don't want to bump into Fahim.'

'Stay there,' I said. 'When the meeting's over I'll come to you.'

'This situation has got to be resolved, Mr Lomax. I can't allow myself to be exposed to this sort of thing. If you can't deal with it, I'll have to find someone who can.'

I glanced at Fahim. He was studying the deed plan and thoughts were gelling in my mind. 'I understand what you're saying, Miss Macfarlane, but I don't think that's going to be necessary. Just hold on there and I'll be with you shortly.' Cradling the phone, I looked across at Fahim. 'Sorry about that. Mrs Feinburg's maid's having problems with her car. I think you said you had an option on the other properties that make up the block?'

He nodded. 'A firm option. I can call it in at fairly short notice.'

Flicking open the folder again, I lifted Abraham's list to the top of the pile. 'You're referring to the dozen or so properties that were owned by a man called Zhang Shensu?'

He eyed me warily. 'That's correct. Shensu owns the rest.'

I smiled at him. 'Did own, Mr Fahim. Ownership was transferred to Abraham Feinburg more than a year ago. Abraham didn't keep the properties long; he broke up the holding and sold it on to four or five other parties.'

'You must be mistaken, Mr Lomax. Everything except the corner plot is owned by Zhang Shensu and we have a binding agreement to—' His voice tailed off when he saw me slowly shaking my head, then shock froze his handsome features and he gripped the arms of his chair so tightly his knuckles turned white.

'I'm certain my facts are accurate, Mr Fahim. Perhaps when you've contacted Zhang Shensu and verified what I've told you you'll get back to me and confirm you still have an interest in the corner property?'

'Confirm an interest—' Dazed eyes flickered over my face while he struggled to collect himself.

I picked up the phone, keyed in an internal number and Edward's voice purred calmly down the line, 'Havers speaking, sir.'

'Mr Fahim is leaving now, Edward. Could you come through and show him out?'

'Certainly, sir.'

Arms trembling, Fahim levered himself out of the chair. I rose, reached over the desk, retrieved the plan, and grasped his hand. It remained limp in mine while I did the shaking. Wide, shocked eyes stared blindly into mine. Together with Abraham's corner property, his investment portfolio would have made him millions. The sudden knowledge that he'd lost it all must have been devastating.

'You'll get back to me regarding the corner plot?' I beamed at him.

He nodded vacantly, then the door opened and Havers glided in.

'Could you show Mr Fahim out, Edward?'

* * *

I asked Edward to fill a flask with brandy and find Alice Macfarlane, Marlena's maid and companion. I figured a little alcohol and some female company might help her get over the ordeal. Alice ran out of the back door, a red tartan car rug over her arm, a silver flask in her hand. I opened the passenger door of the Jaguar, she slipped inside, then I walked round and got behind the wheel.

'Have they had an accident?'

'Sort of. They were waylaid by Zhang Shensu.'

'The Chinaman?'

I nodded. 'He upset Mrs Feinburg pretty badly. Lewis managed to drag him off, but—'

'Drag him off!'

'He'd climbed into the back with Mrs Feinburg and was being abusive about some business dealings he'd had with her husband.'

It took fifteen minutes of fast driving along winding country lanes to get to Stanhope. As we cruised more sedately past the general store, I saw the Daimler parked on the square of grass in front of St Edmund's, the church where Mrs Brody ministered to tiny tots. I pulled up alongside. Alice swung her legs out of the car as soon as it stopped, ran over to the Daimler and climbed into the back. Lewis was standing by the driver's door, his cap under his arm, looking pretty shaken. I went over and asked him what had happened.

'Chinaman must have pulled up behind us when we were at the junction with the Retford road. I was watching the traffic lights, waiting for them to change. First thing I knew he had the back door open and he was climbing inside, yelling at Mrs Feinburg. Then he started saying all sorts of filthy things I certainly wouldn't want my missus to hear. I tried to drag him away but he was so big he got jammed in the door, so I had to punch and kick him until he came out. I shoved him on to the verge, then I got back behind the wheel and drove off. Mrs Feinburg asked me to park here where the villagers could see us. She was too upset to go on to Tanglewood and too scared to let me drive her home.'

'Thanks, Alan,' I said. 'You don't mind if I call you Alan?'

'Don't mind at all, sir. I'd rather you did.'

I put my head and shoulders into the back of the limousine. Alice had unfolded the tartan rug and spread it over Marlena's legs, and she was unscrewing the cap on the flask. When she began to fill a thimble-sized silver cup, Marlena shook her head, took the flask from her and put it to her lips. Her face was grey with shock.

After she'd handed the flask back to Alice, she turned accusing eyes on me. 'This should never have been allowed to happen, Mr Lomax.' It was Mr Lomax now. We were no longer on Christian-name terms. Showing displeasure demanded formality.

'Perhaps we could go back to the house and talk about it there?' I suggested.

Alice began to tuck the rug around her mistress's knees. Marlena reached for the flask, took another mouthful and grimaced when she swallowed. 'What if that brute waylays us again?' She coughed as the spirit burned her throat.

'Miss Macfarlane and Lewis will be in the car with you. I'll be close behind.'

'I want you inside, sitting beside me.'

'I'll be keeping close behind,' I repeated gently. 'That way, if anyone tries to stop you I can deal with it while Lewis drives on and gets you out of trouble.'

Too distressed to argue, she snapped, 'Oh very well. But make sure you stay close.' Then she took another angry sip at the brandy flask.

Nodding at the chauffeur, I said, 'We're heading back to the Vicarage, Alan. You lead and I'll follow.'

TWELVE

Mrs Feinburg's distress had mutated into anger by the time we arrived at the Old Vicarage. She felt I'd let her down, that I should have foreseen the risk and warned Lewis; better still, ridden with them in the car. Recalling the threats Zhang Shensu had made when he visited the office, I had to admit to myself that she had a point.

'My husband wasn't ungenerous, Mr Lomax.' She was pacing up and down the large sitting room she used for music practice, hips swaying in that genteel way, her high heels stabbing angrily into the carpet. 'And he paid you in advance.'

I was tempted to tell her that if she read her bank statements she'd find I'd not cashed his cheque, but I let it go. She must have been desperately scared back there in the car and she'd every reason to be angry. Suddenly stopping in front of my chair, she scowled down at me and snapped, 'You're going to have to move in here, Mr Lomax. Stay until you've dealt with everything. And don't talk about going to the police. I'm not prepared to humiliate myself by telling them every sordid little detail about Abraham's dealings with Shensu.'

'All you need tell them is that a man's become dangerously obsessed with you. They wouldn't find that hard to believe.'

'And when they went to see Shensu he'd say all sorts of vile things about me. That's why my husband engaged you, Mr Lomax. I really must insist that you move in here.'

'When your husband engaged me he thought he had longer to live. He understood I'd have to clear outstanding business before I could devote myself full time to this. There's just one case I'm working on. I thought I'd cleared it up, but there's been a problem.'

'It's Maria Brody's boy, isn't it?'

'You know about that?'

'Of course I know. It's all she wants to talk about. She told me you saved Jason's life.'

'Relief makes worried mothers exaggerate.'

'You obviously hadn't told her you were engaged by Abraham to protect my interests.'

'I regard who I'm working for as strictly confidential, Mrs Feinburg.'

Determined to make me take notice of what she had to say, she stepped closer, rested her hands on her hips and leaned towards me. 'I want you looking after *my* interests,' she hissed. 'I want you watching over *me*. I want you to move in here, and I want you to travel with me when I go out in the car.'

'I'm pretty sure the Zhang Shensu problem's going to be taken care of. Just a couple of days and—'

'Pretty sure? A couple of days? The wretched man's insane and he's as big and strong as an ox. He could break in here during the night. He threatened to abduct me back there in the car. And he shoved his hand up my skirt while he told me all the lewd things he wanted to do to me. He assaulted me, Mr Lomax. The brute sexually assaulted me!'

She flicked her hair with her hand and turned her back towards me. She was using her body to display her anger. The tiny jacket of the suit was short and the grey material of her skirt was like a second skin over very shapely thighs. Rounding on me again, she snapped, 'There's not just me. I have to think about Alice, too. When Havers and his wife go to their flat across the yard we're alone in this rambling old place. You must move in here for a while. Go and collect what things you need and come back before Havers serves dinner.'

I gazed up at her. I could understand her distress and anger, but I'd promised Maria Brody I'd drive over to Birmingham and search for Jason. 'I'm sorry, Mrs Feinburg, but—'

'Sorry! Is that all you can say: sorry?'

Rising to my feet, I got my eye-level above hers and kept my voice gentle as I said, 'I'm sorry you had the fright this morning. I'm sorry you have these problems. I'm sorry your husband's died. But I think I've dealt with the Shensu problem. We'll know in a couple of days or so.'

'How can you have dealt with it? You've been spending all your time chasing Maria's son.'

'Trust me, Mrs Feinburg. I'm pretty sure it's sorted. But I can't move in this afternoon. I've—'

'*I'm frightened*, Mr Lomax.' Anger was seething in her voice now. 'I have never been so frightened in my entire life. If you won't move in here I'll have to terminate your engagement.'

'Of course I'll move in, but there's something I have to attend to first.' She opened her mouth to object, but I ploughed on. 'Why don't you and Miss Macfarlane move out of the house, just for tonight, or maybe a couple of nights? Perhaps stay with Mrs Brody. No one would know you were there, and tomorrow or the day after I'd move in.'

Her expression began to soften. 'Maria's husband's gone away for a couple of days,' she said thoughtfully. 'Some model engineering exhibition in London. She might welcome the company, especially if she's worrying about Jason. I'll go and call her.' Marlena crossed over to the door, then glanced back. 'But you've got to drive over with me to Tanglewood. And I expect you to have moved in by tomorrow evening.'

'I'll tail along in my car and hold back when you're within sight of the house,' I said. 'If I ride in the Daimler, Mrs Brody's going to know I'm working for you.'

She smiled at me, then stepped out into the corridor and I heard her calling for Alice Macfarlane as she headed towards the stairs. It was smiles and Christian names again. The prospect of spending a night at the Brodys seemed to have pleased her, suddenly calmed her and lifted her spirits.

After she'd left to arrange things with Maria Brody and pack an overnight bag, I went into Abraham's study, intending to retrieve the camera. Fahim hadn't said anything incriminating; recording the meeting had been a waste of time. I was dragging a chair over to the bookshelves when the phone began to ring.

Havers sounded breathless. 'I'm pleased I've caught you, sir. When you weren't in the front sitting room I thought you might have left. Mr Fahim is on the line. He's extremely agitated. He's asking for Mrs Feinburg, but I think you should take the call.'

'Don't tell him she's not available, Edward. Just put him through to me.'

'Thank you, sir.'

'After a few seconds the line clicked. 'Mr Fahim?'

'Lomax! I presume Mrs Feinburg's still out?'

'That's correct, Mr Fahim. How can I—?'

'I'm back in Leeds. I've just left Zhang Shensu. He confirmed he no longer owns the property he was holding for me. He also told me how the Feinburgs tricked him out of it, then denied him the chance to win it back. Abraham Feinburg was a scoundrel, Mr Lomax, and his wife's no better than a whore if she'd allow herself to be offered to another man in a wager, no matter how much money was involved.'

'She'd no idea what her husband was doing. And as far as the card game was concerned, Abraham won it, fair and square. Shensu accepted that. He wouldn't have signed over the deeds if he thought there'd been any cheating.'

'It was an ongoing game. He was expecting a chance to win it back. And the woman deliberately set out to distract and seduce him.'

'Gambling and women, Mr Fahim: was it wise to trust your investment to a man with those weaknesses?'

'We grew rich together. He helped me import from the Far East, brokered many deals for me. I had every reason to trust him. Abraham and his wife tricked him.'

'What's the bottom line, Fahim? Why are you phoning?'

'I want to tell you you're not dealing with Shensu now, you're dealing with me. I have powerful friends. I have influence. I have considerable resources. Tonight I'm dining with the Home Secretary; tomorrow I'm meeting the Secretary of State for Industry. On Thursday—'

'I didn't ask for your credentials, Fahim. I asked why you're calling?'

His rage snarled at me out of the phone. 'I want restitution. It took me years to acquire the property; I invested millions in it. I want the corner office block Mrs Feinburg owns conveying to me for a nominal sum and I want the twenty million Shensu was demanding.'

'I'm going to tell you what I told Shensu: there's no way I can recommend that to Mrs Feinburg. Zhang Shensu willingly disposed of property that was registered in his name. If you want redress, take it up with him.' I slammed down the phone.

* * *

Birmingham was in the throes of the evening rush hour and commuters were stopping and starting in the long crawl home.

Traffic flow didn't improve until I'd driven past the university campus. A hundred yards further on, I made a left into the network of residential streets; they were almost deserted. I was trying to remember the way to Harroven Road and the house that overlooked the park. After a few wrong turns I saw the expanse of grass and trees, got my bearings from the children's play area, and pulled up opposite number 34.

I lowered the window and sat there for a while, watching the house and the street, listening to the sound of children playing. Beyond the city the sun was drowning in a haze of red and gold, and the upper windows of the house gleamed in the last of its light. No one went in, no one came out, so I ambled over and hammered on the door. When no one answered, I turned the knob and pushed. It opened. I listened to the silence in the hallway for a while, then climbed the stairs and rounded the landing.

The door to Jason's flat was hanging open. A cheap music centre had been tossed in a corner, books tipped out of shelves, papers scattered, bedding strewn across the floor. Jason couldn't be this untidy. The place had been trashed.

I walked back along the landing and tapped on the door to the flat at the rear. No one answered. Hearing a faint sound, I put my ear to the panel. Someone was moving around inside. 'Anyone home? Name's Lomax. I'm looking for Jason Brody.'

A latch clicked, the door opened, and a red-haired youth with a lot of freckles peered out at me. 'Who did you say you are?'

I plucked a card from my top pocket and handed it over. He stared at it for a long time. Eventually he looked up and said, 'Jason called here a couple of hours ago. When he saw someone had made a mess of his flat, he cleared off.'

'Did you see who trashed it?'

'Four Asian guys; two nights ago. They were looking for Jason. When I told them he wasn't here any more they kicked the door down and started throwing his stuff around. They were wild: really scary.' He peered at me with nervous eyes. He was wearing black jeans and a black T-shirt. Vividly red female lips, pouting and parted for a kiss, had been printed on the shirt. It made me think of Marlena.

'Did Jason tell you where he was heading?'

The youth blinked at me vacantly. 'He just said he was looking for a girl; that he'd been searching all morning.'

'The girl – was she called Halima Fahim?'

He shook his head. 'He said he was looking for Caron Summerfield.'

'Thanks,' I said. 'If he comes back, could you call me on my mobile?'

'Is he in some kind of trouble?'

'Family business: his mother wants to contact him urgently.'

He glanced down at the card again. There was a fuzz of red hair above his upper lip and the beginnings of a beard on his chin. 'I'll tell him to phone you if I see him.'

'I'd prefer it if you phoned me. He's upset about something and he might not bother.' As I headed down the stairs I called back, 'And keep the front door locked; anyone could walk in.'

'It's the guy in the ground-floor flat. He's always leaving it on the latch. I'll tell him.'

Back in the car, I scribbled Caron Summerfield in my notebook, then pulled out and headed for the student-let Jason had shared with the two girls; I didn't have any other address to try. Semi-detached houses gave way to long terraces when I turned right on to the main road. Less than a minute later, I swung the Jaguar into Shinley Street and found a clear stretch of kerb close to number 78. Someone was still practising the electric guitar in the house opposite; the sound of clanging chords drifted down from an open attic window. Closer at hand, music with a heavy beat was pulsing from a hi-fi system that was being driven pretty hard. Heaving myself out of the car, I crossed the pavement and rapped on the faded green door. It opened almost immediately and a slender girl, wearing jeans and a yellow cotton blouse, looked out at me.

'Name's Lomax,' I said, raising my voice above the music. 'I'm trying to locate Jason Brody.'

Her generous mouth slowly widened in a smile. 'The private investigator. Julie told me you'd called.'

'Julie?'

'We share the house.'

Remembering, I said, 'Julie: the girl with the gorgeous blue eyes. And you must be Samantha?'

She laughed. 'I'll tell her you said that. Haven't you found him yet?'

'Found him and lost him. I'm searching again.'

'You'd better come and talk to Julie. She's been in the kitchen all afternoon, getting ready for the barbie. If he's been here, she'll know.' The girl called Samantha moved aside and I stepped into the narrow hallway. Closing the door, she said, 'Go on through,' so I strode on, crossed the communal sitting room where the hi-fi was playing, and entered a tiny kitchen. Worktops were stacked with cans of beer, bowls of salad, buttered rolls and paper plates. Plastic knives and forks were wrapped in paper napkins. It seemed unusually neat and orderly for a student bash.

'Fancy a drink?'

I turned. Samantha was smiling at me. 'Driving,' I said. 'Best not.' The back door was open. I headed out into a high-walled back yard. Julie, very fetching in a white dress with a pleated skirt, was sipping at a paper cup, enjoying the lingering glances of a couple of tall, muscular young men who were forking charred things around on a barbecue. A pall of blue smoke and the smell of burning meat hung over the yard. I strode towards them, down the side of the kitchen projection. Julie frowned at me as I approached. 'Lomax,' I said.

Her face brightened. She pointed at me with her paper cup and laughed. 'The private investigator! Don't tell me you're still looking for Jason?'

'He's gone missing again. His mother's distracted.'

'Mothers! Can't she leave him alone?'

'There are issues,' I said vaguely. 'She's got reason to be worried. Have you any idea—?'

'He was here this afternoon, about three. He'd been to his flat in Harroven Road. Someone had broken in and messed it up. He asked if he could stay here the night; left his things and went off again.'

'Went off?'

'Said he was going on to the campus. He was trying to find someone called Caron Summerfield.'

'And why would he be looking for her?'

'She was friendly with his girlfriend, Halima. Caron visited her once or twice when she was ill, took course notes and books to her. Jason said he had a lot of Halima's things and he wanted her address so he could return them. Seems Halima's packing in her course and going home.'

Young men and women, talking and laughing, holding paper plates and cans, were emerging through the back door and drifting down the yard.

'What time did Jason hope to get back here?'

She shrugged. 'He's left his rucksack and a couple of carrier bags. He said he'd try to come back for the barbie. Do you want to wait? Have a beer and burger?'

Glancing around the small back yard at the growing crowd of laughing, chattering students, I suddenly felt like a stranger in a strange land. And the lunch Havers had served before Marlena left for Tanglewood was still more than a pleasant memory. 'Kind of you,' I said. 'But I have to check a few things out. Maybe I'll call again later and see if he's here.'

I headed back through the house, moving against the flow of new arrivals eager to grab a can and a paper plate and join the crowd around the barbecue. It was too early in the year for alfresco dining, but the day had been unseasonably warm and students wouldn't be troubled by the chill in the air.

When I stepped out of the front door I stood for a moment, gazing down the long perspective of the darkening street. If Jason had found the Summerfield girl and persuaded her to tell him Halima's term-time address he'd have headed for the Cheema residence. I climbed into the car and began the drive across the city.

* * *

Spring foliage, unfurling on the trees in Burbank Avenue, formed a canopy that screened the light of the street lamps, and the shrubs and rough grass on the narrow central island were in deep shadow. After parking the car, I began to stroll past the big Victorian houses. They were shrouded in darkness pierced, here and there, by a light behind an uncurtained window.

When I was almost opposite the Cheema residence, I saw a tall figure standing in the shadows beneath the trees. A few more paces and I could make out untidy hair, broad shoulders, the glimmer of light on spectacle lenses. It was Jason. He was staring at the house, his arms held rigidly by his sides, his fists clenched. Suddenly his body tensed. Throwing back his head, he roared, '*Halima, Halima, Halimaaa.*' Tendons stood out on his neck as he hurled his lover's name into the night, creating a volley of sound that echoed to and fro across the street. '*Bastards!*' he roared. '*Bloody murdering bastards!* You've killed Halima. *You bloody murdering—*'

Darting beneath the trees, I grabbed him and dragged him back. He began to struggle and throw punches.

'Jason,' I shook him. 'It's Lomax. Your mother sent me. For God's sake keep quiet or you'll get yourself killed.'

'Don't care,' he snarled, still struggling. 'I don't fucking care. I want to die.' Then, jerking free, he roared, '*Bastards*! You killed Halima. *Bastards*! *Fucking murdering bastards*!'

I got hold of him again and began to drag him towards the car. Glancing back, I saw the Cheema's front door crash open and a stocky, heavily built man appear and stare across at the trees. Other men were pushing past him and running over.

Jason stumbled. I helped him up, made him run with me to the car, then bundled him into the passenger seat. Four men emerged from the line of trees, saw me circling the car, and began to run towards us. I slid behind the wheel and keyed the ignition, but all I got was the tired drone of the starter. They were closing on us, angry eyed, tensed for violence. Pumping the accelerator, I tried the ignition again, heard the engine splutter, fire, then roar into life. The men were all around us now. One was tugging at my door, another was standing, arms outstretched, in front of the car. My door swung open and hands grabbed at my jacket as I crashed the engine into gear and let out the clutch. The car lurched forward, the man in front bounced over the bonnet and his head thudded against the windscreen. His friend lost his grip on my arm but managed to cling to the door pillar. He screamed when I slammed the door on his fingers. When I slammed it again, it closed. I began to move up through the gears, accelerating hard. Wide-eyed with fright, the man on the bonnet suddenly rolled off and I felt the rear wheels bounce. At the junction with the main road, I glanced in the mirrors. Two men were kneeling beside a prostrate figure; another was staggering around, clutching his hand and howling.

Horns blared when I turned out and cut into the flow of traffic moving towards the ring road. I kept checking the rear-view mirrors. We weren't being followed. Jason was hunched in his seat, sobbing helplessly. After we'd cleared the city, I pulled into a lay-by on an unlit stretch of road and turned towards him. He seemed unaware that we'd stopped. I said, 'You're going to get yourself killed, Jason. You're going to get me jailed for grievous bodily harm.'

'Halima's dead,' he moaned. 'They can kill me; I don't care.'

'Better ways to die than having your throat cut. And what about your mother? She's distracted with worry.'

His shoulders heaved with a fresh wave of sobbing. He let his head roll against the door and began to mutter, 'Bastards. Fucking murdering bastards.' Hardly language Wordsworth would have used, but Larkin might have cheered him on. 'She was so beautiful,' he whimpered. 'I loved her so much, and she's dead. Bastards! Murdering—'

'How do you know she's dead?'

'She'd have found some way to contact me, or get a message to me by now if she was alive. And it's what they'd do to her. You know about these things. Don't you think she's dead?'

The lights of an approaching lorry penetrated the interior of the car and I got my first good look at him. He was badly in need of a shave and tears and mucus had plastered his long hair over his face. Misery shaped his mouth and all the anguish of the world was in his eyes. Sighing out my weariness with the whole business, I said, 'Yes, Jason, I think she's dead. And if you stand outside the Cheema house, yelling up at the windows, you'll end up dead, too.'

'I can't live without her.'

'Trust me,' I said. 'You'll get over it.'

'God, you're just like Father,' he sobbed. 'You've no soul. You're dead inside.'

'You'll be dead all over, Jason, if you don't let go.'

We sat in darkness while another lorry and a couple of cars swept past. Then he choked out a sob, and said, 'Are you taking me home?'

'Yes, I'm taking you home. Have you eaten today?'

He didn't answer, just wiped his nose on his shirt sleeve and snuffled into his chest.

'Shall we stop somewhere and get a meal?'

'Did my Father go to the engineering exhibition?'

'He's staying over; spending a couple of days there.'

'Then please take me home.'

Making some excuse about wanting to check the car for damage, I climbed out, slammed the door, then wandered round to the boot and dialled Jason's mother. I'd almost given up on her when a voice gasped, 'Maria Brody.' She was panting into the phone. She dragged in a breath, then panted some more.

'Lomax, Mrs Brody. Are you OK?'

'I'm fine,' she gasped. 'You ... woke me. I was having a rather vivid dream. Jason? Have you found—?'

'He's in the car. We're about ten miles out of Birmingham. I should have him home in a little more than an hour. He's in a pretty bad way.'

'He's been hurt?'

'Not hurt; mentally unstable. I found him outside the girl's house, yelling abuse, saying they'd murdered her. He's almost over the edge, Mrs Brody.'

Her panting slowed into heavy breathing, then she said, 'He's been very distressed since the girl disappeared.'

'This is more than distressed. If you have a doctor you can talk to, I think you should have him at the house when we arrive.'

'I'm not sure I know what you mean, Mr Lomax: a doctor I can talk to?'

'The doctor might want to section him.'

'Section him?'

'Refer him to a mental hospital whether he wants to go or not. I don't think you'd like that. And maybe he wouldn't care to start out on life with that on his medical records.'

'I'll phone our doctor now and ask him to come over. You'll be here in about an hour, I think you said?'

I peered at my watch. 'Maybe a little before ten.'

As I tugged open the driver's door I was thinking it was early in the evening for Maria Brody to be having vivid dreams. Maybe worry had exhausted her. I got behind the wheel and glanced across at Jason. He was slumped in his seat, arms folded across his chest, eyes closed. When I touched his shoulder he turned his head and peered at me through the darkness. 'I want you to promise me something, Jason.'

'Promise you what?' he sobbed.

'That you'll walk away from this; that you won't go back to the Cheemas' place in Burbank Avenue.'

He didn't say anything, just gazed at me with sad, desolate eyes.

'Halima's dead, Jason. Nothing's going to bring her back. You're distressing your mother and putting yourself in danger.'

'They're going to get away with it,' he said bleakly.

'Let it go, Jason. Be kind to your mother. Help the living: you can only mourn the dead.'

THIRTEEN

A sudden gust of wind fluttered papers on the desk. I pushed my chair back, stepped beneath the sloping edge of the ceiling and closed the dormer window. There was a chill in the air. The early spell of warm weather seemed to be over. Through the gap in the parapet I could see the church tower. The clock showed 10.30 and the sky was as grey as the lead on the spire.

Days were passing. There were still no letters of instruction in the mail, no cheques. And Melody hadn't left any notes about calls from prospective clients. Running my eye over the Brodys' account, I remembered I'd agreed with Daniel Brody that I'd bury the cost of checking out Maria in the cost of finding Jason. I added four hours' time and fifty miles travelling.

Later that morning I had to report for protection duties at the Old Vicarage. A spare suit, a couple of shirts, some changes of socks and underwear were in a case in the boot of the car. Dressing-gown, shaving gear and toothbrush were in an overnight bag. No pyjamas. I don't wear pyjamas. When I'd packed that morning I'd felt like a criminal getting ready to surrender to a jailer. Still, the meals and all the other creature comforts would make the sentence bearable. And after acquainting Fahim with the loss of his property, I was hoping my stay would be short. The desk phone began to ring. I dug it out from beneath the papers and muttered, 'Lomax.'

183

'Paul! I was expecting your surly secretary.'

'She's not my secretary, Marlena. She's a friend who takes messages. I was about to head out to the Vicarage.'

'Then I'm glad I've caught you. Maria's asked me to stay on at Tanglewood until the end of the week. She needs the company.'

'I thought her husband was coming back from London.'

'She phoned him last night, told him you'd brought Jason home and suggested he spent another couple of days at the exhibition. Jason doesn't get on all that well with his father and Maria felt she could cope with him better if Daniel was out of the house. And I've lost Alice for a few days. She's visiting her sister in Perth.'

'How is Jason?'

'Devouring a cooked breakfast. The doctor sedated him last night; said he had to be fed well this morning, and he'd call in again before noon to sedate him again.'

'You'll phone me if you need me?'

'Of course. But you are trying to unravel this dreadful mess, aren't you? You're not running around after another client?'

'Now Jason's home, you're my only client.'

'I should hope so.'

A cloud had lifted. I was still a free man. Easing back the swivel chair, I tugged at the bottom drawer of the desk, groped around under a carton of ball-point pens and pulled out Abraham Feinburg's cheque. It was time to deposit the funds. When I stepped out on to the landing the phone started ringing again. I toyed with the idea of ignoring it, decided not to, and unlocked the door and dashed back. When I got it to my ear I heard Melody's husky voice saying, 'There's a young woman at my reception window; she wants to see you.'

'Does she have a name?'

'She won't give it. She's wearing long black robes, a black head-scarf and a worried look.'

My pulse quickened. 'Tell her to come up.'

The phone clattered down, I heard the faint sound of a conversation, then Melody was back on the line. 'She asked if there was a woman in your office. When I told her you were on your own, she said she couldn't come up.'

'Don't let her leave. Whatever you do, don't let her leave. Can I talk to her in your office? Keep the door open so she can see you and the girls?'

'Reception, answering service, coffee, sandwiches; now you want to take over my office?'

'This one's important, Melody. Show her into your office and tell her I'm coming down.'

I took the attic stairs at a run, slowed as I rounded the accountant's landing, then descended to the entrance lobby at a dignified pace. Stepping around Melody's reception counter, I made my way between the desks and machines in her main office. Half-a-dozen girls were keeping busy, pecking away at keyboards, staring into computer screens, operating copiers, binding documents. Melody was standing just inside her office with her back to the door; the girl was sitting in front of the desk. I tapped on the glass partition and stepped inside.

'Miss Cheema? Miss Ghinwa Cheema?'

She didn't contradict me; just gazed up at me with dark frightened eyes, and said, 'You gave me your business card. You said I should contact you if—' Her eyes slid from mine to Melody's. Melody turned, gave me a grim little smile, and walked out. She went far enough into the main office to be out of earshot.

'I'll leave the door open,' I said. 'That OK?'

She nodded. There was a big brown-leather zip-up bag beside her chair. Blue jeans and gold-beaded sandals were visible beneath the hem of the ankle-length black over-dress she was wearing. Its sleeves were gathered around her wrists, and the small pink patches on her hand, where the skin had no pigment, had been hidden with dye or make-up. A black hijab covered her hair and throat. Only the dark oval of her face was exposed. Her huge eyes were luminous; her features refined and quite beautiful. Suddenly realizing I was intimidating her by standing there, I moved behind the desk and sat in Melody's crimson leather chair.

Leaning forward, I put my arms on the desk, smiled and made my voice gentle as I said, 'How can I help you?'

She glanced through the open door, satisfied herself that no one could hear above the low hum and clatter of the machines, then frowned at me. 'You obviously know I'm not Halima Fahim.'

I kept up the encouraging smile.

'How did you know?'

'Jason Brody gave me a photograph of your cousin. You're very much alike, but there are differences. The small patches of pale skin on your right hand were the real give-away. Jason confirmed Halima didn't have any marks like that.'

'I usually hide them.'

'And you've come all the way from Birmingham to tell me you're not Halima?'

She looked away from me, gazed through the open door at Melody and the girls busy with keyboards and copiers. After what seemed like quite a while, her eyes found mine again and she said, 'I suppose I came because I'm frightened. I was on my way to Leeds. I saw the Barfield signboards on the station and got off the train. It was a spur of the moment thing, not something planned. Then I walked up here. It's not far. Normally, one of my brothers would have travelled with me, but Asif and Bilawal were hurt last night and Mian had to make deliveries to the restaurants. So they sent me on my own and I was able to break the journey. If Uncle Nawaz says I'm late, I'll tell him I got off at the wrong station and had to wait for another train.'

'Your uncle's Nawaz Fahim, the wealthy businessman who's standing for Parliament?'

She blinked slowly. 'How did you know that?'

I ignored her question and asked her another. 'Is that why you're scared?'

Looking down at her hands, she whispered, 'I think I'd better begin at the beginning.' Then big brown eyes swept back up and her voice became stronger. 'About two weeks ago I found out that Halima was in love with a white boy called Jason Brody. When you called, I guessed he'd hired you to find her. I couldn't imagine the university being bothered. They didn't send anyone to check during her second year, and she was away ill for more than a month then.'

'What was she suffering from?'

'Depression. The doctor said she was working too hard and worrying about exams. Looking back, I think she was worrying about the consequences of becoming involved with a white boy.'

'And why did she suddenly disappear a couple of weeks ago?'

'Bilawal saw her coming out of a house with the boy. He told my father, my father called Uncle Nawaz, and he drove down from Leeds. There was a dreadful row. They blamed me. I'd been told never to leave her alone while she travelled to and from the university. When father was dragging me upstairs to beat me, Halima started screaming, saying it wasn't my fault. She told them she'd missed lectures, slipped off during the day to the boy's flat. She said I couldn't possibly have known. My father was still angry with me. You see, it was so shaming for him.'

I raised an eyebrow. 'Why shaming for your father?'

'Because Halima had been entrusted to him. It was his sacred duty to take care of her and protect her. It was an arrangement made so Halima could go to university. She would live in my father's house and there would always be someone to escort her across the city.'

'And who escorted you?'

'Escorted me?'

'When you came back home after you'd dropped her off?'

'Asif or Bilawal or Mian drove us there in the car; I would walk the short distance to the campus with her and whoever was driving would wait until I came back to the car. Uncle Nawaz was still worried, but he accepted it was the best that could be done. Most families would have let her travel with a male cousin, but Uncle Nawaz insisted that I go, too.'

I looked at her across Melody's desk. It was an uncluttered desk: just a red leather blotter, a neatly stacked pile of invoices in a red plastic out tray, an empty in tray, a bright red telephone, a black telephone, and a red sculptured arrangement for holding pens and paper clips. The black phone was the extension on my line that Melody used for taking calls when I was out. I was thinking Jason and Halima must have been pretty careful or they'd have been found out sooner.

'Anyway,' she went on, 'they took Halima up to her room. My father and mother held her across the bed while her father beat her. They closed all the doors and told me to stay downstairs in the back room, but I could still hear her screaming and Uncle Nawaz shouting at her, making her swear she was still a virgin. She kept on saying, "Yes, yes, yes. What kind of a daughter do you think I am?" And he was yelling, "This God-forsaken country has corrupted you. I should never have listened to your mother. I should have followed my instincts and said no to university, found you a husband who would keep you out of trouble".' Ghinwa closed her eyes. Distress was beginning to curve her beautiful mouth into an ugly shape. 'Please,' she whispered, 'could I have a drink of water?'

There was a dispenser alongside a storeroom door at the far end of the outer office. I fetched her some in a plastic tumbler and set it on the edge of the desk beside her chair. A slender hand reached out and picked it up. She began to take tiny sips.

After passing a pink tongue over her lips, she said, 'They locked her in an attic room. They wouldn't let me see her. She was disgraced, you see; she would be a bad influence. The room was just above mine. All night I listened to her crying. And then my mother saw she'd been vomiting. Every morning she was vomiting. My father was scared the beating had injured her in some way and he phoned Uncle Nawaz. Uncle Nawaz arranged for a doctor to call.'

'Couldn't they have got their own doctor to take a look at her?'

'Uncle Nawaz is a very important man. The family is very proud of him. He daren't expose himself to criticism, so he sent a doctor who would be understanding and know how to deal with the situation.' She drank what was left of the water, then said, 'The doctor examined her and tested her. He said she was no longer a virgin and she was pregnant. No one told me this. I heard my mother screaming at Halima about it. My father was too shocked to say anything. He was beside himself. Halima was his brother-in-law's child and she'd been entrusted to him. Her shame was his shame.'

Ghinwa held out the plastic tumbler. 'May I have some more water?'

'Sure.' I crossed the outer office and got her a refill. On the way back, Melody gave me a questioning look. I just shrugged, returned to her inner sanctum, and handed the water to the girl.

She sipped at it gratefully, then said, 'My mother and father were arguing all day. In the end, my mother persuaded him to telephone Uncle Nawaz. I thought Uncle Nawaz would drive over, but he didn't. The next morning, when I started to put Halima's breakfast tray together, my mother told me not to bother. She said Halima had stayed overnight at Uncle Khazir's because she was going with them to Pakistan for a holiday and they were flying out early. She said they wouldn't be back until the end of June.'

'This Uncle Khazir: where does he live?'

'Allott Street. I can't remember the number, but the house is very brightly painted: green walls and a blue door and red around the windows. Uncle Khazir's liking for bright colours is something of a joke amongst the family.'

'Allott Street: didn't your father own a house near there, a house that was burned down?'

'That's right, Father's house was in Faxby Road. Sometimes members of the family would sleep there for a few nights; relatives over from Pakistan for weddings and funerals. You know how it is when there's a family gathering; there's never enough room for people to sleep.'

I nodded. I'd no idea how it was, but I didn't want to stop her talking. I said, 'The day I called at your home, then came back and handed you my card, that was the day your father's house burned down?'

She nodded and gave me a puzzled look. She obviously thought the talk about the burned-out house was irrelevant.

'After I'd called back and given you my card, was it very long before your parents came home?'

She sipped at the water. 'Not long. Ten minutes perhaps. Does it matter? I remember my father was angry when they came back and my mother looked worried. More than worried; frightened. Dad reminded me to tell any strangers who called that I was Halima. He kept going on and on about that. Then he drove off again to make a delivery to one of the restaurants. He came back about half an hour later, unloaded some supplies into the basement, then the police called to tell him his house in Faxby Road was on fire. They wouldn't let him go to it, and they stayed for ages asking questions. They asked to see Halima's passport.'

'Passport?'

'Two of them kept looking at me and looking at the photograph in the passport. But Halima and I are very much alike. Perhaps it's because our mothers are first cousins and they married first cousins.'

I gazed at her; said nothing. She hadn't picked up on the passport still being in the house when Halima was supposed to be on her way to Pakistan with her Uncle Khazir. I didn't point it out to her. I didn't want to interrupt the flow.

'The police called again the next day, and the day after that. Dad was very angry and uptight. Mum told me to watch what I said and only speak when they spoke to me. She said I was called Halima now and my father was Nawaz Fahim and I lived in Leeds and I'd decided to give up university and go home to be married. Mum was scared; really scared.'

'When we began talking, you said that you're scared,' I reminded her.

She looked down at her hands for quite a while. I began to wonder if she was weeping, but when she looked up her eyes were dry. 'The boy came last night,' she said softly. 'The boy Halima was in love with. He started yelling up at the windows. He was swearing and saying we'd murdered Halima. He was like a crazy man, shouting so loud the whole street must have heard. Dad went to the door, then my brother, some of my cousins and an uncle came through from the kitchen and went out into the street. They said he had a friend with him and they got into a car and drove off. Asif tried to get inside but the driver slammed the door on his hand and broke his fingers. Bilawal blocked the road but they just drove at him. He's got a fractured pelvis and a broken leg; he's been kept in hospital.' Dark eyes searched my face, then she said, 'I've been worried and scared ever since they told me Halima had gone to Pakistan. Last night I began to think that what her lover was yelling might be true. After he'd driven away, they sent me up to my room, but I could hear them talking about it while they waited for the ambulance to come for Asif and Bilawal. They sounded really scared.'

'They didn't call the police?'

She shook her head. 'Just the ambulance. It came very quickly. Then my father phoned Uncle Nawaz. They were talking for ages. This morning my mother came up to my room and told me I had to go to Leeds and live in Uncle Nawaz's house. From that moment on I was to be Halima. I was no longer Ghinwa. I felt certain then that Halima was dead. I think Uncle Nawaz told my father and my brothers to kill her when the doctor said she was pregnant.'

'An honour killing?'

She ignored that; just went on recounting events. 'This morning they gathered up my birth certificate, my health card, my passport, my school certificates; everything they could find that had my name on it, and burned it. Then they put all of Halima's papers into a big envelope and gave them to me to take to Uncle Nawaz.' She paused, but kept her eyes on mine. Through the open door came the murmur of female conversation, the rhythmic clatter of a big machine, a peal of laughter. Ghinwa's voice was little more than a whisper when she went on, 'I am to be married. I will meet my future husband and his parents next week. His family are rich and greatly respected in the community. I have seen his photograph. He is tall and quite good-looking.'

'Does that please you?'

'I'm too frightened to be pleased. And I don't know what to do. That's why I came here.'

'You could walk away from it all: walk away now. There are organizations that protect women from forced marriages. I could make some phone calls, take you to a refuge.'

'It wouldn't be a forced marriage, Mr Lomax. When we meet next week, he might decide he doesn't like me, or I might say I don't care for him.'

'It's a safe bet he's going to like you, Ghinwa. And Uncle Nawaz could get upset if you get picky. The question is, is that what you want?'

'I don't think I could live the lie.'

'If you won't walk away—'

'I'd lose everything if I walked away. And I'm not like Halima. I couldn't live outside the family.'

'How do you get on with your Uncle Nawaz?'

'He's always been pleasant and kind to me. He's refined and polite. You would call him cultured. And he's always well groomed and immaculately dressed. Halima was so critical of her father. She thought he was shallow, forever seeking out and befriending the right people, publicizing himself, making donations to politicians; bribes she called them. She broke his heart long before this business with the boy. I'm sure Uncle Nawaz only agreed to let her go to university because she was so argumentative and difficult he couldn't stand her in the house.'

'And your aunt, his wife?'

She smiled. 'Nice. Very gentle. Very much the fine lady.'

'So, living with them, being part of the household, wouldn't be a problem for you?'

Her eyes clouded. 'I'm sure Halima's dead, Mr Lomax. She was incredibly stupid behaving the way she did, but she didn't deserve to die. I'd feel I was betraying her. I'd feel I was profiting from her death.'

Giving her a questioning look, I said, 'What is it you want me to do? Seems to me your conscience won't let you go along with the plan, but you couldn't bear to be cast out of the family if you don't.'

'I hoped you'd tell me what to do,' she said bleakly.

I gazed at her across the desk for a while, then said, 'Go along with it. Go and stay in your uncle's house and pretend to be his daughter, but don't agree to marry a man who thinks you're Halima. You'd be breaking the law and you could end up in trouble yourself if you did that.'

'But where would that leave me?'

'It would give you a breathing space; buy you some thinking time.'

'You really do feel I should go to my uncle's?'

'If you won't let me find you a place in a refuge where people would help you, what else can you do?'

'I hoped you might be able to do something.' She gazed across at me. There was a helplessness and disappointment in her eyes and in her voice. She held out her hands, palms up, then shrugged fragile-looking shoulders. It was a gesture of despair.

'Halima's dead, Ghinwa. I can't wind back the clock for you.'

Reaching down, she began to gather up her bag.

'Does your father own any other houses apart from the one that burned down?' I asked.

She rose to her feet. 'He had about six more, further down Faxby Road, but the council declared a clearance area and demolished them. Dad got money, but he said his valuers had stood by and let the council cheat him.'

'He has restaurants?'

'Four. One not far from the burned-down house, the others in the suburbs on the far side of the city.'

'So, the house you live in, the house in Burbank Avenue, is the only habitable place he owns?'

She nodded. She'd already told me what she really wanted to tell me and she was losing interest in the conversation. I took her big zip-up bag and we headed into the main office. Curious eyes followed us as we rounded the reception counter and stepped out into the entrance lobby. She turned towards the front door.

'Don't go that way,' I said. 'Go out the back way and across the rear yard.'

She gave me a puzzled look.

'Someone who knows you might see you walking down the pedestrianized area. It's not likely, but you never know.'

She was still giving me the look.

'Your brother saw Halima; someone could see you.' I led her through the back door and down a long yard. When we emerged into the access roadway, I handed her the bag then pointed towards a street of small shops. 'Go down there, keep on to the end, then turn left. Walk on for another hundred yards and you'll see the station forecourt.'

She smiled at me. It was a frightened smile; the first smile she'd given me. 'Thanks,' she said.

'Don't thank me. I haven't done anything. But call me if you change your mind about the refuge, or if you think I can help.'

She turned and headed off.

'And Ghinwa—'

She glanced back.

'Memorize the phone numbers, then tear my business card up. Don't hang on to it.'

The sky was still overcast. Spring had regressed into winter. I watched the slight figure, the cold wind tugging at her black over-dress, trot past a baker's, a key-and-heel bar, a chemist's and a charity shop. Then I went back into the building and began to climb the stairs. An intelligent young woman, she hadn't needed me to spell out her options, but perhaps she'd felt a desire to tell someone outside the family what had happened, just for the record, and going to the police would have meant the end of life as she knew it. So she'd told me; told me about the dark things that had scared her, told me about going to a new home and assuming a new identity.

FOURTEEN

They turned and stared at me when I stepped back into the office. They weren't smiling. One of the waiting room chairs had been dragged through. Detective Chief Inspector Manson from Barfield CID was sitting in it. I didn't recognize the other plain-clothes cop sitting in the usual visitor's chair. Manson muttered, 'This dump's not been cleaned and tidied since I was here a year ago, Lomax.'

I grinned affably. 'Don't think it's ever been cleaned and tidied.'

He nodded towards his companion. 'This is DCI Hughes, Leeds CID. We'd like to ask you a few questions.'

I got behind the desk. 'Always a pleasure to assist the police.'

Manson sneered, then said, 'Where were you last night, between six and eight?'

'Birmingham.'

'You can prove that?'

'Plenty of people saw me there.'

'Surprised you had the nerve,' Manson said.

'Nerve?' I kept up the affable grin.

'To go back to Birmingham after the bother you caused. Coppers' wives and kids are still complaining about the stink.' Manson gazed at me for a while, then asked, 'What took you to Birmingham?'

'Missing person. I was hired to find him and bring him home.'

'Who?'

'That's confidential. Family's a little embarrassed about the whole business. You know how it is.'

'Did you?'

'Did I what?'

'Bring him home?'

I nodded. The cop from Leeds hadn't said a word. He'd just sat there, listening with ears that had heard too many lies, watching with cold, dead eyes that had seen things no man should ever see. My gaze drifted from one expressionless face to the other. Unblinking eyes stared back. Across the paved area, the church clock struck eleven. It took quite a while for it to chime eleven.

Manson said, 'How do you cope with it, Lomax?'

'Cope?'

'With the mess, the din: working in this untidy rat-hole where every hour there's bell chiming loud enough to shake your fillings loose.'

'You get used to it. And I'm out most of the time.'

'Do you know a man called Zhang Shensu?' It was the first thing Hughes, the cop from Leeds, had said.

I frowned, then made my face brighten. 'The kung fu film star; the guy who prances around doing karate moves?'

Manson let out an exasperated sigh. 'Don't take the piss, Lomax.'

Hughes reached inside a folder on his lap, took out a glossy ten-by-seven, and tossed it across the desk. 'That's him,' he said. 'Do you know the guy?'

I stared down at the clear, sharp, black-and-white enlargement. Abraham Feinburg's gambling partner, his shapeless mouth grinning out of a flat face, his homburg hat tipped over almond eyes, stared back at me. Shrugging, I said, 'Never seen him before.'

'He knew you,' Hughes said. 'Your name and phone number were pencilled in his diary; last Friday.'

'Maybe he was thinking about hiring me.'

'You've never met the guy?'

'Not that I recall.'

Hughes reached over the desk and made a give-it-back-to-me gesture with his fingers. I handed him the image of the smiling Zhang Shensu. He slipped it back in the folder, then took out another photograph and held it up for me to see. It was Marlena and Alice in the dress shop fitting room: a big black-and-white enlargement of one of the colour prints Shensu had been carrying around in his wallet. 'How about her?' Hughes said. 'Do you know her?'

'The smallish woman holding the cup and saucer?'

Manson sighed out his irritation. 'Don't push it, Lomax. The woman in her best black satin smalls, stepping out of the dress.'

'Looks familiar.' I grinned across at them. 'Actress: she's been on television, in some drama series.' I raised an eyebrow. 'No?' I took another look at the photograph. 'Fashion model: she's a fashion model.'

'You're taking the piss again, Lomax. When did you last see a fashion model? The woman's got too much shape, too much flesh on the bones, to be a fashion model.'

'Then I can't help,' I said. 'Sorry.'

'You're not sorry, Lomax. You don't give a shit,' Manson muttered.

Hughes slipped the photograph back in the folder and glanced at Manson. They rose to their feet. 'We'll probably ask you to verify that you were in Birmingham last night, Lomax. Don't start whining about client confidentiality.'

I watched them head out. They hadn't wasted a goodbye on me. They were big men and their big feet thudding down the attic stairs almost drowned out the sound of the ringing phone. I picked it up.

'Am I talking to Paul Lomax?' I said he was. 'The Paul Lomax who represents Mrs Marlena Feinburg, widow of the late Abraham Feinburg?' I admitted that, too. 'I'm Bernard Blossom of Blossom and Blossom,' he went on, in a rather effeminate voice that was menacing in its friendliness. 'You may have heard of us. We're known as the Blossom Brothers.'

'Doesn't ring any bells.' I was lying and my spirits were plummeting. Debt collection, recovering losses, dispute resolution, even restoring wounded pride: Blossom and Blossom were leaders in the field, their success built on extortion and intimidation, their clients people who wanted the kind of quick and certain result the law can never provide.

'We're debt collectors.' He chuckled affably. 'In a very big way, of course. We wouldn't contemplate sums less than a million unless the client was well known to us. We're currently acting for Mr Nawaz Fahim. I understand you've met our client?'

I said I had.

'He's instructed us to recover twenty-five million pounds from the estate of the late Abraham Feinburg.'

'It was twenty million at the last count.'

'Twenty if a property mentioned to you by Mr Fahim is conveyed to him for a nominal sum. Twenty-five otherwise.'

I took a deep breath. 'I can only say to you what I said to Fahim: recover from Zhang Shensu. He and Fahim had the gentleman's agreement. Shensu reneged on it.'

'Enforcing gentlemen's agreements is a service we're particularly proud of, Mr Lomax. Shensu's already made restitution for the breach. He has nothing left to give.'

'Fahim has no claim on the Feinburg estate,' I said. 'The properties were registered in Shensu's name and legally conveyed.'

'I don't think you can be very well acquainted with the way Blossom and Blossom do business, Mr Lomax.' The voice was pouring charm down the line. 'Although we're a much larger organization, we function in a similar way to yourself. We're very much the agency of last resort; the firm people come to when they can't obtain redress from the police or in a court of law.' He let that hang in the air for a while, then cleared his throat and said, 'Twenty-five million, Mr Lomax. Talk to the widow. Tell her it would be in her best interests to pay. And yours too, of course, but you probably wouldn't want her to know that. You've got forty-eight hours to persuade her to transfer the funds. I won't call you again.'

The phone went dead. I stood there, holding it, trying to collect myself. I knew what I had to do, but forty-eight hours might not be long enough. Tomorrow I might have to swallow my pride and tell Marlena to pay or run. I got out of the building before the phone could ring again.

* * *

The NatWest Bank's Barfield branch is located in a vast echoing hall that's tricked out with fluted columns, deep cornices and coffered ceilings. I joined the roped-off queue winding towards the tellers and let my thoughts wander over the events of the morning. Ghinwa Cheema was heading for Leeds to enter the home of Nawaz Fahim and assume his daughter's identity. Maybe Jason Brody's performance outside the Cheema residence had scared them all, made Fahim realize he had to get Ghinwa into his house in case questions were asked about Halima. Zhang Shensu was almost certainly dead. There was no other reason why the cops would pay me a call and show me pictures they'd found in his wallet. And Fahim had called in the Blossom

Brothers. He hadn't wasted any time. They'd expect a big cut, but they'd be swift and ruthless: Zhang Shensu had already paid. Soon they'd be leaning on Marlena. I decided not to warn her. I daren't. If I did she'd want me close at hand, round the clock, and I had to be free to try and sort out the mess. And she might want to buy Fahim off. Abraham hadn't hired me to encourage his widow to do that.

When the queue shuffled forward my mobile started bleeping. I patted my jacket, found it behind my wallet, and keyed it on.

'What's Mr Pick-Axe-Handle doing?' The voice was low pitched and mockingly seductive. There was laughter in it.

'Making a deposit.'

'I've caught you in the men's room?'

'In the bank.'

'You're doing a dump in the bank?'

'Depositing a cheque.'

'Thought you might be excreting.'

I moved out of the queue and stood behind one of the massive columns. 'And what's DCI Houlihan doing?'

'Taking a long hot bath and wondering if you'd care to join me. It's my rest day. I've just got up.'

'Bath's going to be cold by the time I get over. How about dinner?'

She let out a throaty chuckle. 'I was hoping you'd ask. How soon can you get here?'

A huge clock on the back wall of the bank showed five to twelve. There were things I had to do, so I said, 'Just before the evening rush-hour; four, four-thirty.'

'Sounds good. We could have a drink before we go out.'

'Wear the yellow dress.'

'You've got a thing about that dress.'

'I've got a thing about the woman who wears the dress.' When I heard her laughing I switched off the mobile and rejoined the queue.

FIFTEEN

Helen Houlihan stirred when I untangled my legs from hers and eased myself into a sitting position. I drew the duvet over her shoulders, gently tucked it around her, then swung my feet to the floor. I sat on the edge of the bed for a while, listening to her breathing. It was slow and regular. When I was sure I wouldn't wake her, I rose, gathered up my things and crept into the living room. It was almost 2 a.m.

We'd dined earlier at a classy place called Birds of Paradise. She hadn't worn the yellow dress, but she'd filled a red sweater in a rather spectacular way. Black silk trousers had swirled around her legs, almost like a long skirt, and the pointed toes of her red and black shoes had kept peeping out as she trotted along beside me. In that outfit, with her hair cut and styled, she got plenty of admiring glances from the other male diners. Dinner was pleasant. The three hours we'd spent together before she fell asleep in my arms had been memorable.

My overnight bag was behind the sofa. I took out black jeans, a pair of black boots with soft rubber soles, and a black anorak. When I'd dressed, I folded my suit and packed it in the bag together with my best Oxfords and a tie I'd bought specially. Picking up the bag, I switched off the light and let myself out of the flat.

Finding Halima's body was the key to it all. Her cousin, Ghinwa, had been sent to Leeds to assume her identity so Fahim could convince the curious that his daughter was alive and well and contemplating matrimony. With Halima's body parts laid out on a mortuary slab and DNA tests done, he'd have to start explaining why he was passing Ghinwa off as Halima. The police would cling like limpets and Blossom and Blossom would abandon a client who was under such close scrutiny. With Shensu dead and Fahim otherwise occupied, Marlena could relax again.

The women who'd caught me staring up at the bloodstained laths would have phoned Cheema at the restaurant. They'd have described me and he'd have guessed I was the phony university welfare officer who'd called at his home. That would have scared him; made him decide to take the bags out of the bin at the back. He wouldn't have risked hiding them elsewhere on the premises and his other restaurants were too far away for him to have taken them there and got back to Burbank Avenue so quickly – Ghinwa had told me her parents had arrived home, scared and agitated, not long after I'd dropped off my business card. Her father had gone out again, returned half an hour later, maybe after he'd started the fire in the terraced house, and unloaded things from the car into the basement. The police had called that day and the next day. The Cheemas would have felt they were being watched. They wouldn't have dared take body parts from the house and dump them somewhere.

The police didn't search Cheema's home. His brother-in-law, Nawaz Fahim, had exerted influence, threatened to make complaints about harassment. And with a girl assuring the police that she was Halima, and Fahim saying his daughter was alive and well and returning home, no magistrate would have signed a warrant. The more I thought about it, the more sure I became that the blue sacks containing Halima's dismembered body were in the basement of Cheema's house.

Police cars prowled, taxi cabs ferried revellers home, and groups of young men and women sauntered along brightly lit streets as I drove across the city. I parked the Jaguar in front of an old Methodist chapel that had been converted into a Sikh temple, walked a hundred yards along the main road, then turned into Burbank Avenue. Silent in the rubber-soled boots, I kept in the shadows beneath the trees as I approached the Cheema residence. A small jemmy, a wallet of lock picks, a glass cutter wrapped in a hand towel, and a couple of pairs of surgical gloves were zipped up inside the anorak.

The family's white Mercedes was parked in the road: the house pre-dated the age of the car and there was no driveway, just a narrow path down the side. A light glowed dimly behind the decorated glass panel in the front door. The rest of the house was in darkness. I studied the place for a couple of minutes. There were no alarm boxes; no signs of life.

Leaving the belt of trees, I crossed over and padded silently down the path to the rear of the house, drawing on a pair of surgical gloves as I went. A flight of steps led up to the back door; another disappeared into a basement light well. After climbing down, I calmed my breathing and listened. A dog was barking a couple of streets away and there was the faint rumbling, like distant thunder, of a plane crossing the night sky. The house was silent.

Small windows were set on each side of the door at the foot of the basement steps. I shone the torch inside; played its beam over a white-glazed sink, a launderette-sized washing machine, a big dryer, and a couple of ironing boards. Neatly folded table cloths and napkins were piled on a bench. I was looking at the laundry facility for the Cheema chain of restaurants.

The door had a cylinder lock and an old dead lock. When I turned the knob and pressed my knee against the panelling, the door gave a little and the gap where it met the frame widened: the old lock wasn't being used. I took a square of flexible plastic from the wallet of picks, slid it into the crack above the latch and dragged it down. The sneck slid free, the door swung open, and I stepped inside.

After checking the laundry, I headed along a central passageway. On my right, stone steps led up to the ground floor. The door at the top was shut, so I risked switching on lights in some of the windowless rooms. Supplies for the restaurants were stored everywhere. In a large cellar at the front of the house, four chest-type freezers formed an island in the middle of the floor and metal shelving lined two of the walls. It was stacked with tinned foods, cartons of spices, packs of bottled water, soft drinks.

One by one, I lifted the lids of the freezers and poked around amongst plastic-wrapped meat, frozen sauces and cartons of ice-cream. There were no blue plastic sacks, no frost-encrusted bundles that, when pressed with the fingers, could be anything other than poultry. I checked the walls, the stone-flagged floor, the position of the freezers, for signs of disturbance. Finding none, I clicked off the light, returned to the passage, and went through another door into a smaller chamber. In the light of the torch, I could see a chute leading up to a grating at the side of the house: the room had once been a coal cellar. A new-looking gas boiler, sprouting pipes and a flue, stood on a concrete plinth. Gas and electricity meters and fuse boxes were mounted on the opposite wall. It was all neat and tidy and free from clutter. No one had lifted the old stone flags that covered the floor. No one had disturbed the walls.

When I stepped out into the passageway, the door at the top of the cellar steps rattled open. I clicked off the torch, darted back into the boiler room and stood behind the open door. With my eye close to the narrow gap under the hinge, I saw Cheema, wearing a

T-shirt, boxer shorts and a pair of flip-flop sandals, descend the steps and head towards me down the passageway. I held my breath; watched him turn and enter the cellar with the chest freezers. I heard him tearing at plastic wrappings, the hiss of a bottle being opened, thirsty gulping, a belch; then he muttered something I couldn't understand and his sandals flip-flopped back into the passageway. Pausing, he took another drink from the bottle, belched again, then returned up the steps. The light went out and the door rattled shut.

I stood in darkness, listening. After a while I heard the faint sound of someone climbing carpeted stairs and I left the boiler room and began to check the passageway. Beneath the cellar steps, a hole, big enough for a man to crawl through, had been cut into the wall at chest height. Shining the beam of the torch into it, I saw a shallow void that extended under the floor of a large room. I got my head and shoulders inside. Nothing had been hidden behind the opening; the rubble-strewn concrete beneath the floor hadn't been disturbed; but new-looking electrical cables snaked across it and disappeared into the room above. Electricians had been doing a rewiring job.

Sacks of flour and rice were stacked on timber racking arranged around the walls of a cellar next to the laundry, but they were too small to contain the limbs and torso of a young woman. I wandered back through the cellars again, checking white emulsion-painted walls and stone-flagged floors. Nothing had been disturbed. Everything was clean and tidy. Cheema had a very orderly approach to his business and he bought basics in bulk.

I toyed with the idea of going up into the house, then dismissed it. It was too risky: Cheema and his wife, and probably some of his sons, would be there. Leaving the basement, I climbed out of the light well and returned to the avenue.

Cheema's white Mercedes was parked outside the house. There

was always a chance he'd left the sacks in the boot. It was an old car, not likely to be fitted with an alarm, so I slid the jemmy from my anorak and shoved the sharpened end into the gap beneath the lock. I put my weight against it, felt metal crumple, then pressed down. The lid sprang open. In the faint light from the street lamps I could see a nylon tow rope, a set of jump leads and cans of Coca Cola in shrink-wrapped cardboard trays. No blue plastic sacks. The house was still in darkness. I lowered the boot lid and crossed over to the trees.

Back in the Jaguar, I began to wonder if the police had made a proper search of the rubbish tip; if they'd gone to the right tip. It was almost 3.30 and tiredness was taking hold of me. I'd got absolutely nowhere. Closing my eyes, I tried to recall the conversation I'd had with Ghinwa in Melody's office. She'd mentioned a house in Allott Street, owned by an uncle; a brightly coloured place. Halima was supposed to have gone with the uncle and his family to Pakistan and they wouldn't be back for weeks.

I tugged off the gloves, wiped perspiration from my hands and keyed the ignition. Ten minutes later I was cruising past Cheema's burned-out house. The front door and ground floor window opening had been boarded up. Through a gap where the bedroom window had been, charred roof timbers made black bars across the sodium glow of the night-time city sky. I turned right, cruised past the ends of terraces, then turned left into Allott Street and let the car roll down the gradient.

The green-painted house with its red window frames and bright-blue door stood out from its neighbours like a parakeet amongst a flock of crows. I drove on to the end of the terrace, then made a left and parked the Jaguar near the mouth of an alleyway that ran behind the houses. After pulling on a fresh pair of gloves, I climbed out of the car and entered the narrow passage, counting gates as I headed back up the hill.

The gate to number 55 was bolted, but the gate to the adjoining yard opened when I tried it. A rabbit hutch had been built against the boundary wall. Clambering on to it, I swung my legs over the copings and dropped down into Uncle Khazir's back yard.

The door was secured by a decent lock. I was too tired to pick it and forcing it would wake the street, so I played the torch on the sash window. There was no security device, just the old swinging fastener that stopped the sashes sliding. The hand towel was soft against my chest, inside the anorak. I drew it out, unrolled it, caught the glass cutter as it fell. When I'd scribed a saucer-sized hole at the top of the lower pane, I laid the folded towel over it and pressed hard. There was a dull crack, followed by the tinkle of breaking glass; the disc had shattered on a television set beneath the window.

I stood in the cold misty darkness, holding my breath. Nothing stirred in the adjoining houses. From a great distance I could hear the rhythmic clatter of a train and, closer, the rush of a fast-moving car. Passing my hand through the hole, I reached over the frame and slid back the catch. The sash creaked when I heaved it up. I waited and listened. Everything was steeped in silence, so I climbed inside.

Switching on lights could have alerted a neighbour, so I used the torch to search the place. It was a small house. A flight of steep and narrow stairs was sandwiched between the two ground-floor rooms, and a tiny kitchen projected at the rear. I wandered through. Furnishings were sparse: just a sofa and an armchair in the front room, a long sofa facing the television in the back, and a small dining table and chairs in the tiny kitchen. Letters and junk mail were piling up behind a door that connected the front room directly to the street.

Uncle Khazir's liking for bright colours extended to the interior: wallpapers were red, gold and green, doors were bright blue, and coloured rugs had been scattered over the plastic-laminate flooring. It took less than a minute to make sure there were no blue plastic sacks in the kitchen and living rooms.

The sofa in the back room obstructed a door. When I dragged it clear and tugged the door open, I felt a rush of damp musty air. Worn steps took me down to what had been a small coal cellar at the front and a tiny chamber for storing food at the back. A crazed china cheese dish and the decaying remains of a child's cot were the only things down there. The brick walls and floor were covered with a powdery white efflorescence that sparkled in the light of the torch. It hadn't been disturbed.

I climbed back to the living room and took the stairs to the first floor. Two sets of bunk beds, a chest of drawers and a wardrobe were crammed into the bedroom at the front. A double bed, a wardrobe and a leather-covered wooden trunk were arranged in a smaller back bedroom that led to a bathroom. The trunk held sheets and blankets. What remained of the family's clothes after they'd packed for their long holiday were on wire hangers in the wardrobes. A door in the corner of the back bedroom opened on to a cupboard. An old television set, battered toys, rolls of wallpaper and pots of paint, were stacked inside. No sacks.

Almost as an afterthought, I swept the torch beam over the ceilings and saw an access hatch above the tiny landing at the top of the stairs. I dragged the trunk from the bedroom, stood it on its end, climbed up and pushed the wooden cover aside. With my head and shoulders through the opening, I played the torch over slates, old roof timbers, a water tank and the brick walls between the houses. Loft insulation, like a thick fall of dirty snow, undulated across the dark space. Reaching out as far as I could, I patted it, felt shapes in the troughs between the joists. When I folded it aside, I saw two of the blue plastic sacks: the smallest and the largest.

I had to be sure. I dragged the smaller sack towards me. The plastic was too tough to tear, so I gripped the torch in my teeth and fumbled with some sticky tape that sealed it. Eventually I got the sack open and peered inside; saw what looked like a mass of black wool, glistening with slime. I grabbed it and drew it out. I was holding a woman's hair and staring into her face. One eyeball had collapsed, leaving a weeping slit; the other was swollen beneath its hooded lid. White and perfect teeth seemed large in the sagging mouth.

A stench of rancid blood and putrefying flesh suddenly hit me. When I recoiled, the trunk swayed, then toppled and crashed down the stairs. I slid out of the hatchway and dropped on to the tiny landing; lay there, dazed, while Halima's head bumped softly down, from tread to tread.

The torch was lying in the bedroom doorway. I clicked it off and listened; heard voices in the adjoining house speaking a language that was strange to me. Then a child began to cry. I crept down the stairs, ears straining for any sound. A woman was speaking calming words. A man's voice was loud and angry. After a while, the talking and the crying stopped. I crouched in the darkness and the silence for a few minutes, then switched on the torch. Its beam glistened on a swirl of slimy black hair. Halima's face was winking up at me, the flesh at her throat ragged where they'd hacked her head from her body.

The appalling stench overwhelmed me again. Retching, I dashed to the raised window in the back room, leaned over the sill and breathed in cold early morning air. The sky was becoming lighter above the rooftops. When I shone the torch on my watch I saw it was almost five.

I keyed a number into my mobile. It seemed to ring for a long time, then a sleepy voice said, 'Houlihan.'

'I've found Halima Fahim's body.'

'Paul!' There was a pause while she checked the bed. 'Where the hell are you?'

'Allott Street; number 55.'

'You crazy bugger, you'll—'

'Send someone,' I said, interrupting the invective. 'The body parts are in blue plastic sacks just inside the loft hatch. The head's at the foot of the stairs.'

'At the foot of the stairs?'

'I dropped it.'

'You're crazy. You're absolutely crazy.'

'I'll leave the back window open. You can say it was a tip-off from a shocked burglar. And keep it under wraps. Nawaz Fahim had the girl killed. Her cousin's been sent to live with him in Leeds. She's been told to say she's Halima. You've got to get Fahim to pass Ghinwa off as Halima before he finds out the body's been recovered.'

'Stay there. I'll get someone to pick you up. You'll have to make—'

I started laughing. 'You've got to be joking, Helen. I'll watch the house to make sure it's not disturbed, but I'm clearing off when I see your boys driving down the hill.' Suddenly remembering, I said, 'One last thing: Fahim organized the murder of a guy called Zhang Shensu. An outfit called the Blossom Brothers handled the killing. DCI Hughes from Leeds CID will want to question him about that.'

'Paul ... Paul, wait there. Wait until—'

I switched off the phone.

SIXTEEN

It was a few minutes after twelve noon when I wandered into the office. I'd showered, shaved, changed into a light-grey suit, a blue-striped shirt, and the blue silk tie I'd bought the day before. There were no message slips on the blotter. That morning's mail amounted to no more than an offer to fit cut-price double glazing, a free kitchen if I allowed my home to be used as a show house, and an option on a time-share flat in Marbella. Dropping it all in the bin, I reached under the desk for the office bottle. A glass was lurking somewhere amongst the papers. I found it, blew out the dust and poured myself a couple of fingers. Lack of sleep and the events of the night before had left me feeling in need of a bracer. I took a couple of sips, then leaned back in the chair and closed my eyes.

'Sleeping on the job now, are we?' I heard a disapproving sniff and opened an eye. I must have been dozing. Melody was lowering a tray on to the desk. She wrapped a napkin around the handle of the coffee pot and began to pour. Her black suit had a faint red pinstripe and she'd clipped tiny red studs to her ears.

'I've asked you not to stare at me like that,' she said. 'And what's made you so tired and ill looking?'

My gritty bloodshot eyes had been lingering on the deep 'V' between the lapels of her jacket. Ignoring the reproach in her voice, I stifled a yawn and said, 'Spent the night in Birmingham. Didn't get back until almost nine.'

'A tryst with your Brummie girlfriend, was it? Little Miss Hooligan?'

'Houlihan.' I went on gazing at Melody while she added sugar and put the cup on the blotter. She'd made it painfully clear she wasn't interested in any sort of a relationship, but she had to go on making these caustic comments. Maybe she was just trying to wind me up. 'I was on a case,' I said. 'Playing handball with a severed head.'

'That's a very sick joke, Paul.'

'Wish it was. The thing was putrefying.'

Melody shuddered. 'Do you know whose head it was?'

'An Asian girl called Halima; cousin of the girl who called here yesterday.'

'And you actually touched it?'

'I was holding it when I fell and dropped it down some stairs. This is all very confidential. Don't tell a soul.'

'Can't bear to think about it,' she said. 'The last thing I'm going to do is talk about it.' She grimaced again.

'Fabulous suit. You look stunning.' I had to change the subject. Thinking about the head was making me feel nauseous.

She gave me a half-pleased little smile but her big blue eyes were still reproachful. 'I've told you so many times, Paul. I'd rather you didn't look at me like that.'

'Can't help it.'

'I'm talking about the little-boy-lost look, not the lecherous stares.'

'I'm trying to get over it.'

'I didn't realize there was anything for you to get over.' She turned and strutted towards the door. As she was moving through the waiting room, she called back, 'Just ask yourself, Paul: what woman in her right mind would get involved with a man who throws severed heads around?'

Still feeling shivery and cold, I tipped the remains of the whisky into the coffee, sagged back in the chair and began to sip it. The ringing phone startled me out of another doze. I groped for it under the papers.

'At last! I've been trying to reach you since yesterday evening.' It was Marlena. 'Maria's husband got tired of the exhibition and came home, so I've returned to the Vicarage. Alice is back from Perth and Maria Brody stayed with me last night, but we need a man in the house. I want you to come over.'

'The situation's completely changed, Marlena. I—'

'I'm very frightened, Paul. My husband engaged you, my husband paid you, and I want you to come over. I want you to come over now!'

My recording gear was still hidden in Abraham's office. I decided I may as well motor over to the Vicarage, recover it, and explain things to Marlena, face-to-face. 'Be with you in about fifteen minutes,' I said.

* * *

Marlena was otherwise engaged when I arrived, so I went into the study, dragged a chair over to the bookshelves and retrieved the camera and recorder. The attaché case was where I'd left it, beneath the knee hole of the desk. I'd just pressed the gear into the plastic foam and clicked down the catches when Marlena swept in, her eyes wide and scared, her lips trembling. She was wearing the dress she'd worn when I'd first met her in Mrs Pearson's summer-house: the one with the grey velvet top and a skirt made from layers of filmy grey silk.

Fear made her accent heavy when she said, 'Thank God you've

come. You mustn't leave me until this dreadful business is over. I've just organized a room for you. It has an en-suite. The maid's making—'

'It's over, Marlena,' I said gently, then moved from behind the desk, took her arm and led her to the sofa.

'It's not over,' she snapped. 'And I keep having nightmares about that dreadful Zhang Shensu. Even when I slept at Tanglewood, I kept imagining he was creeping up the stairs.'

'He's dead, Marlena. He can't creep up stairs.'

'Dead! You've killed him for me?'

I smiled. 'Fahim, the rich Asian who was pestering your husband, the guy who called here a couple of days ago: he had him killed.'

'Why on earth would he have him killed?'

'When we met here, I told him Shensu had conveyed his Leeds property holdings to your husband. That was the first Fahim knew about it. Fahim was calling because your husband was the long-time owner of another property in the block, and he was trying to persuade him to sell.'

Marlena looked bewildered. She hadn't grasped the significance of my having told Fahim what Shensu had done.

'Fahim spent years gathering it all together,' I went on. 'He only needed the corner plot your husband owned to have a portfolio that would have made him millions, and Shensu lost it all in a card game. When Fahim found out, he probably tried to get money out Shensu, and when he realized he'd little or nothing to give, he had him killed.'

'He'd have Shensu killed for that?'

'People are murdered for a lot less, Marlena.'

She sank back into the sofa, the filmy material of her skirt drifting over the cushions. Nodding towards an inlaid cabinet, she said, 'There's whisky in there, Paul. Would you be very sweet and get me one. And get yourself one, too.'

I did as she asked. As I was handing her the glass, her eyes suddenly widened and she began to look scared again. 'This Fahim man: he's had Shensu killed, he might harm me.'

'He's not going to be in a position to harm anyone, Marlena. Trust me. It really is all over.'

She gulped at the whisky and left a lot of lipstick on the rim of her glass. Her dark hair had been drawn back tightly and gathered into a chignon. The bodice of her dress was low; grey velvet, clinging to her breasts, rose and fell with her agitated breathing. 'I don't understand,' she said. 'Why won't Fahim be able to harm me?'

'Because last night I exposed his involvement in another murder. He's probably in custody.'

'Do the police know my husband gambled with Zhang Shensu?'

I studied her pale, almost perfect face. Zhang Shensu was dead and Fahim wasn't likely to talk to the police about the disastrous card game his associate had played a year earlier: he'd be revealing too much; he'd be telling them he had a motive for the killing. So I decided not to worry Marlena with talk about Shensu's photo-graphs and the visit from the police. 'What is there to know?' I asked. 'Two men can play a game of cards.'

She shivered, drained her glass, then held it out to me. 'Would you be very sweet and get me another, Paul?'

I crossed over to the elegant little cabinet, poured out an even more generous measure and brought it over. She smiled up at me. 'I can't believe it's over. And no one will ever know about my involvement in all this?'

I raised an eyebrow and sipped at the single malt. 'Your involve-ment?'

'That night,' she explained, 'in this room, wearing the dress that distracted Shensu, being my husband's stake in the game?'

'You're being paranoid, Marlena. A woman can wear an expensive dress. Shensu was obsessed; infatuated. He'd have been distracted if you'd worn a boiler suit. And he's dead. He's not going to talk about anything.'

'Maria Brody's son was involved with a girl called Fahim. Was she related to the Fahim who called here?'

'She was his daughter.'

'Jason told Maria he was sure the family had murdered the girl.'

Feeling a need to be careful what I said, I studied her for a moment, then asked, 'What else did Maria Brody tell you?'

'She said Jason was deeply in love; that the girl was carrying his child.'

'Then you'll know why she died.'

'One of those honour killings?'

'Don't talk about it, Marlena. Don't even discuss it with Mrs Brody. The police will come looking for you if it gets about that you know something.'

There was a tapping on the door and Maria Brody bustled in. 'Mr Lomax! I'd no idea—'

I downed the whisky and stood up. 'It's OK, Mrs Brody. I was just leaving.' Turning to Marlena, and giving Mrs Brody a reason for my being there, I said, 'I gathered together all of your husband's papers on the corner property and put them in a folder. It's in the bottom drawer of the desk. Don't be in a hurry to sell it.' I picked up the attaché case.

Marlena rose, went over to Maria and linked her arm in hers. Maria said softly, 'I have to go. Do you think Lewis could drive me back to Tanglewood?'

'I'll take you,' I said. I wanted to talk to her about Jason; warn her to keep him quiet when the papers got hold of the Halima story.

'Would you?' Maria Brody beamed at me. She looked bright eyed, radiant, much younger. Maybe it was because she was no longer quite so worried about Jason.

When we reached the front door the two women puckered their lips and pressed their cheeks together. Marlena watched while we crossed over to the Jaguar. I opened the passenger door for Maria, then Marlena ran towards us. I thought she was going to give me a grateful embrace, but she swept past me, wrapped her arms around Maria and hugged her. When Marlena released her, she took her hands in both of hers, beamed, and said, 'Tomorrow we must choose the music for our next concert.' Then she drew Maria close again and kissed her on the lips.

'We should include Debussy's G minor quartet,' Maria gasped, breathless after the kiss.

'Opus 10? But of course! It gives one such a feeling of rapture.'

'Passion and tenderness: it soothes the trembling heart.' Maria laughed happily, then let go of Marlena's hands and climbed into the car.

Marlena waved as we drove off. A faint breeze was stirring the filmy grey material of her skirt, making it swirl like smoke around her endless legs.

* * *

I peeled foil from cartons then tipped the take-away curry on to a plate. The attaché case containing the camera and video recorder was beside me on the dining table; just where I'd left it a week earlier. On a sudden impulse, I clicked it open, took out the disk and slid it into the player under the television. I keyed the remote, then began to fork up chicken tikka masala while I watched a replay of my meeting with Nawaz Fahim, enjoying all over again his expression of outraged disbelief when I told him Shensu had gambled away his property. Fahim would be feeling even more outraged and disbelieving now. The day before he'd been charged, along with Cheema and two of Cheema's sons, with the murder of his daughter, Halima.

And Fahim wasn't alone in feeling outraged. That morning the bank had returned Abraham Feinburg's cheque with a brief note saying he'd died and the question of payment should be raised with his executors. If I hadn't been brooding because Melody Brown had given me the brush-off, if I'd kept my mind on the business instead of Helen Houlihan, I'd have remembered Abraham's account would have been frozen and taken the cheque to Reed and Russell instead of wasting my time standing in the queue at the NatWest.

Movement and body heat activated the surveillance camera. I watched myself leave Abraham's study after the meeting with Fahim, then the picture vanished and grey lines flickered across the television screen. A second later I was back on display, taking the call from Fahim after he'd returned to Leeds and spoken to Shensu.

Grey lines appeared again. I reached for the remote, thinking the recording had ended, but the screen blinked into life once more. Maria Brody and Marlena Feinburg had entered the study. I watched Marlena close the door and lock it, then move over to dark windows and draw the curtains. I checked the date-and-time signature in the top left-hand corner of the picture. The camera had picked up an event that had taken place the night before I'd recovered the gear. Marlena switched on a couple of table lamps and the image was suddenly bright and sharp.

Maria Brody said, 'I was hoping we'd be able to go into your bedroom.'

Marlena crossed over to her and took her hand. 'Alice is moving around up there and I think she suspects. I think that's why she decided to visit her sister when I came over to Tanglewood. And Havers usually checks the sitting rooms before he goes to his flat. Abraham's study is the only place I can be sure we won't be disturbed.' Her voice was low and a little tense; maybe she was afraid that Shensu might be prowling around, or maybe it was excited anticipation. They kissed. It was a tender teasing and caressing of the lips that went on for quite a while. Marlena took her mouth away, then slowly pulled down the zip at the back of Maria's dress and slid soft dark fabric over her shoulders. Maria closed her eyes, allowed her head to fall back, and Marlena began to kiss her throat.

'I don't care any more,' Maria breathed. She ran her fingers into Marlena's hair and they exchanged a swift, passionate kiss. 'You're all I think about. I think about you every minute of every hour of every day. I'm driven mad by longing. When I'm holding you, when you're caressing me, I'm in ecstasy.' Her voice began to shake. 'I'm lost, Marlena, utterly lost. I've even lost my soul. Sometimes, when I'm at the altar rail, taking communion, I can smell your perfume on my hands and in my hair. I'm hopelessly adrift on a wild, dark, ocean of love and desire.'

'Don't talk,' Marlena whispered. She eased the dress over Maria's narrow hips and let it fall around her ankles. 'Don't wallow in guilt. Just abandon yourself to the wonderful mystery of it all.' Taking Maria's hand, she led her to the leather sofa where they fell, sprawling, along its length. Maria unbuttoned Marlena's blouse, freed it from the waistband of her skirt, then peeled it open.

Too engrossed to chew and swallow, I began to choke on a piece of chicken. Coughing and spluttering, I keyed the remote and ejected the disk. Daniel Brody had got the sex of his wife's lover wrong, but his instincts had been right. I recalled Maria's graveside glances, her reflections on the nature of love, her heavy breathing that last time she'd answered the phone when Marlena had been staying with her. I'd missed these and all the other signs. I'd not looked beneath the surface. I'd let Daniel Brody down.

I was sipping cold beer, trying to clear my throat, pondering on whether or not I should tell him what I'd seen, when the phone began to ring in the hall. I padded, bare foot, down the dimly lit passage and picked it up.

'Don't you ever answer your mobile?'

'Sorry. It's in my jacket on the bed.'

'I had a lot of trouble finding your home number. I was beginning to think you might be two-timing me with a wife.' Helen Houlihan sounded more than tired.

'I don't have a wife. I told you that.'

'Men tell women anything,' she said, then her voice suddenly brightened. 'I suppose you know Fahim and the Cheemas are in custody?'

'I heard it yesterday, on the six-o'clock news. You'll be in line for a promotion.' I heard a cynical laugh. 'A commendation, then? Surely they'll give you a commendation?'

'Chief called me in and gave me a reprimand. Reminded me he'd sent word down the line that this one had to be left alone. Blathered on about the sensitivities of ethnic minorities; said it was his primary duty to work for social cohesion and ensure stability and calm in the community.'

'Turn a blind eye to murder?'

'We think the Home Secretary's handed out some monumental arse-kickings, here and in Leeds. Fahim was a major donor to the party and he'd been nominated to stand in a Parliamentary by-election. That's what's really pissing the politicians off. They've lost a candidate who was big in the Asian community and they're scared the press are going to make a meal of it.'

'How did you finger Fahim?

'Female DI visited with a social worker; insisted on talking to Halima. Said they'd been advised she'd returned home and they'd called to make sure she was OK and he'd no worries about her. Fahim's wife brought Ghinwa in and they both passed her off as Halima. Rest of the team went in then and made the arrests.'

I listened to her breathing for a while, then said, 'You OK?'

'Not really.' Her shaky voice sounded tearful.

'Want me to drive over?'

'Would you?'

'Two hours. I'll be with you in a couple of hours.'

'Thanks, Paul. I don't want to be alone tonight: too many muti-lated bodies. Halima's was the last straw. I've started sleeping with the light on.' She let out a tearful laugh. 'Jesus, I'm a little girl again, afraid of the dark.'

It was at that moment I decided, for some reason I can't explain, not to tell Daniel Brody about his wife's affair. Keeping my voice low, I said, 'It's not the dark, Helen, it's what lies beyond the dark that scares the hell out of me.'